PIECES
AND
PLAYERS

BY

BLUE BALLIETT

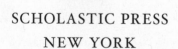

SCHOLASTIC PRESS
NEW YORK

2/16

LIBRARY OF CONGRESS CONTROL NUMBER: 2014947736

ISBN 978-0-545-29990-9

10 9 8 7 6 5 4 3 2 1   15 16 17 18 19

Printed in the U.S.A.   23 ☐☐☐ First edition, April 2015

Book design by Marijka Kostiw and Elizabeth B. Parisi

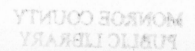

FOR BILL AND FOR MATTEO,
WHO BOTH UNDERSTAND THE BEAUTY OF
A CLICK BETWEEN PIECE AND PLAYER

FOUR-AND-TWENTY CHAPTERS ▢▢▢

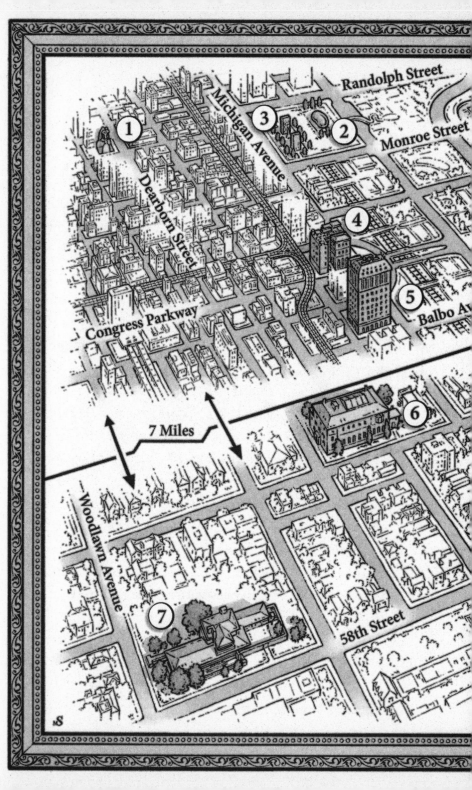

CHICAGO

Map Key

1. Picasso Sculpture
2. The Bean
3. Crown Fountain
4. The Fine Arts Building
5. The Blackstone Hotel
6. The Farmer Museum
7. Robie House
8. Mrs. Sharpe's House
9. Calder's House
10. Petra's House
11. Powell's Books
12. Monument Cracken's House
13. Early's Apartment

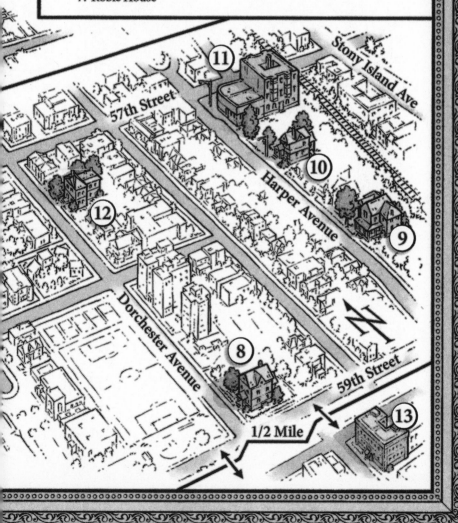

ART IS NOT WHAT YOU SEE, BUT WHAT YOU MAKE OTHERS SEE.

◻◻◻ EDGAR DEGAS

CHAPTER ONE   STUNG

❏ ❏ ❏ The man startled awake, stung by a jolt of pain in his neck. "Serves you right, you old fool," he muttered to himself.

Lumbering to his feet, he glanced at the monitors that recorded each floor of the building. Dawn slid smoothly along the terra-cotta tiles, past carved stone and wood, the glow of old paintings, the shimmer of gold leaf, lacquer, and glass.

But what was this?

A draft ruffled the giant ferns in the courtyard. *Air moving.* It was too early for the relief guard to be arriving. And besides, he'd never leave the door ajar.

Something is wrong, the man thought.

Tossing empty bottles into the trash and covering them with a newspaper, he grabbed his cell phone and burst out of the security room, heart thudding.

"Hel-lo?" he called out, hurrying toward the inside garden.

"Shouldn't have fallen asleep," he growled. "Bad idea, celebrating St. Patty's Day."

As he stepped through an arch and into the open, a breeze poured down from above, stirring blossoms, vines, and even the edge of one of the tapestries. Next he heard the familiar creak of a broken window on the fourth floor, followed by the wail of wind moving through hinges, dragging the cracked storm casement open and then shut. *Scree-ka-ka-thunk!* Still, it didn't make sense — not that much of a draft. His scalp tingled and the hair rose on both arms.

There was the ghost, of course. He shook his head; what a load of hogwash. Some thought she opened that pesky window in her old bedroom upstairs when she wanted to attract attention.

"Why can't they just keep up with the repairs?" the guard grumbled.

Straightening his glasses, he rounded the corner to the Dutch Room — and froze.

He couldn't believe what he was seeing.

Or rather, what he *wasn't* seeing.

His cell phone fell and the case shattered, the shards of red plastic skittering brightly through shadow. Trembling, he sank to his knees, realizing that his life, as he knew it, was over.

CHAPTER TWO   AN UNLIKELY THREESOME

□ □ □ Tommy Segovia followed his feet into the bathroom, head down and braced for the next shock.

He was stuck in foreign territory, and the worst part of it all was — he was home. He clicked on the bathroom light and peered into the mirror.

"Tommy!" His mom's voice was losing patience.

"I'm *up*," he called back, and his voice broke and shot up on the word *up*, which would have been funny a few months ago.

Stray hairs were appearing all over this spring, as if his body was a nightmare garden. Garden was too nice a word: How about *glob of dirt*? There was a black spear at the corner of his mouth this morning, and a small volcano was starting over one eyebrow. And his nose, meanly, seemed to be spreading across his face, melting into a larger and larger lump with each passing day. His nostrils looked like tunnels.

He stuck out his tongue — then knocked his toothbrush off the sink. Bending down to pick it up, he noticed that his right leg seemed to have more black, curly hairs than his left. Great. And he'd have to put on gym shorts today.

He stood up quickly, cracking his head on the edge of the sink. A bad word shot out just as the bathroom door opened and his mother's face appeared.

He was still in his underwear, an old pair that looked more like Swiss cheese than anything else.

Reaching out, he slammed the door closed. There was too much going on here, and none of it felt good.

"See you later, honey," his mom said apologetically.

Honey? Tommy sighed.

Becoming a man was ugly stuff.

🂠🂠🂠 Tommy and his mom lived in Chicago, in the Hyde Park neighborhood. They were caretakers with their own little apartment in the Robie House, a magical home built ages ago by the famous architect Frank Lloyd Wright. Tommy was only a few minutes' walk from his school, and his mom was four blocks from her job at a University of Chicago library. There were big trees, generous gardens, deserted streets, and a great deal still to be uncovered. After all, many famous and wacky people had wandered through Hyde Park over the years, and must have dropped or hidden plenty of loot. Not long ago, living here had seemed like a dream to Tommy — he wondered why it didn't still feel like one.

"Good, my life is good, and I'm lucky," Tommy muttered to himself as he trudged down the block. He thought about his best friends, Calder Pillay and Petra Andalee. They lived down the street, and the three had done some amazing detective work. They'd rescued a stolen Vermeer painting a couple of years before — well, Tommy hadn't exactly found it, it was the other two, but that wasn't *his* fault — and had then saved the historic house he was now living in, in part because of his fearless digging and trespassing skills. The three had also had a big adventure with an Alexander Calder sculpture in England, and his buddy Calder had almost died. Because of all this, their names had been in the news and they'd been interviewed on TV and the radio.

The problem was, months had now gone by and no one was thinking of them as special anymore. When a terrible, terrible art robbery happened last week at the old Farmer Museum, in the nearby neighborhood of Kenwood, nobody had asked for their help, or even for their opinion. The heist had drawn instant national and international attention — reporters and media trucks had flooded the area just blocks away. Someone had managed to get into the museum and turn off the alarms and security monitors for a short period of time without waking the guard, who'd apparently been asleep. They then left with armloads of art.

It had all happened practically around the corner, Tommy thought with a twinge of guilt, and the three of them weren't even *trying* to help. A few months ago, they would have talked about it nonstop and jumped into an investigation of their own without a second thought, but now it didn't seem as if they'd be able to add much, and no adults, not even the ones they knew, had suggested they get involved.

Tommy figured life was easier at eleven and twelve. Thirteen was such an obvious, unpredictable mess. Didn't everyone who looked at them feel like running? Tommy could see the headlines: "Teen Detectives Blunder onto Crime

Scene and Act Really Awkward." Or, "Unbeautiful Teens Fail to Find Beautiful Art."

The people who painted the stolen masterpieces had probably never ever heard of a zit. Maybe bad complexions hadn't even existed when that old stuff was being painted. *No wonder it was so valuable*, Tommy thought bitterly. This was art from the Perfect Skin days, kind of like painted mummies from the Egyptians or marble statues from the Greeks. The thought of the three of them discovering and handling a Vermeer or a Rembrandt — getting photographed by reporters at this stage in their lives — was ridiculous. A bad joke.

It happens to everyone, Tommy reminded himself as he kicked at a large brown stone. *At least in this century.*

Oh, *scaz*! It wasn't a stone — he must need glasses now, on top of everything else. The smell of fresh poop drifted up as Tommy stared down at the toe of his sneaker.

"SCAZ!" he growled aloud. It definitely helped. He and Calder and Petra had stumbled on the word a few weeks ago; an online slang dictionary said it meant someone so uncool that eventually they're cool.

"That," Petra had said, "is us." They had fist-bumped three ways, muttering *scaz* each time. It felt good to use as a private swear, one which didn't make grown-ups mad. The word was even beginning to spread at school. Yesterday Tommy overheard someone mutter it angrily after running headfirst into an open locker door.

"Scaz," Tommy repeated as he wiped his sneaker viciously on a patch of grass. He wondered what else could possibly happen.

Now I smell and look hideous, I'm hairy as a dog, and I'm going blind, he thought to himself as he stomped up the stairs and into the University School.

The day was off to a horrible start.

⬚ ⬚ ⬚ At lunch, Tommy sat with Calder and Petra. Calder was quite a bit taller than him now, and although his hair was always greasy these days, he didn't seem to have as many skin disasters, which Tommy thought was very unfair. Petra did share Tommy's predicament, and on bad days she had stopped tying back her hair and chose to peer out from between two dark, corkscrew curtains. Sometimes, Tommy thought unkindly, she reminded him of an egg with a black triangle for a head, at least from behind. Her rear end had grown this year, and when she turned around — well, things didn't always stay in place in the front when she ran. It was hard not to notice.

They made an unlikely threesome. Tommy was short, he had a chipped front tooth, and his head was as round as a marble. A finder and scavenger, he was great at spotting street treasures of all kinds, but school was not his strong point. Once a teacher started talking, Tommy's mind floated away like a fish in a current — or, as Calder had put it, like something going down the toilet bowl.

Calder was thin and his hair stood up in scrub brush formation. Numbers and mathematical shapes made more sense to him than people, and most of his thinking happened with his set of pentominoes. He stirred the twelve pieces around and around in his pocket, and everyone who knew him was used to the clacking sound. Sometimes he pulled out a pentomino and muttered something aloud. Each piece had its own letter-name from the alphabet, and one or another letter could put the world into focus like a pair of glasses. Plus, the pieces somehow connected to puzzling stuff in Calder's life, although not in a way most grown-ups understood.

An only child, Calder lived with his mom and dad, and although the three of them were happy, he envied bigger families. The idea of being ignored was delicious. His mom taught mathematics and his dad had a job experimenting with which plants worked where in cities. Both numbers and leaves could grow in strange ways, he pointed out to his mom when she suggested they find out why one of his feet had gotten bigger than the other this year.

Petra was the oldest of five kids and her household was loud, busy, and jumbled. She loved the deliberate quiet of words. Whenever possible, she'd disappear into her notebook, where she could be the boss of her own ideas. She loved the way a sentence, once written, stayed where you put it. Her dream was to become a famous writer one day but that now felt unlikely. No, impossible. After all, homework took more and more time and wasn't about to get easier as school went on.

Why did anyone think kids liked the word *responsible*? Petra told Calder and Tommy that she thought it had a clumsy, squashed feeling, like a hand-me-down winter boot. A real writer should be able to sit quietly in a peaceful spot, eating popcorn or staring out the window until they got a description right. Sometimes it felt like life was all about interruptions. That, or trying to dodge all mirrors.

This morning, Petra had a small white-topped mountain range on her chin. Every time Tommy looked at her face, he thought about the time bomb getting ready to erupt just north of his left eye. It might as well be Krakatoa, a volcanic island that destroyed everything within miles when it blew up. He and Calder had built a model in third grade, and it had sprayed goo — watery oatmeal propelled by a shaken soda — across a substitute teacher's face. They'd been heroes for a while there.

Not anymore.

The three were silent for a moment, and then Petra said, "I can't stop thinking about the Farmer heist. They announced on the news that it was the biggest art robbery ever to happen in the United States. And that gorgeous Vermeer is now the single most valuable stolen painting in the world! The three of us should be doing something."

The other two nodded uncomfortably, avoiding each other's eyes. Tommy scratched his nose, although it wasn't itchy.

Petra had recently gotten green-and-black glasses, and they made her look like a cross between an army general and a parrot. *Someone should tell her*, Tommy thought.

"Hello, you three." Rescued! Their old teacher Ms. Hussey stood at the end of the table and grinned at one face after another, as if they weren't looking as hideous as they truly were. She leaned toward them.

"Something big has come up. An opportunity. No, wait — that's not the right word. It's a once-in-a-lifetime challenge — and one that could rescue each of you from current distractions."

The table of three froze, all mouths open. Were they that obvious?

Luckily, Ms. Hussey could say anything and they wouldn't mind. And although she was sometimes puzzling, their old teacher never lied. When she sounded this way — as if everything that was about to happen mattered — it was important not to miss a clue.

"I would give anything, to tell you the truth, to be in your shoes," she blurted suddenly. "To be a kid and to be given this — this — gift of confidence." Was that a tear glinting in the corner of Ms. Hussey's eye? Still standing at the end of their table, she turned her head to one side and in two swift movements shook her hair loose and then swirled it back into a bun. Pulling a pen from her back pocket, she stabbed it through the coil of hair.

"Our old friend Mrs. Sharpe isn't getting any younger. In fact, she's been feeling awful since the robbery — well, we all have, I know — and I'm worried about her. She's calling a meeting in order to talk with you at her house. She's also invited a couple of kids you don't know. They're around thirteen, too, and have both done some incredible detective work. Remember hearing in the news about that boy, Zoomy Chamberlain, who is legally blind and found a notebook belonging to one of the most famous thinkers of all time, in his town in Michigan? And the girl — her name is Early Pearl, and she rescued her family and identified a diamond theft with the help of Langston Hughes' poetry."

Before Tommy, Calder, or Petra could wrap their heads around this, Ms. Hussey continued. "All of you have spring break coming up at the end of this week, which will mean you have some free time. I'll see you after school this Wednesday, four o'clock at Mrs. Sharpe's house." It wasn't a question.

As she swished away, the three were quiet.

These two new kids sounded way too smart. And Mrs. Sharpe had apparently invited them over first. What was going on?

"I wonder what she thinks five kids can do," Petra said, one hand covering the landscape on her chin. After a moment she added fiercely, "It'll just mess things up, having two strangers along for the ride. I wish she hadn't done that."

Petra's mouth hardened into a line, a line with a fleck of potato chip at one end, like a sideways exclamation point. Calder's mouth was still open and he stirred his pentominoes, a sign that he wasn't sure whether things were headed in a good or a bad direction. For his part, Tommy wondered if Petra was going to think these new kids were way cooler than him. Of *course* she would. He hoped they wouldn't show up, but didn't want to say that out loud. Instead he passed his bag of Goldfish to Petra and Calder, who both grunted thanks. The three ate in silence.

As he crunched the empty bag in his fist in what he hoped was a manly way, Tommy mumbled, "Scaz," allowing the *z* to fizz for a long moment. Calder repeated it. Then Petra said it. The word drew a sort of stay-away triangle around them, and suddenly life felt a little better.

CHAPTER THREE   STOP, BOY!

☐ ☐ ☐ Petra, Calder, and Tommy trudged the two blocks from the University School to Mrs. Sharpe's house on Wednesday afternoon. It was a cool March day, gray with a smudge of green. Calder's pentominoes clacked in his pocket and Petra was silent. The sidewalk wasn't wide enough for three, so Tommy walked behind, realizing that as a group they looked close to pathetic — either stick-thin with nasty hair, dumpy, or boasting a pimple that belonged in the *Guinness World Records* book. Well, there was no way out now. Mrs. Sharpe and Ms. Hussey would be waiting, as well as these two super-accomplished kids.

Why hadn't the three just said no?

Even as he thought it, Tommy knew none of them could ever say that to Ms. Hussey, who had been their better-than-best sixth grade teacher. She was brave, unpredictable, and often made decisions *with* her class — even if they didn't always work out. She fessed up to mistakes and she never seemed bored, which matters when you're a kid sitting for hours at a desk. Sometimes she wore clothes with weird colors or exciting patterns to school — Tommy remembered a skirt covered with exploding firecrackers and a pair of pants with diving mermaids on the back pockets. Sometimes she even brought them doughnut holes, breaking all the rules. Plus, she was a loyal friend to confusing old Mrs. Sharpe, who had gotten to know the kids and helped them through some of their most difficult and thrilling investigations.

The thing about Mrs. Sharpe, Tommy thought, was that you were never quite sure where the mystery stopped and she started. You knew she was hiding stuff, you could *feel* it, and you were never 100 percent sure it was for the right reasons.

You never knew who was fooling whom.

Mrs. Sharpe lived in a Victorian house that was gray with plum trim and boasted a huge wisteria vine over the front porch. Without leaves, the vine looked threatening, more like a boa constrictor than anything else. The house was bigger, fancier, and less homey than the places the kids lived. Plaster lions reared up from the garden as you walked to the front entrance, as if reminding you to feel uncomfortable.

The door flew open after one knock. It was dim inside, and Ms. Hussey's voice was subdued. "She's not feeling too much like herself," she half whispered to the kids. "Come on in."

"Uh-oh," Calder said.

As they stepped in, Petra reached quickly into one pocket and pulled out a hair clip. Tommy didn't see her elbow coming and it poked him right in the eyebrow, the one located beneath the volcano.

"Ow!" he yelped. Calder turned around just as Petra stepped to one side, and the two bumped bellies. Both moved away in the same direction, pressed together in a dreadful dance.

Petra was the first to recover. "Hello, Mrs. Sharpe," she said. "We're here," she added . . . and then wished she hadn't.

Mrs. Sharpe's voice rose from a small red velvet sofa in the corner.

"That is evident. I should have known you three would arrive in style."

The old bag sure knows how to make a bunch of kids feel at home, Tommy thought to himself.

Immediately Ms. Hussey cleared her throat with a businesslike *chuh-chuh-chuh-hum* and introduced the other two kids in the room.

Tommy couldn't help but stare at this kid Zoomy. He was like someone from another planet. First of all, he was super small — sitting down, his feet didn't even touch the floor. He had glasses that were so thick they looked like a part of a Halloween costume. When Zoomy was introduced, he began tapping his chin and didn't stop. Everyone got silent for a moment, watching.

Ms. Hussey reached across the coffee table and touched Zoomy's arm. "Got something to write on?" she asked.

Zoomy nodded, stopped tapping, and pulled a small notebook and a purple pen out of his pocket. Leaning close to his knee, he wrote several words.

Maybe he's weird like Einstein, Tommy thought.

Next came Early, the girl. The first thing Tommy noticed was how tidy she was. A thick black braid clung to the back of her head like a giant caterpillar. Her jeans had a crease down the front and her sweatshirt looked as if it had been folded five minutes ago. And what was that lilac smell? Couldn't be Mrs. Sharpe, who only smelled like grown-up perfume, and it wasn't the other four — Ms. Hussey always smelled like vanilla, that spoonful just before it went into making French toast.

Next Tommy noticed that Early looked ready to run. She was sitting as straight as Calder's N pentomino, back and shins parallel, eyes darting around as if she'd landed in a crowded fishbowl. Suddenly, in a flash, Tommy realized that it would be nice if he and Calder and Petra helped the other two feel comfortable. Plus, if he made the first gesture, maybe this new girl would like him. After all, it was dark in Mrs. Sharpe's living room and his Krakatoa might be less visible. He wished he'd washed his hair that morning. Reaching quickly for a plate of cookies on the table, he passed them to Early.

"Stop, boy!" Mrs. Sharpe's voice cut like a knife. Tommy froze and three of the cookies kept going, landing with a plop in Early's lap.

Tommy heard her suck in her breath, surprised.

Ms. Hussey laughed, somehow making it all better, and bustled around, straightening Mrs. Sharpe's blanket and passing paper napkins to the kids. The napkins each had a fancy crest on them — two lions standing up on either side of a red-and-black shield with a crown on the top and three silver *X*s running down the center. Long words in some other language decorated a scroll beneath the shield.

Petra reached an open hand toward Early, who gratefully gave her two of the cookies and a cautious smile. Tommy wanted to kick himself. *Oh, well*, he thought. *Since when have my plans for girls worked out?* He slumped back into his seat. Petra passed the third cookie to Calder.

"They'll be careful," Ms. Hussey assured her old friend as she passed around heavy glasses of lemonade. "Now. Should we cut to the chase? I'm sure these kids are wondering why on earth we've called them all here this afternoon."

Ms. Hussey, Tommy noted, was the only person he'd ever met who could be normal with Mrs. Sharpe.

All eyes were on the old woman, who closed hers for a moment as if to gather strength. "I have called you here because you are all rather extraordinary. Mentally," she added, with a hawk-like glimmer. She paused, as if to let that sink in. "Each of you has done some detective work that the adults around you were incapable of doing. Three of you have already worked together. My hope is that the five of you will be able to rise to even greater heights." She paused for a shaky sip. Ms. Hussey reached to help her with the glass, and didn't seem to mind when Mrs. Sharpe forgot to say thank you.

The old woman continued, her voice quavering. "I had

hoped that within the past week you five would have begun an investigation on your own. That you'd have asked for my help. But perhaps, at this stage, you've been too busy trying *not* to be what you are and *disguising* things as opposed to revealing them. It's a pity that children mature in such predictable ways."

Tommy had thought Mrs. Sharpe was going to call them *disgusting* when he'd heard that *disg*. She'd said the word slowly, like she'd wanted them to think that. Tommy popped upright and glanced at Petra, who also looked shocked and embarrassed. *No pleasing some people,* Tommy thought to himself. He felt sorry for Zoomy and Early, who'd never met Mrs. Sharpe before. If he were in their seats, he'd be scouting out the nearest exit.

Tommy tried to peer at Early out of the corner of his eye. Was she even breathing?

Mrs. Sharpe cleared her throat. "One of the thirteen pieces stolen from the Farmer is irreplaceable." She paused. The room was now silent. She cupped her hands together, as if in prayer, then anchored them in the saggy web beneath her chin. Stones sparkled from between swollen knuckles and veins.

Her skin is worse than ours, Tommy thought, and he wondered if any of the others had noticed the same thing.

"I speak of an extraordinary work of art, and there's no need to say which one. Quite truthfully, this crime has destroyed me, in part because I feel responsible, as one of the trustees of the museum. As trustees, we are the people in charge of the institution and its future. But for the past year, we have been dillydallying around and arguing about whether the place could be restored or whether the collection should go to Washington! Those of us who were in charge should . . . should . . ." Mrs. Sharpe's cheeks were flushed, and she now stabbed the back of the couch with a closed fist, as if holding a dagger. Even Ms. Hussey jumped.

"This is a crime so *heinous* that it must be resolved, and quickly." The old woman closed her eyes. "There's no excuse for endangering this collection the way we did. The thirteen missing pieces belong to each one of us in this room and to — to — the future of humanity. To millions of people all over the world. And to the wonderful spirit who collected and displayed them for the public —" Mrs. Sharpe broke off, ran her tongue around her lips, and patted them with her napkin.

She's not a normal old person, Tommy thought to himself. *She's more like a bloodthirsty dog that would give anything to bite down on a plump squirrel.*

Mrs. Sharpe was speaking again. "Suffice it to say that I am horrified by the loss of every item that was taken that night. Three are by the incomparable Dutch master Rembrandt, and he is considered to be one of the greatest artists of all time. I confess, however, that the one painting I referred to earlier, *The Concert*, has haunted my dreams since the moment it was stolen. You all know it, of course."

"Not me," interrupted Zoomy, staring up at the wall over Mrs. Sharpe's head. "But I know you mean the Vemmer painting."

"That's Ver-*meer*, emphasis on the second syllable," Ms. Hussey said quickly, not giving Mrs. Sharpe a chance to respond.

Calder, Petra, and Tommy all grinned, and Tommy leaned toward Zoomy and whispered, "I like *Vemmer* better." Ms. Hussey frowned at him.

Zoomy nodded and Tommy thought he caught the tiniest smile on Early's face. *Score*, he thought happily.

"To tell you the truth," Mrs. Sharpe went on, raising her voice, "I have my suspicions about who took the art but truly don't *care* to know who the thieves were or are. It's the thirteen objects — every single one — that I want. If all are returned safely, I shall die in peace."

There was no response. Somehow, it wasn't possible to tell Mrs. Sharpe that she shouldn't think about dying — she'd probably think it was rude. Calder dug one hand into his pocket, making a sudden clacking sound.

"Thirteen and seventeen, the art and the date of the robbery. Both prime numbers," he blurted. "And so is five. One of a kinds, if you know what I mean."

"Mmm, well put, boy." The old woman's face creased into a shape that was almost friendly. "Oddly fitting. A prime crime." She paused for a moment, as if waiting for someone to comment. No one did. "Not possible to divide by multiples," the old woman finished curtly.

"Fewer red herrings." Ms. Hussey nodded, and Mrs. Sharpe lifted her chin, as if to say, *Exactly.*

Their old teacher cleared her throat. Reaching for her computer, she gave the group a slideshow glimpse of the thirteen pieces, from the interactive FBI website. She passed the screen extra close to Zoomy.

First, the delicate, dreamy Vermeer . . . next, a ship filled with panicky faces . . . portraits of well-dressed people . . . a friendly self-portrait by Rembrandt . . . a scene of the country with a tall, skinny tower and a bridge . . . sketches of horses and dancers and musical instruments . . . a man writing at a table . . . then two objects, one a brass eagle from the top of a flagpole, the other a heavy-looking drinking cup.

The kids had seen some of the pictures in the news, but not all of them. Calder, Petra, and Tommy whispered comments to one another, partly because Zoomy and Early were listening.

"Jeez, how did they handle so *much*? I hope they didn't put that eagle in a bag with the Vermeer!" Petra said.

"Or the cup in with the big landscape!" Tommy added. "That'd be a bad move!"

"Whoa, nasty storm: nightmare waves, even for a surfer dude. Those guys are saying, 'Lemme outa here!'" Calder observed.

Mrs. Sharpe raised her hand for quiet. "Don't assume everyone old is hard of hearing. Some of us are robins who never miss a worm. Let us hope that the five of you can stop trying to impress each other long enough to get to work." Mrs. Sharpe dropped the last three words as if they were tissues she'd just used for blowing her nose.

Instantly the room was quieter than silent.

Wasn't she *just trying to impress* us? Tommy wondered. He didn't like adults who were nice one moment and nasty the next — or were unjust. After all, Zoomy and Early hadn't said a thing.

Mrs. Sharpe now looked around at the group, who squirmed on their chairs. She sighed. "I wouldn't ask you five to engage in this investigation if I didn't believe that you will make an extraordinary, *unexpected*, and *understated* team. A team that no one will notice."

Forgetting his Krakatoa, Tommy lifted his glass the tiniest bit in Calder's direction, like an adult doing a toast after a speech. After all, how could no one notice them if they'd been invited by a rich grown-up to do something cool? It was a joke.

At that moment, Tommy's lemonade slipped from his grip and descended in slow motion, the glass bouncing on the thick carpet beneath.

"Scaz!" he gasped.

CHAPTER FOUR **CHAOS AND MURDER**

⬚⬚⬚ Everything happened very quickly after that. Ms. Hussey dropped her laptop on the sofa and hurried into the kitchen to get a towel. Mrs. Sharpe tried to sit up straight but began to tip off her seat, and Petra reached to help just as her hair clip popped from her head and shot beneath the coffee table. Zoomy chin-tapped, and Calder cracked heads with Early as both reached to grope around for Petra's missile. Ms. Hussey, kneeling to sop up the sugary mess, yelped in pain as her knee connected with the metal clip.

An odd creaking sound came from the sofa. Was Mrs. Sharpe laughing?

"That's it," she wheezed. "Spilling and purposeful chaos! Children! A natural asset in any sting." She paused. "Infallible timing," she added under her breath, her voice suddenly distant. She closed her eyes and leaned back against a cushion.

Tommy had no idea what she was talking about but felt a tiny bit better. The word *infallible* sounded important. But wasn't a sting some kind of criminal setup?

He remembered a great film called *The Sting* that he'd watched once with his mom. One bunch of gangsters had tricked another, and in such a way that the audience was also fooled until the very end. Well, Mrs. Sharpe probably never watched movies and didn't know what she was saying. Maybe she was thinking of bees. Hyde Park was full of them in the summer. Chaos would certainly distract you if you got a nasty sting.

He then realized that Zoomy's notebook had slipped out of sight in the excitement and that he was chin-tapping again. Tommy leaned toward the smaller boy, retrieved the notebook, and said, "I just made a horrible mess with my lemonade. And we all got clumsy and smashed into each other."

Zoomy nodded and said, "Sometimes I get jittery-splat when I'm nervous." He paused to write for a moment in his notebook before adding, "And I'm great at falling down."

Jittery-splat? Tommy wondered. He glanced at Zoomy's notebook and saw that he'd written, *-big farming theft.*

It was then that Ms. Hussey took Mrs. Sharpe upstairs to rest. She returned moments later.

"Exciting, huh?" She looked around at the kids. "Think you can tackle this?"

Four of the five glanced at one another. Zoomy held his notebook with both hands and looked straight ahead. Early said quietly, "Is this for real? Does she really want our help?"

"Absolutely," Ms. Hussey said. "She realizes that kids your age can be problem solvers who are far more observant — and less likely to be watched — than the adults around them. Plus, as every kid knows, you guys are often misjudged or underestimated. This can be an advantage. Sometimes it's best to be overlooked, you know? Not only does she want your help, I believe she's *counting* on you."

"I'm in," Petra said. The others nodded while Zoomy raised his notebook and tapped himself lightly on the head with it.

"Bonk," Tommy whispered, and Zoomy grinned.

Ms. Hussey stood quietly in front of the group, tightened her ponytail, and lowered her voice to its listen-carefully-or-you'll-miss-it level.

"This is truly a compliment, Mrs. Sharpe wanting you five to work with her on this robbery. This matters more to her than I can tell you.

"Zoomy and Early, you may not know this, but Mrs. Sharpe's husband was a Vermeer scholar, and he was murdered many years ago. In Amsterdam. Shot in the back on the steps of a big museum. He'd told her the morning before his return flight that he'd uncovered something huge, but that he couldn't yet share it. And then, *poof!* Tragically, he was gone.

"Mrs. Sharpe has tried unsuccessfully to solve that crime. The police wrote it off as a random act of street violence. She never believed that, having heard the edge of excitement and nervousness in her husband's voice. Obviously he hadn't felt it was safe to share this news over the telephone.

"Mrs. Sharpe has replayed this moment a million times in her mind, and devoted much of the rest of her life to trying to retrace his last steps and uncover whatever her husband had found. This has meant learning a great deal about Vermeer's work and following the controversies that surround it. Perhaps he discovered new information on the artist's life, or a lead on a long-lost painting — she made it her business to learn so much about Vermeer's work that she's even become known in the US as something of an unofficial Vermeer expert. I know she thinks that she could have done more when her husband hinted that he'd made a discovery; that she could, somehow, have pressed him to share his secret and in doing so saved his life.

"In the thirteen years since her husband was murdered, Vermeer's mysterious legacy has remained her primary focus. She and Leland always adored *The Concert*, an absolute gem painted at the height of Vermeer's powers, and felt more than lucky to be living near it. As a trustee of the Farmer Museum, Mrs. Sharpe told me that she's stopped after each and every board meeting to visit the painting before heading home: for herself, for her husband, for their mutual love of that great work of art. And now this! It's the heartbreak of a lifetime.

"Here," Ms. Hussey said, tapping her computer screen and passing the painting around again. "Somehow, Vermeer is always with you once you know his work."

The five kids leaned in, studying the painting. Two women, one playing the harpsichord and the other singing, flanked a man who sat with his back to the viewer. The women were serene and absorbed in the moment, their pearls and hair ribbons shining in the light, their outfits an elegant mix of yellow, pebble-gray, and cream. The man between them looked oddly out of place and somehow disturbing.

Was it his powerful shoulders or the red, flag-like square on the back of his chair? The image was awash in peace and the flow of music, despite the figure without a face — as if Vermeer had wanted to challenge the viewer and say, "All is right with the world here . . . or isn't it?"

Petra sat back. "Funny, the picture pulls you in, but it also makes you hesitate, like you might not be welcome. And it makes me miss the lady in *A Lady Writing*. In fact, I think it's her playing the harpsichord, don't you, Calder?"

Calder nodded, and Tommy felt left out. Calder and Petra had found the stolen Vermeer painting she mentioned and had returned it to the world. They had actually held it. Tommy hadn't been in Chicago at the time, which still felt unfair. He looked down and picked at a hangnail.

"Think those three grown-ups are having a good time?" Zoomy asked suddenly.

"I think the women are," Early said. "And the man's a mystery."

Ms. Hussey nodded and sighed. "A mystery is right. This whole thing is a horrible mystery. I believe Mrs. Sharpe would happily — no, joyfully! — give her life if this painting could be returned tomorrow."

Tommy shifted in his seat. *Hard to imagine the old lady doing anything joyfully*, he thought to himself. *Much less having a husband.* He practically gagged at the thought of Mrs. Sharpe being involved in any romantic activity, then tried to get the thought out of his head by examining his sneakers.

"Don't you think, Tommy?" Ms. Hussey finished, and Tommy could feel himself blushing.

"Huh?" he asked.

She sighed. "I'm not trying to put you on the spot. I'm just reminding you guys to pay attention to the right stuff whenever you're in the same place at the same time. In teamwork of this kind, all progress can depend on it. Mrs. Sharpe is giving you each an information packet, just to get you started. You'll find one of the short histories of the museum and a color printout of what I showed you on the FBI website, meaning a photograph of each stolen item. Thirteen pages. Soak up these images. Look at them before you go to sleep. Look at them when you wake up. Live with them. See if they speak to you."

Ms. Hussey sat back and beamed. "You five, I'll bet, are the first kids to tackle this. Good luck! And, Early and Zoomy: Welcome to Hyde Park and to this awesome team. Don't be afraid of Mrs. Sharpe. She can sound a bit frightening, but she's really a pussycat."

This last was followed by a faint meow. Ms. Hussey smiled and murmured, "Well, hello! The neighborhood is full of cats. They're everywhere in Hyde Park."

Yeah, and not pussycats like these two, Tommy thought to himself, glancing at the snarling lions on his chair.

▯ ▯ ▯ The five left the house ten minutes later, each with a large, sealed envelope in hand. A plan had been made to get together on Saturday, the first day of their weeklong spring break. Ms. Hussey had asked them to meet her on the street outside the Farmer Museum. Mrs. Sharpe would, by then, have gotten permission for the kids to visit the crime scene. The old lady and the other trustees were meeting there at the same time, which seemed less than great. Tommy wondered if there was anyone in Chicago who *didn't* do what Mrs. Sharpe asked.

Early lived and went to school in neighboring Woodlawn, which was a short walk from Mrs. Sharpe's house. Zoomy lived with his grandparents in a small town in southern Michigan, Three Oaks, and his grandma had brought him to the meeting today. Mrs. Sharpe had invited them both to stay in a bed and breakfast down the street when they returned on Saturday.

Gam, as Zoomy called her, had shown up at the door just as the kids were getting ready to leave.

"It's great to have you on our team," Tommy found himself saying to Zoomy, maybe because his grandmother was standing right there, but maybe for some other reason. Tommy raised his arm for a fist bump. Zoomy was confused for a second, then bumped him back.

Tommy, Petra, Calder, and Early watched with interest as Gam and Zoomy headed toward an ancient pickup truck. Gam was cozy, relaxed, and had comfortable eyes. Zoomy, they realized, could see a short distance around him, but not far at all. They could hear Gam's voice saying, "Curb coming up, now straight ahead . . ." as they walked side by side.

The scene in Mrs. Sharpe's living room suddenly seemed unreal.

"Is — well, not to be rude, but is Mrs. Sharpe kind of crazy?" Early asked. "And is she on the right side of the law? She said something about a 'sting.' I can't get dragged into anything bad — my family's had enough trouble."

"Yeah, I noticed that word, too," Tommy said quickly. "She's an old wreck, probably thinking about bees and the *bzzzzt* shock of a sting, you know?"

"Huh," Early said.

"I think she likes to sound romanti — I mean, *dramatic*," Tommy added. "One of those 'atics."

"How about *fanatic*?" Calder said.

"Yeah," Petra agreed. "She's kind of obsessed, but not in a bad way. If Ms. Hussey trusts her completely on this, I'm sure we can, too. And Mrs. Sharpe *is* truly a Vermeer fanatic. The world only has thirtysome of his paintings, and this is the only one that's missing. Mrs. Sharpe understands that Vermeer's work is not only irreplaceable but also kind of alive, and I love that about her. Those people in his paintings *breathe*. Calder and I rescued *A Lady Writing* a few years ago, and I still feel like the woman in that painting says things to me sometimes. Like a dream, but not."

Early nodded. "I hear you. When I was hunting for my dad last year, some of Langston Hughes's poetry popped into my head at tough moments, as if someone was whispering clues to me. Like Langston came alive and helped me out."

Petra looked at Early with new interest. "Yeah, art can be weird that way — it can step right into your life. Mrs. Sharpe knows that, too. She scares me sometimes, but underneath it all she's —"

"Thirsty for blood," Tommy said quickly, adding, "Nawww, just kidding," when everyone laughed.

"Huh," Early said. "I think I've met people like that. Life made them prickly and then they try to frighten everyone. But that's not the whole picture."

"Exactly." Petra nodded. "And Mrs. Sharpe has some powerful reasons. Her husband's murder and all."

"Well," Early said, zipping her jacket under her chin and stamping her feet. "It's getting late. And cold. Gotta get going." She glanced around as if half ready for something dangerous. "See you guys."

She turned south as Calder and Petra headed east to their street and Tommy west to his apartment.

"Hey!" Calder called out over his shoulder. "Zoomy went north, which means we're covering all four directions."

"Good sign!" Early and Petra called back at the same moment.

Tommy chuckled loudly and waved one hand as if to say, *I already noticed the directions stuff.*

It had been a while, but he knew he'd get back in the game.

CHAPTER FIVE   A PILEUP OF PRIMES

❐❑❐ Tommy and his mom lived with Goldman, who had been part of the family for many years. Goldman just got wiser and more orange with time, and Tommy loved giving him surprises to investigate.

Sprinkling a pinch of fish food into his bowl, Tommy peered in just as Goldman did a quick whish around the territory.

"Nothing much today, old buddy," Tommy said. "Nothing new but us trying to solve the hugest art crime in US history. Gotta figure this one out. And it's all tied into the nutcase down the street." A shiver ran down his back, as if he shouldn't have said that. "The old lady," he muttered. "You know, Mrs. Sharpe. And she wants us three to work with two other kids, although I bet I'm the only really good finder."

Goldman swiveled one eye in Tommy's direction and flipped his tail. He opened his mouth, sucking in some food. He spun around, fixing Tommy with the other eye.

"What?" Tommy asked.

Goldman dove for the bottom and then shot straight up to the top, scattering gravel. "Okay, I admit it doesn't look all bad." Tommy described Zoomy and Early. "But five is a weird number."

The fish shrugged his fins and swirled behind a large

china dragon. "Something to do, you're right." Tommy watched Goldman looking carefully at the dragon's spikes. He seemed to be counting them.

"Why was *spilling* good, though? What was Mrs. Sharpe talking about?"

At the word *spilling*, Goldman shot madly around the bowl. "Oops," Tommy said quickly, remembering the terrible day a couple of years ago when Goldman's world got smashed in a break-in and he spent some time on the floor.

He placed one knuckle against the glass and Goldman came over and bumped it with his nose. Tommy then opened the envelope Ms. Hussey had given him and held each picture up to Goldman's bowl.

"Take your time, man," he said. "Check this out." Goldman was calm about each image except the Rembrandt storm at sea. At first sight, his eyes got even bigger and he darted behind some weeds at the back of his bowl. He stayed there for some time, the greens quivering.

Tommy apologized. "I'll never show you that one again. Sorry, old buddy."

Goldman returned when Tommy showed him the Flinck landscape. It had lots of peaceful trees that looked almost like seaweed. By the time Tommy turned on the family computer and typed in *Farmer Hiest*, Goldman was following with one eye.

The browser corrected Tommy's spelling, and he began to read. His mouth fell open — experts were speculating that the stolen art was worth well over *500 million* dollars.

"Man," Tommy muttered.

The hugeness of this adventure was beginning to sink in.

◻◻◻ On his way back to Michigan, Zoomy talked to his best friend, Lorrol, on the family cell phone. She had moved to Boston a few months earlier, but they still called each other a lot. He told her about the meeting and described the theft as happening in some kind of garden place in Chicago, not far from Hyde Park.

"Dang, Zoomy!" she shouted, so loud that his grandma could hear over the roar of the truck. "That's the Sarah Chase Farmer Museum! And that's the most tragic and awful art theft in the world! You are so lucky!" Lorrol said that every kid in Boston knew about the Farmer heist.

Zoomy's eyes were blank, but he smiled happily at the windshield. It was hard to imagine either the museum or the coming investigation with the other kids, but the fist bump — something Lorrol had taught him — with the boy named Tommy! Now, *that* was a first.

◻◻◻ Early Pearl's home was a ten-minute walk south from Hyde Park. She lived in a small apartment with her mom, dad, and little brother. Her dad was going to school to be a librarian while working at the huge public library downtown.

Her mom helped in the cafeteria in her school and her brother was in first grade. They had lived in that building all her life except for a few terrible months a couple of years ago when lots of bad stuff had happened, her dad had disappeared, and they'd had to leave their home. She didn't like to think about it.

Her mom and dad had checked out Mrs. Sharpe's invitation to visit. Thinking it might be exciting for Early to meet some other detectives and make a friend or two in Hyde Park, they helped her plan a safe walking route from home to Mrs. Sharpe's house. Ever since her family's terrible adventure, she'd had fears she couldn't shake, and didn't seem to have as many friends at school.

On the way home that afternoon, Early noticed an unfamiliar man in a black leather jacket sitting on a bench in the Midway, an open area with grass and trees between the neighborhoods of Hyde Park and Woodlawn. Cell phone in hand, he glanced up casually as she scurried by.

That evening, Early looked up the words *heinous* and *infallible*, and entered them in the family Word Book. The Pearls collected words the way other people collected coffee mugs or T-shirts. Next came *sting*. Webster's gave many meanings, all having to do with a sharp, quick pain. You could be stung by insects or stung by words. The final definition was "an elaborate confidence game," especially one "worked by undercover police in order to catch criminals." Early felt a sudden jolt of panic and had to remind herself that for most people, setting up a sting simply meant playing a trick on someone in order to win something.

Not wanting to worry her parents, she decided to stay away from *sting* and didn't write it down. But why would Mrs. Sharpe use this word?

Of course, the Farmer heist was giving those who loved this art the sting of a lifetime . . .

🔲🔲🔲 Walking north on the Harper Avenue block where both Calder and Petra lived, the two friends were quiet. Petra thought about Early and Zoomy, and what a strange group the five of them made. Calder thought about his pentominoes. When he stirred them around in his pocket, he sometimes came up with an unexpected answer to a problem. Just now, the Z and C had popped into his hand together. He pulled them out, palm up.

"Huh. Z for *Zoomy*?" Petra asked.

"Maybe this is Z minus C, the twenty-sixth letter minus the third, which equals twenty-three. Another prime, but why?"

"You are a fabulous weirdo, Calder," Petra said, and high-fived her friend. Calder was now a foot taller than Petra, which meant she held her hand up at shoulder level. She got a whiff of sweaty pits when they smacked palms. Someone should tell Calder about deodorant.

Her stomach growled. "See you, Calder," she muttered as

she hurried up her steps, hoping her mom had made macaroni and cheese for dinner.

"Later," he said, the pentominoes back in his pocket. Walking away, he pulled out the T.

T for *trap* . . . but why not T for *theft*? He looked up and down his street.

⧫ ☐ ☐ Calder phoned Petra that night, after checking in with Tommy.

"It adds up in several ways," he said, without even saying hello.

"What are you talking about, Calder?" Petra asked, over a bloodcurdling scream. "Cut it out!" she shouted. "Oops, sorry to yell in your ear."

Calder didn't seem to have noticed. "The twenty-third letter in the alphabet is *W*. That's what I got when I subtracted the Z pentomino from the C, remember? But the C could also be a U, which has a value of twenty-one. If you subtract twenty-one from twenty-six instead, you get five. That'd be us kids. If you spin the W upside down, it could be an M, the thirteenth letter — and possibly a thirteenth pentomino, like the thirteen things that were stolen. It's as if the primes that keep appearing fit the crime: three, five, thirteen . . ."

"Hey, that's Mrs. Sharpe's rhyme." Petra clicked her fingers. "A prime crime, just in time."

"Then there's W for *watch* and M for *murder*," Calder went on. "Plus T for *trap*. Came out of my pocket after you left. Maybe Early had a point. We should be extra careful. I'll let Tommy know," he added, and hung up the phone.

The three were so used to one another that they didn't have to explain much. Petra realized that might change with Zoomy and Early on the team.

Tommy whispered the words to Goldman that night: *Watch. Murder. Trap.* His buddy froze for a moment in the center of his bowl, then dipped and spun neatly in place, as if giving a careful message about the clues.

☐ ☐ ☐ That night in the neighborhoods of Hyde Park and nearby Kenwood, thirteen people lay awake. Five were kids, all around thirteen years old.

One of the adults puzzled over the pileup of primes — numbers that couldn't be divided by anything but themselves and one. There was the age of the kids, their number, the one younger adult, the number of stolen items and then the number of adults responsible for the Farmer Museum: 13, 5, 1, 13, 7. The numbers drifted and bumped in the dark.

Down the street, another grown-up worried that this investigation could go very, very wrong.

Of the six remaining adults, only an old man watched the moon rise between dark, leafless trees. He pulled the covers up to his ears. There was a face on the moon tonight and it looked worried. As if it were watching him. No, reproaching him.

Hey diddle diddle, the cat and the fiddle, the cow jumped over the moon. Funny how soothing those old nursery rhymes could be.

He'd been rash and careless about much in his life, and might do things differently if given a second chance. He hoped the blackbirds would behave; they'd be fools to do anything else. *When the pie was opened, the birds began to sing.*

Just at that moment of worry, he felt a burning pain race through the left side of his body. *Help! Oh, help me!* He felt himself spinning backward in time, to the day he'd fallen into a hornet's nest as a child.

About the bush, Willie,
About the beehive,
About the bush, Willie,
I'll meet thee alive.

Groping for the bedside light, his hand fell short. He was alone in the house and suddenly filled with a deadly clarity.

He'd been stupid. Stupid, stupid, stupid! His last thought, before blanking out, was an apology.

So sorry . . . you trusted me . . .

□ □ □ Tommy's mom opened her newspaper the next morning and gasped. She spun the laptop sideways so Tommy could see. Cold cereal bulging in both cheeks, he read: *William Swift Chase, Director of Farmer Museum, Rushed to Hospital.*

"Jeez," he said, a glob of wet Cheerios landing on the table. "The old lady didn't tell us anything about the other trustees. Can you read it, Mom?"

Goldman swam closer and Tommy stopped chewing so as to hear.

"The man who is both the director and head of the board of trustees of the Sarah Chase Farmer Museum is now in intensive care, having suffered a stroke. Mr. Chase is the great-nephew of Mrs. Farmer . . . ya-de-ya, one of the other six trustees, Carolyn Crunch, states this has been a 'desperately upsetting' week. None of the others were available for comment."

Tommy's mom shook her head. "Such a terrible thing to happen, I still can't believe it . . . and I'm so glad you five are going to jump in. They need you. Hey, listen to these names, Tommy — they're marvelous. The trustees are Mr. Chase, Ms. Crunch, Mr. Hershel F. Hurts, Mr. Monument Cracken, Ms. Winnifred Whacker, Mr. Hurley Stabbler, and then your Mrs. Sharpe. What a lineup." His mother smiled. "And they all live in this area, either in Hyde Park or near the Farmer Museum, in Kenwood. You'd better believe they all have money and connections. Trustees almost always do."

"I'm not sure I get why they're all fighting — to move or not move the museum, that stuff," Tommy said, swallowing. "I mean, I was doing research after our meeting yesterday but . . ." He shrugged.

His mom looked at him over her glasses. "Serves you right for not reading every word," she said, reaching across the table to ruffle his hair. He pulled back, leaving her hand hanging.

"Just tell me," Tommy pleaded.

"Well, you know the building's in bad shape. Leaks, a ton of repairs needed. Plus, it's hard to get to, there's hardly any parking, and it's now only open a couple of days a week. The National Gallery of Art, in Washington, wants the collection and has offered to build a new wing. They'd make it a replica of the current Chicago building and name it after Sarah Chase Farmer. Yup, Mrs. Farmer's collection is incredible — or was, horrible to have to say this, before the theft. The seven trustees have apparently been fighting like cats and dogs about whether or not to move. This has gone on for ages now, ever since the National Gallery made its offer. And then everyone's nightmare: a robbery."

Tommy nodded and looked over at his fish, who was whooshing one way and then the other, stirring up the gravel in his bowl. The break-in last year in their apartment sure had been traumatic, and he'd almost lost Goldman.

"Yeah," Tommy murmured. "And what'll happen if the old man dies?"

"The six remaining trustees will have to come to a decision, clearly. But meanwhile, you kids will be hard at work. I think it's great that Mrs. Sharpe reached out to you. It's nice for you to have something to do over spring break."

Tommy bristled. "What, you think she called us in just to be nice? She's *never* nice. She meant it when she told us we could help."

Tommy's mom was reading again and didn't seem to notice his tone.

"I'm sure you guys will make an extraordinary team," she said absently.

Tommy looked at Goldman and rolled his eyes. *Wasn't that what Mrs. Sharpe had said? Not so easy to be extraordinary when you look like us. I mean, Early doesn't have zit issues or anything, but she has being-afraid issues. Anyone can see that.* His goldfish now swam slowly toward the surface, pausing to roll his eyes in turn.

Goldman always got it.

▯ ▯ ▯ Before school that morning, Tommy phoned Calder, who phoned Petra, who phoned Early. Then Tommy called Zoomy. There was something about that kid that he already knew he liked.

Everyone was sorry for Mr. Chase, and could imagine how doubly rotten he must have felt all this past week. First this robbery of his world-class family collection, then the unfriendly roar in the news — everyone in the world, it seemed, was now pointing fingers at the trustees. After all, was there any excuse for keeping priceless art in a run-down mansion? Was there any excuse for only having one night guard, someone both past retirement age and worn out from his St. Patrick's Day partying? *Irresponsible* and *careless* were some of the words being used by the press to describe the management of the place. And then it came out that Mr. Chase had chosen the trustees himself, as his great-aunt's relative, and had allowed the guard, a retired family chauffeur, to stay on at the museum. He was at fault all over again.

"Scaz, the old man must feel like what I stepped on the other day," Tommy remarked to Calder.

"If he even knows," Calder said. "My dad says a stroke is serious stuff."

Tommy happened to walk by Ms. Hussey's classroom at the end of the day and stuck his head in the door to say hello.

"Hey!" Ms. Hussey called. "Come here a sec, Tommy." She plunked down the armload of notebooks she was carrying and sat on a desk. Her hair was in a loose braid, a bedraggled crimson ribbon clinging to the end of it.

"Oof! I'm tired." Ms. Hussey sighed. "What a week it's

been. Just knowing that that heavenly Vermeer is in the wrong hands. It's sickening."

Tommy nodded. "Yup. I've been thinking about when Calder and Petra rescued *A Lady Writing*, and how she's now safely back on the wall at the National Gallery. Too bad the people in Vermeer's art can't talk to each other, and that the Lady in the painting can't ask some questions and then tell us where the people in *The Concert* are hidden, you know?" These were actually Petra's thoughts, but Tommy thought he'd borrow them.

"Well put, Tommy." Ms. Hussey's voice was grim. "I got a call from Mrs. Sharpe just a few minutes ago. She shared some information with me, all pretty shocking. It's funny how you think you know someone, but you actually never know all the pieces of their past." Ms. Hussey paused and glanced at her old student. "I guess it's okay to share some of this with you," she said, swinging her legs.

Tommy sucked in his cheeks and blinked several times.

Ms. Hussey continued. "Mrs. Sharpe is an old, old friend of William Swift Chase. She and he were on opposite sides of the fence about what to do with the museum. He had wanted everything to stay right where it was, in the neighborhood his great-aunt, Mrs. Farmer, loved so much. He was in favor of accepting advisory help from some of the big museums who offered it — the Art Institute, which of course is right here; the Metropolitan, in New York City;

the Getty, in Los Angeles — and then hiring professionals to organize a massive fund-raising campaign. So much is needed. They have to repair and tastefully modernize the building, plus buy a neighboring piece of land for surface and underground parking. We're talking about many millions of dollars in improvements and even after all that, Kenwood isn't a neighborhood that's easy to reach by public transportation. Mrs. Sharpe, much as she loves Chicago, felt it was time to accept the National Gallery's offer and know that the art was forever protected and accessible to the world."

"So were they friends or enemies?" Tommy asked. It really wasn't clear to him how you could be both.

"They were friends who disagreed about something important," Ms. Hussey answered, "which is never an easy thing. Mrs. Sharpe went to visit Mr. Chase in the hospital today. His speech is very bad right now. She asked him if he had any ideas about the theft. He became visibly upset and frustrated, and kept saying, 'F— F—' but couldn't seem to get the rest of the word out."

"Huh!" Tommy said, imagining the worst.

"Mrs. Sharpe, being the resourceful soul that she is, grabbed a pen and paper and gave it to him, but he was unable to write. Then she wrote out the alphabet, and asked him to point to the next letter. He did. It was *A*. Then he said something garbled and closed his eyes, too tired to continue. He was instantly asleep, and Mrs. Sharpe, sitting by his side, said he still looked disturbed. Troubled even when unconscious, as if whatever he'd needed to say was urgent."

"Awful," Tommy agreed, in what he hoped was an adult tone.

"So we all need to think about *F* followed by *A* and what that could mean. A word? Someone's initials? Something relevant to the stolen art or the Farmer Museum, which of course begins with *Fa*? Mrs. Sharpe didn't know, nor do I, but I'm thinking."

It occurred to Tommy that *F* followed by *A* could certainly spell something. Tommy tried it out in his mind, picturing a feeble old man in a hospital bed whispering a word that would make Mrs. Sharpe and the nurse both rock backward in embarrassment.

When his phone rang a moment later, he dove for it.

"Sure, Calder! Meet you outside," Tommy said after his friend had told him where he was. "See you in a few."

Ms. Hussey patted Tommy on the shoulder. "I want you to share this information with the others, as time is of the essence here. Do the grapevine thing by phone. And remember that prime numbers — like five — are only divisible by themselves and one."

She grinned reassuringly, but when Tommy left, he turned back to wave good-bye and saw his old teacher scowling as she straightened her desk. Her hair ribbon had fallen off entirely, and Ms. Hussey, who rarely had untidy hair, didn't seem to notice. She was muttering to herself.

Good grief, what next? Tommy thought as he stepped quietly down the hallway, not wanting his old teacher to know he'd lingered.

Who was Ms. Hussey mad at? And what *hadn't* she told him?

❑ ❑ ❑ "Even the best grown-ups can be weird," Tommy said as he and Calder trudged toward Harper Avenue. "Like Ms. Hussey just said, you think you know them and then you don't. She was definitely acting funny."

Calder nodded. "Sometimes my parents seem angry or unfriendly, and then I find out they're just worried."

"Yeah, exactly. So we have to tell the other three about the *F-A* business. I promised Ms. Hussey we would." Even though he and Calder and Petra went to the same school, by eighth grade they had schedules that sometimes kept them apart all day.

Calder pulled out his phone and hit Petra's number.

"Funny you called," she said immediately, without even a *hi* first. Familiar with the extreme decibel level in Petra's household, Calder held the phone away from his ear. "I'm about to meet Early at Powell's Books. She's walking over here with her little brother. She has him for the afternoon since her mom's still at work. *Hey, stop that! You can't have a chocolate milk fight in here! If you spill on Dad's computer, you'll be in trouble for the rest of your lives!*" Calder and Tommy then heard a muffled, "*NO, you* can't *come this time, we're having a* meeting."

"Seems like Petra hates being the babysitter," Tommy said, after Calder ended the call.

"Yeah, the other kids are even more of a handful, now

that they're big," his friend said. "I used to envy her having all that company, but not so much lately."

Tommy called Zoomy as they headed for Powell's. He was back home, and said he was studying the envelope of pictures and reading about the museum. Both could picture him working his way through the art, his nose inches from the page. He'd be back in Hyde Park the day after tomorrow.

"He sounded kind of sad that he's not here now," Tommy remarked to Calder as they pulled open the door to Powell's.

The store was a maze of narrow passageways between old, wooden bookshelves that reached to the ceiling. Ladders squeaked and leaned; footstools were dragged into corners for comfortable browsing or a subdued chat. Employees never glared at kids and left customers alone unless they asked for help. Aside from the rattle of old fans in the summer and the clank of radiators in the winter, the place was quiet — a treasure trove for those who liked hanging out with the printed word, which most people in Hyde Park did.

Both Tommy and Calder had delivered books for Powell's in the past, but neither were big visitors. Petra, on the other hand, was always stopping by on her way to get groceries for her parents. It was her home away from home. Sometimes she started a book there, left a hidden bookmark, and returned again and again until she'd finished it.

Stepping inside, Tommy and Calder heard Petra before they found her.

"Here's the book of Sarah Chase Farmer's ideas, Early," she was saying. "The one I found this morning. This has *much* more than the museum booklet Mrs. Sharpe gave us. You've gotta hear some of this."

Then they heard a shrill, "Earl-ee! Earl-EEE!" Rounding a corner, the boys found Petra next to Early and her little brother, who looked like he was about six. Jubie wasn't about to let the girls talk, at least not yet.

"Hi, guys." Petra nodded in their direction. "Almost ready here."

Scanning the shelves, Early crouched next to her brother. "We're looking for picture books. Just for you, Jubie. Exciting ones, so you can be busy while we're busy."

"Yeah, I want *crimes*. Gangstahs. Pow!" he roared.

"Shhhh . . ." Early said. "You know Dash and Sum don't like those books. How about books on digging machines?"

"Tough guys! Pow!" Jubie shouted.

Petra tried to help. "Hey, Jubie," she said. "My brothers like these books over here. There's a ton on people doing hard stuff, like climbing mountains, scuba diving, blasting dynamite holes in rock to build roads . . ."

"Boom!" Jubie appeared satisfied. "With weapons!"

Early sighed and shrugged. "This might not work," she said to the other three.

"Who are Dash and Sum?" Tommy asked.

"Our parents," Early said. "We say that instead of Dad and Mom. And hey, this is Jubie. Jubie, meet Calder and Tommy."

"*HI!*" shouted Jubie. "Our family writes *Dashsumearlyjubie* inside our *spesh-all* books," he said, bobbing his head like mad. "It's *looooong!* And I can write my full name superfast, Ju-bi-la-*TION!*"

"Great," Tommy said.

"Good for you," Calder added.

"He thinks he likes scary stuff more than he really does," Early said behind her hand.

"Gaangstahs! *Now*, Early! Not this construction book!" Jubie began to bounce.

Just then a man poked his head around from the Folklore section.

"I like tricky stories, too," he said to Jubie.

The man's face had sad lines but also a sparkly smile. Early noticed bluer-than-blue eyes and dark curls. He had a black leather jacket and a soft hat that looked familiar.

"I'll read you something," he offered. "How about, hmmm, oh look: *The Real Mother Goose*. Ever hear of that?"

Jubie shook his head violently. "That's for babies!"

"Wait!" the man said quickly. "It's really not. Ever thought about going to sea in a boat that's too small or getting stuck on a shelf because you can't spell? Running away from someone with a knife? Falling from a great height? Uh-oh, Humpty Dumpty looks terrified! I wouldn't want to be on that wall, either." The man was now on the floor, flipping through pages.

"Okay, let's get to the dangerous part," he said as Jubie leaned closer. "Now see, these guys look kind of like bad guys. And oh, boy, this kid is on his own! And the dogs are barking, which usually means trouble."

"Uh-oh," Jubie agreed. "But those guys *won't* break stuff or hurt the doggies." He popped one finger into his mouth.

"We'll find out," the man said.

Early watched them for a moment, hesitating, and then told Jubie she'd be over in the corner with her friends. Jubie nodded and the man looked up with a quick smile, as if to say, *We're fine.*

"Look, something bad's coming." The man now seemed as absorbed as Jubie. "Animals are smart. See, they're trying to get the right people to pay attention."

The four older kids sat on the floor in the Art Criticism section, where they could keep an eye on Jubie. "Okay, tell us Ms. Hussey's message first," Petra said. "Then I've got something pretty cool here." She waved a small red book in the air.

Tommy spilled what Ms. Hussey had said about Mr. Chase's friendship with Mrs. Sharpe, the Farmer Museum's choices, and the *F-A* puzzler.

"Yikes," Petra said. "Poor man, that's horrible. So frustrating."

"Could be the name of the museum," Calder suggested. "Or a person's initials."

"How about a publication like *Farmer's Almanac?*" Early said. "I've seen that in libraries. Or Flying Aces — they were fighter pilots in World War Two. Oh ... I don't know." Early broke off happily, just glad to be part of a group of kids her own age, kids who seemed to have had adventures that were as scary as hers and didn't mind sharing doubts or strange ideas.

Calder was scrolling on his phone. "*Functional Acknowledgement,*" he read. "Means an electronic acceptance."

"Whatever." Tommy glared at his friend. "It could be a place. I have an aunt in Fayetteville."

"There's Fayyūm, in Egypt," Petra added. "One of my grandmas lives near there."

"Or maybe it's part of a word. A not-polite one," Tommy said, looking around. "You know, old people get nutty sometimes ..."

Early said, "Maybe it was something personal that Mr. Chase needed to tell Mrs. Sharpe, especially since they were friends who'd had a squabble. I hope all the other trustees *do* show up tomorrow at the museum; it'll be good to see what they look like, now we know they've been fighting." She giggled. "Somehow, it's funny to picture old, rich folks whacking each other with canes."

In truth, the whole disagreement seemed silly to Early, who understood that having enough money made many problems go away. These were rich people fighting over rich things. There was something about Mrs. Sharpe, though —

Early understood her determination, and knew that having a mission was important to keep you going, especially when things were hard. Mrs. Sharpe might be wealthy, but there was also a part of her life that was sad.

Tommy sucked in his cheeks, picturing the trustees fencing. *I knew Early was awesome*, he thought to himself.

"How about the old folks have a pillow fight?" he suggested. "Then they'd just get feathers stuck in the wrinkles."

"Gross!" Early laughed. Tommy thought he'd never felt so happy.

"My dad said it's been gruesome at the Farmer for ages now." Petra's voice was serious, bringing them back to business. "Some of the trustees were interviewed in the news. Each one is convinced he or she knows what's best here, both for the city of Chicago and the art. My dad says they know what they're doing when they talk to reporters, and have tried to use publicity to pressure each other. Those folks each want what they want and — my dad says this is a biggie — they don't have all the time in the world. He says some old people don't care what anyone thinks, not anymore. And in this case, they're old people with lots of power over world-class art."

"But less power over it once the art is stolen," Early pointed out.

"You mean, they're all suspects," Calder said slowly.

Early frowned. "Not exactly. But I see what you mean: If you steal the art, that means someone else can't move it."

"Or else it gets very *easy* to move — only not in public," Petra pointed out. "Either side could have done it."

Calder scratched his head with the M pentomino. "My parents said old people with money can be very ruthless."

Tommy suddenly remembered Mrs. Sharpe hitting the sofa with her fist. *Ruthless . . .* he'd thought of that word, too.

"Like Mrs. Sharpe," Tommy blurted. "I can picture her stabbing someone, can't you?"

Petra elbowed him. "You're a freak, Tommy." For all Mrs. Sharpe's bark, Petra couldn't imagine her hurting anyone.

Early wasn't so sure. She definitely sensed that being on Mrs. Sharpe's bad side was a bad place to be. The old woman had been hunting her husband's murderer for years now, and without much help from the police — someone like that had to be both tough and tricky.

Calder stirred his pentominoes and now pulled another one from his pocket. "Perfect. M for *money* and F for *fight.* And Mr. Chase's *F.*"

"F for *freak,*" said Tommy, his words ending in a ghastly squeak.

"*Ferocious,*" Early added.

"And Mr. Chase is part of Mrs. Farmer's family," Petra mused. "He must feel extra bad. This little book, *The Truth About My Art,* is packed with ideas his great-aunt had about her art and her home. It sounds like she was an awesome person — I wish I'd met her! She's like a much less spiky Mrs. Sharpe."

Tommy tried to imagine what a less treacherous Mrs. Sharpe would be like.

He couldn't picture it.

"Listen to this." Petra opened the book. "Here's what Sarah Chase Farmer says about Vermeer's *The Concert*." She read the passage aloud:

"Three faces, two of which are unselfconscious and absorbed, making music in the light. One is forever hidden, but clearly a part of the trio. Because his face is hidden, the viewer returns to thoughts of him again and again. Without a face to decode, the viewer feels a touch of anxiety. Perhaps that is part of Vermeer's spell: He wants you to worry about what might be coming. He wants you to wonder, What if he turns?

"It's the story of life. We never see all that we know is there. Art keeps us wondering, and while we wonder, we're not alone."

Early looked sad. "That's haunting. I kind of know what that feels like," she said. "*What if he turns?*" Instinctively she looked over at Jubie and the man. Neither of them turned.

Calder thought of the thieves who'd stolen the paintings from the Farmer. They must have felt the same way about the sleeping guard. *What if he turns?*

Tommy wondered if the man with his back turned had some reason he didn't want to be seen. Maybe he had an adult-sized Krakatoa, and Vermeer didn't want to paint it.

Petra was still reading. "Whoa," she said. "It sounds as if Mrs. Farmer knew what it was like to have hard times. Here in the introduction, written after her death in 1924, it says that she lost her only child when he was a baby and that her husband died suddenly in 1898, just as they were about to begin construction of the museum. She'd inherited a ton of money from her father, who was in the Chase meatpacking business. The museum was opened to the public in 1903, and Mrs. Farmer lived in an apartment on the top floor. The rest of her life was devoted to enjoying and sharing the treasures that made her happy, and to writing this book, which was published in 1930. I'll bet she loved doing that."

Even as she said it, Petra wondered if this was too easy. Then she reminded herself that art had once made *her* feel happy and filled with dreams. Not much lately, but once — when she was younger. When she wasn't thirteen.

Shoving these thoughts away, she went on, "You guys — what Mrs. Farmer says could be giving us *clues* about where the art has gone. Especially if the person who planned the theft knows this little book. Like the trustees, right? I'll come back here with my notebook."

Early saw signs of restlessness in Jubie and knew she'd have to leave. "Read us some more, Petra. Quick, before I have to take Mr. Pow-Gangstahs to the playground."

She's one of us, Tommy thought happily.

"Okay. How about this," Petra said.

"Welcome to my collection. I truly hope that it will give as much to you as it has given to me. While living with great art is one of the deepest privileges a person may have, I do believe that one only needs to meet and fall in love with a masterpiece in order to call it one's own. In this way, what's mine can become yours.

"The people in my art are my friends and family. They speak, filling my life with their presence. I respond. I love to think that others may visit my home and do the same.

"What you see will be different from what I see; a thousand people can love the same painting in a thousand ways. Such is the cycle of life, as art reaches out beyond the will of its maker or owners.

"Great art will live, given a chance."

"Bit nutty-bananas," Tommy commented.

"Not if you're truthful with yourself," Petra snapped. "And not to someone who loves art and might feel a bit lonely. This is generous and *honest*. She's a guide. Lots of us who look at art think about stuff like this, but who *says* it? And maybe by believing the art could talk back to her, that it was kind of alive, she made it happen. Maybe what she says in this book *can* change the people who read or hear it. Maybe there's some magic here. Some power. Just like athletes before a big game psych themselves into winning, you know? They focus extra hard on what they want to see happen because they believe that'll change what they can do. Why is that nuts?"

Tommy gazed at the shelf behind Petra's head, hoping one of the titles might help him. "It's not — it's the good kind of nuts. Like ours." Calder elbowed him in the ribs and Tommy stared back furiously when he realized why. *I hate hanging around with girls. Seems like everything gets twisted into something embarrassing.*

Early, happily, didn't seem to notice. "I don't think any of Mrs. Farmer's ideas are wacky," she said. "It's the opposite — they're more than right! But what I don't understand is, who would steal from a museum like this? I know we said stuff about the trustees taking the art from each other, but the truth is that a theft like this would be done by someone pretty bad, right? I mean, who *takes* priceless art like this? Are we sure it's safe for us five to be working on it?"

"Mrs. Sharpe wouldn't pull us into something really dangerous," Petra said, although she didn't look positive. She glanced around and then added, "I don't think. And Ms. Hussey would know if it was something we shouldn't be doing. I think."

Early rolled her eyes unhappily just as Jubie popped to his feet and trotted over. "All done, Early. No puppies got hurt."

When Early turned to thank the man who'd been reading to Jubie, she found he was already gone. Another man in a black leather jacket, someone younger and scruffier, was running his finger along the titles in a nearby aisle.

"Hey, black jackets are big around here, aren't they?" she half whispered to her new friends.

Sliding the slender red volume back onto its shelf, Petra shrugged. "Haven't noticed."

A shadow crossed Early's face. As if reading her mind, Tommy said, "Make you think of blackbirds baked in a pie? Next thing we know, someone's nose will get snapped off."

Calder elbowed Tommy, knocking him sideways. Jubie imitated the two big boys, staggering sideways into a shelf.

"Yeah, snapped off!" Jubie shouted. "No nose!"

Early bent down to pick up Jubie's hat, then grabbed his hand. "See you," she said — mostly to Petra, and a little to the boys. She was out of the store before they could say good-bye.

"You scared her," Calder said to Tommy.

"I don't think so," Petra said. "It was like she saw something."

The three scanned the area Jubie and the man had been sitting in.

"No one," Calder said. They walked through the bookstore together, even ducking under water pipes in the basement to check out Mysteries and Science Fiction, but they couldn't find even one black jacket.

"Doesn't mean they're not here. This is an easy place to change directions and hide, there're so many loops," Tommy said, thinking of Goldman and his underwater palace.

Before leaving, Petra muttered, "I wish I could take Mrs. Farmer's book home, that it wasn't so expensive. It's twenty-five dollars. Wait, just a last look," and stepped back to check the shelf.

The others heard her gasp.

The book was gone.

☐ ☐ ☐ "But if no one bought it, where did it go?" Petra's voice was shrill in the quiet store.

Mr. Watch, behind the front desk, scratched his head. "You sure that's what you were looking at today? Someone asked for it earlier this week and I couldn't locate it. Show me where you found it."

Petra stomped back to the shelf, Mr. Watch and the others following.

"Could you have put it back in the wrong spot?" he asked.

Petra's face was thundery. "Not a chance."

"Tell you what, I'll look around in my spare time today. Sometimes people duck in and out, spending a few minutes before they hop on the train downtown. They pull out a book, then jam it back in the wrong spot."

"It's got a red spine," Petra said. "We walked through the store before we left and didn't see too many people . . ."

"I know you, and you know I'll check," Mr. Watch said. He snapped his suspenders, as if that was that.

Leaving the store a moment later, the kids spotted two young men in black leather jackets walking toward the playground.

Without a word to one another, the three followed. Up close, the two looked more like uncomfortable college students than anything else. Early and Jubie were nowhere to be seen.

"I have to be in charge at home this afternoon," Petra said gloomily. "I'll call Early and ask her if she wants to walk to the Farmer with me tomorrow morning. Buddy system, in case she's feeling spooked."

"She'd probably like that." Tommy paused for a beat then shrugged. "Sorry you have to go home. See you, Petra," he said.

As Calder and Tommy crossed the street, another black jacket ducked into the Medici Bakery. Just then, five crows swooped down on a nearby tree, chattering and cawing.

"Maybe the crows are like the prime numbers," Calder said. "Or us. Or the five black jackets. Part of a pattern."

"I dunno," Tommy said. "They might just be birds who needed to stop and poop, and there might just happen to be a few people around here wearing some of the millions of worn-out black leather jackets in Chicago."

"You wouldn't be sounding like such a grouch if the girls were still here," Calder said.

Tommy stopped dead and stared at his old friend.

"I've never heard you talk this way, Calder Pillay! The *girls*! Yeah, we're hanging out with girls who're — you know — not just girls anymore."

Calder punched Tommy in the shoulder, and his buddy staggered happily.

"Yeah, major *detective* work. I know what mystery *you're* working on," Tommy squawked. Neither was quite sure what that meant, but it sounded good.

After several more swats at each other, they walked on, not noticing a curtain that moved in one of Mrs. Sharpe's second-floor windows. It opened a crack as the boys passed on the other side of the street. If either had looked up, they would have seen that the fingers holding it were not those of an old lady.

They were those of a young man.

◻ ◻ ◻ Saturday morning was pearly, the air filled with the promise of spring. Sun warmed the two- and three-story roofs in Hyde Park, and now darted through windows and around stone balconies on the grander buildings in Kenwood. Like an unhappy gift, the Farmer Museum stood wrapped in yards and yards of crime tape, its gray-brown brick stark beneath the yellow ribbon.

Zoomy and his grandma were the first to arrive. They sat in their truck, joining two police cruisers parked at either end of the block.

Tommy was next. He waved to Zoomy, who didn't react. Gam waved back.

Oh, yeah, Tommy reminded himself. *The kid can't see more than a couple of feet.*

Tommy looked around and spotted Calder across the street, then, farther away, Petra and Early. Not wanting to look stupid, Tommy stepped closer to the truck and tapped on the passenger-side window. Zoomy jumped, then grinned.

Tommy rested one arm on the passenger-side mirror, relaxed-man-style. It began to move.

Bam! It ripped off the door and bounced into the gutter.

Even worse: A bad word ripped out of Tommy's mouth. Why hadn't he said *scaz?*

As he was picking up the mirror, Zoomy's grandma rolled down the window and Tommy realized she might not have heard. "I'm so sorry!" he said.

She shook her head. "Old truck, we're good at fixing," she replied.

Early was next to him by then. "Hi, Tommy and Zoomy," she said calmly. She had on a bright red jacket and somehow looked like an advertisement for clean everything.

"Try duct tape," Early said. "My dad says most of the world comes together with duct tape."

Zoomy and his grandma climbed down from the truck just as several limousines pulled up and car doors opened and shut on all sides. The sidewalk in front of the Farmer filled with unfamiliar faces. Fur collars, velvet, tweed jackets, walking sticks. In the midst stood Mrs. Sharpe, wearing a long red coat with sparkly buttons. Ms. Hussey, next to her, had her school backpack over one shoulder and looked very young and out of place.

The group moved in a jingly, perfumed way toward the front door. No one but Ms. Hussey said hello to the five kids and older woman now standing by Zoomy's truck. A policeman opened the door to the Farmer, and the group passed slowly between the two stone lions guarding the front, their canes tap-tapping on the brick walk. Ms. Hussey helped Mrs. Sharpe up three steps and into the gloom, then reached back to the trustees who followed, but no one else took her open hand or even thanked her.

Rich people, Tommy thought to himself. *Spoiled*. He caught Ms. Hussey's eyebrows going up as she closed her hand, said a word to the policeman, and headed across the street toward the kids. Walking quickly, she pulled a long thread off a frayed cuff on her winter jacket and shrugged, as if to say, *Their loss*.

"So," she said briskly, "this is it! I know everyone but Zoomy has been here before. The museum is officially closed and the guards on duty inside know you five are allowed to explore. The trustees are meeting in their room upstairs, on the fourth floor. Mrs. Sharpe will tell them something about you kids, and then hopefully you'll be invited up at the end of our visit."

Calder, Petra, Tommy, and Early hadn't visited the Farmer recently. It had only been open part of the week for years now, and those days were always crowded.

The group stood for a moment, looking up. Oddly, this blocky, rectangular building seemed to look back down, as if excited about keeping so many secrets behind a plain exterior. The only decorative detail was a Υ — or was it a wishbone? — that rose up the middle of the façade. Over the front door was an inscription: C'EST MON PLAISIR.

Ms. Hussey followed Early's eyes and translated the French: "*It's my pleasure.* Lovely, huh? A message from Mrs. Farmer."

Once in the dark entrance hall, Petra hurried ahead past the security booth, which was packed with guards, and stepped into the courtyard. "Empty!" she breathed. "Heavenly, this is what it must have felt like to *live* here."

Anchored by a rectangular garden in the center, the space rose four stories to a delicate glass roof. Countless tall windows bracketed by balconies and decorative arches opened onto the courtyard, giving it an airy, summery feel. The walls were a creamy peach and it all looked old. Very old.

Soon Ms. Hussey had her backpack open on a stone bench and was passing out clipboards. Each had a pencil attached, one piece of paper printed on both sides, and several blank sheets.

"Think I'll settle down here," Gam said. "Got a sore foot from dropping a honey jar on it yesterday. I'll be happy as a squirrel with an acorn." She pulled the *Three Oaks Gazette* out of her purse. "You good, Zoomy?"

He nodded. Ms. Hussey touched him lightly on the shoulder. "Zoomy, I know you're a terrific detective with different eyesight. What's your range?"

"End of my arm," Zoomy said. "After that, it's all deeps.

But if I look close, I can see all sorts of things other people miss."

"Yes, I've heard that about you," Ms. Hussey said comfortably. "Would you like someone to be your partner in the museum here?"

Zoomy nodded. "How about Tommy?"

"Deal," Tommy said right away. It didn't seem hard. But what were *deeps?*

"Calder," Ms. Hussey said, "if you keep clicking your pencil like that, you won't have any lead left to write with."

"Oh, sorry." He plunged the hand with the pencil into his pocket and stirred his pentominoes, still wondering what the trustees were up to. Pulling out a U, he scratched his head vigorously with it.

"*Unhappy* and *unfriendly*," he mouthed. "*Huh?*" he squawked suddenly, slapping one hand on his neck. He poked Tommy with the U piece. "Cut it out!"

Tommy was next to Zoomy. "What? I didn't touch you!"

"Your fingers are freezing and you poked my neck!"

"Did *not*. You saw, Zoomy — I mean —"

"Didn't see but you didn't move," Zoomy said. "Hodillyhum, she likes us."

"*Who* likes us?" Calder asked.

Zoomy shrugged. "The lady."

Calder looked confused.

Is he talking about Ms. Hussey? Tommy wasn't sure — but he also wasn't going to ask.

Early and Petra headed quietly toward the edge of the courtyard.

"Wait, you two, come back here!" Ms. Hussey called out. "A . . . um, friend of Mrs. Sharpe's printed out this reference sheet for you guys yesterday. On one side, you'll see thumbnail reproductions of the thirteen stolen pieces. Beneath that is a typed summary with titles, date, and medium — you know, oil painting or sketch, etc. On the other side is a list of the seven trustees, so that you have their full names. Then all of *our* full names."

"Why does it say *Pieces* on one side and *Players* on the other? Like it's some kind of game?" Petra asked. "This is spooky."

"I don't think it was meant that way," Ms. Hussey said lightly. "This man's name is Eagle Devlin. I met him yesterday at Mrs. Sharpe's house. He runs an art storage business, and he's organized." The kids waited for her to say something more, but she didn't. Gam's newspaper rustled.

"Cool name," said Calder. "Eagle."

"It would be cooler if he was bald," Tommy pointed out. "Is he bald?"

He wanted Early to hear, but she was busy reading. Zoomy, however, thought it was funny, which was some consolation.

"No," Ms. Hussey said. "He is not bald."

Petra looked up. "Check it out, guys. *We* should have done this already." She pointed to the following list, under the Pieces photos:

1 by Johannes Vermeer, *The Concert* (oil), 1658–60.

3 by Rembrandt van Rijn: *Storm on the Sea of Galilee* (oil), *A Lady and a Gentleman in Black* (oil), *Self-Portrait* (etching). 1633–34.

1 by Govaert Flinck, *Landscape with an Obelisk* (oil), 1638.

1 by Edouard Manet, *Chez Tortoni* (oil), 1878–80.

5 by Edgar Degas: 2 sketches of dancers, musicians, musical instruments and boats in a harbor, 2 of racehorses with jockeys, 1 group of people in a landscape (pencil, watercolor, charcoal and color wash), 1880s.

1 bronze Ku, a Chinese beaker for drinking wine, 1200–1100 B.C.

1 brass Eagle: wings half open, finial from top of French flagpole, 1813–14.

"Now for the Players. He starts with the trustees and a few words about each one."

William Swift Chase, age 83, great-nephew of Sarah Chase Farmer, director of the Farmer Museum
Carolyn Crunch, age 79, former CEO of development company
Hershel Hurts, age 73, dental surgeon and inventor

Monument Cracken, age 83, former CEO of
Industrial Recycling Company
Winnifred Whacker, age 79, patron of the arts
Hurley Stabbler, age 89, owner of Stabbler
Metalworks
Louise Sharpe, age 83

"Whoa, eighty-three! No wonder Mrs. Sharpe has more wrinkles than an elephant," Tommy muttered.

Petra chose to ignore this. "Then our five names, all age thirteen, then Ms. Hussey's and Eagle Devlin's. Hey, you and he are both thirty-one, Ms. Hussey. I like the guy who put this together — he's on top of things. But why did he include everyone's ages?"

Calder pulled the P out of his pocket. "That's easy. Primes," he said.

"Maybe," Ms. Hussey said. "If you believe in taking stuff like that into account," she added under her breath.

"There're fourteen names here," Calder said. "If you got rid of one, that'd be thirteen names and thirteen pieces. Maybe the people's ages are there to make things even, because the art dates are there. You know, to play fair. This guy's awesome!"

"Unless he thinks like you, and has to knock one name off to make it thirteen and thirteen," Tommy said.

"All right," Ms. Hussey said. "That's enough of that."

Zoomy was inclined to agree with Calder. He liked people who made lists.

Early also liked lists. But there was something about this one that had her worried. She was used to lists having answers. This one only raised questions.

"Okay, off you go," Ms. Hussey said brusquely. Everyone turned at the sound of a man's footsteps.

"Hello," called a cheerful voice. "It's the kid detectives, right? My name's Steel, as in the metal. I know, bad name for the occasion, but what's a guy to do?" A jolly laugh seemed to startle even the building. The man rubbed his hands together. "I'm your go-to guard for the visit. No touching anything, now. You kids are lucky to be here, so don't abuse the privilege."

Mr. Steel jumped suddenly and rubbed his cheek. "Strange," he muttered. "Cold in here," he said to the group. "Upstairs windows are all closed this morning, of course, but somehow there's a draft . . . I'll check the basement. The other guards are busy adjusting the monitor screens. Ma'am, you'll be with the kids, is that right?"

Ms. Hussey nodded.

"Back in a jiffy!" The guard trotted toward a far door.

The group stood in a silent clump at the edge of the courtyard, looking around. Even Zoomy could sense how much space there was. You had to be *really* rich to have so much room for gardening that inside smelled like outside.

"Makes you feel small but welcome, doesn't it?" Ms. Hussey said softly. "Mrs. Farmer wasn't much of a traveler. I don't believe she ever left Chicago, but she was a huge reader, supporter of the arts, and hostess. The woman fell in love with what she knew of Venice, Italy. The walls of this court-yard were designed to look like the exterior of a Renaissance palazzo, or palace, in Venice, but on the *interior*. Ingenious, don't you think?"

"Kind of an Escher move," Calder said approvingly. "Dizzying."

"Mm." Ms. Hussey smiled. "And perfect for who she was — she turned things inside out. By surrounding herself with so much great art and talent, she met the world on her own terms. And she had an amazing way of blending centuries of creation from many different cultures — everything looks comfortable."

"Like she was the hostess at a huge party and everyone got along," Early said.

"As she often was," Ms. Hussey added.

Petra then told her old teacher about the red book in Powell's and the things Mrs. Farmer had said about her art becoming her family. "The book mysteriously disappeared from the shelf before we left," Petra finished with a frown. "As if someone was watching us and then grabbed it."

"But aren't you smart to have found that! There must be other copies around even though it's old," Ms. Hussey said lightly. "Wait — Tommy, where's Zoomy?"

"Over here," came a muffled voice from under some ferns in the garden. "Investigating the running water."

"Sorry, got distracted," Tommy muttered.

Two fountains, one guarded by a commanding marble woman in a flowing gown, gurgled gently between statues, flowers, fragments of pots, and inviting pebbled paths.

"Oops, not meant to be in there!" Ms. Hussey called. As Tommy dove in to help Zoomy out of the plants, Ms. Hussey looked around appreciatively. "Mrs. Farmer loved to play. Do you see the Medusa? She's Roman, second century — that's a long time to be underfoot."

A young woman with wild hair peered up from a mosaic patio set in the very center of the courtyard.

"You know the ancient myth. If you looked directly at her — see all those snakes around her head? — you'd turn to stone. And this courtyard is filled with stone figures! There's an empty marble chair, right near Medusa, where Mrs. Farmer liked to sit, as if to challenge her. She always dared the children who visited to climb up on that seat, and if they did, she acted frightened and warned, 'Oh, don't look, whatever you do!'

"Of course they did, and then she laughed, rushed over to congratulate them on their bravery, and offered them a snake-shaped cookie."

"She sounds great," Early said. "I wish we could have met her."

Calder looked at the marble chair. "I guess that's one way to make sure your art isn't stolen — make it really, really heavy."

"Check out *these* people," Zoomy said, kneeling next to a huge marble box at the edge of the courtyard. "Couldn't walk off with this, either."

Tommy read the label. "It's a Roman sarcophagus. We're talking thousands of years old." He got down next to Zoomy, then popped up again. "What a coffin! It's covered with teenagers dancing — and a lot of grapevines. Scaz! They're only wearing beach wraps, minus the bathing suits. Come on, Zoomy." Tommy glanced back at the girls and pulled Zoomy toward a lion crushing a howling man, both pinned under a column. "There may be more lions down here. Let's find 'em while those guys are talking."

Zoomy grinned. "She likes excitement, doesn't she?"

"You mean Mrs. Farmer," Tommy said. "I guess. Hey, maybe this is why Mrs. Sharpe has all those lions in her house — you know, the ones outside, the ones on the arms of chairs. She's a *copycat*." A slow grin spread across Tommy's face as he realized what he'd said. "Get it? Lions are cats."

Zoomy, gripping his pencil, was busy making marks on his clipboard. "Check this out, Tommy: I'm starting with the walls. There are old lions *everywhere*. On the edges of old stone window frames! Under furniture! Maybe it's a lion clue."

Tommy had only suggested lions to get away from all the nakedness, but then remembered that even Mrs. Sharpe's paper napkins were decorated with lions. Had she been trying to give them a hint?

Mr. Steel reappeared, rubbing his head. "Funny," he trumpeted. "Maybe the cop unlatched that door this morning before he left, but I sure as heck didn't. Other guards say *they* didn't." He shrugged and marched ahead up the stairs, Calder, Petra, and Early following.

Ms. Hussey stood at the edge of the garden, squinting up at one of the fourth-floor windows. She waved — just the smallest gesture — then hurried after the guard, calling back, "Join us on the second floor in a few minutes, boys, as soon as you've finished your count. Great idea to collect some data."

Scaz, Tommy thought to himself, *now Calder's the only guy with the two girls. No fair. I hope they'll get a whiff of his pits and back off in a hurry. Wait, what am I saying?* Tommy shook his head, glad that his thoughts were private.

"Okay, Zoomy," he said, "I'll scout out the lions in the garden. You stick to the inside walls, then we'll catch up. There's not much furniture here to ambush you, just a few benches."

"Hodilly-hum, I'll be fine," Zoomy agreed. "I like lions, don't you? King of the Beasts. I wish we had this kind of art at home."

Big cats did seem to be hidden everywhere around the courtyard. Soon Zoomy called out, "Twenty-three! Think that's it!" from around a corner. Tommy had found eight, some buried in plants or clinging to stone railings. He also discovered even more mostly naked people. Why didn't women have buttons or zippers in those days, and why did men seem perfectly happy without any underwear on, speaking of beasts? He was glad the girls had gone ahead.

The word *lion*, Tommy realized suddenly, sounded like *lyin'*. Part of being a sharp detective was knowing when someone was *lying* . . . "Zoomy!" he shouted, wanting to share. "Where are you, man?"

He found his new friend on the floor next to a huge stone carving mounted on a wall.

"So was that one of the trustees?" Zoomy asked. "I thought they went upstairs."

"Who?" Tommy said absently, still busy with the idea that Mrs. Sharpe's lions were some kind of lead on *lying* and the theft. And here was Zoomy, *lying* on the floor. He'd never seen double meanings all around before. Was this excellent thinking, or just weird?

Zoomy looked up at him. "I was studying this panel, so close that I could smell it. A woman's boot peeked out from a long skirt. Right here, by my elbow. The toe pointed to this leaping lion way down at the bottom. I said thanks, but then after I'd recorded it, the person was gone."

"Your grandma?" Tommy asked hopefully, his heart feeling suddenly squeezed.

"She never wears skirts. Or has boots with laces," Zoomy said.

"Huh," Tommy squeaked. He hadn't seen anyone, but felt a sudden puff of cool air on his cheek. "Twenty-three plus eight makes thirty-one lions. Whoa, it fits: It's a prime on the list of players! Come on, we'll get in trouble for being down here so long."

Looking around at the empty courtyard, Tommy shot a quick wave to Gam and hustled his friend toward the stairwell.

"Do you think the word *lion* could have a double meaning, Zoomy?" Tommy asked. "Like, the roaring animal and then *fibbing*?"

"Huh. Maybe to someone like Mrs. Farmer," Zoomy answered.

"Yeah," Tommy muttered, thinking that thirteen, an age where you *had* to hide stuff and sometimes lie, was a hard age to be a finder. He glanced at Zoomy, wondering if the two of them were a match for *any* kind of lion.

❏ ❏ ❏ "We're headed down a hallway. I'll tell you when we're near the first step." Tommy, walking next to Zoomy, glanced behind them. The overhead brightness of the courtyard had faded to a sepia gloom.

"That boot — was it solid?" Tommy whispered in Zoomy's ear, covering his mouth with his hand. Zoomy ducked.

"That tickles, cut it out. Of course!" Zoomy said. "Hey, I like the scent of this new place — it's a mix of earth and moss. Like a garden that's never in the sun. Gam calls that a shade nook."

Tommy shivered. "Like in a cemetery," he said — and, right then, tripped.

"Scaz!" He looked down to see what had stopped his foot and bumped Zoomy, who staggered sideways, dropping his clipboard.

"Sorry, man!" Tommy gasped. "Surprise attack," he added, retrieving Zoomy's lists. "Something was in the way."

"Happens to me all the time." Zoomy nodded as they started up the stairs. "I call those *trippers*."

Forgive me, Mrs. Farmer, Tommy found himself thinking. *I didn't mean it, the attack part.*

He glanced sideways at Zoomy to see if he was thinking the same thing, but his new friend only said, "*Scaz.* I like that word."

"Calder, Petra, and I discovered it," Tommy said. He explained what it meant.

At that moment there was a silvery laugh, and Zoomy said, "Oh, I hear them just ahead."

Tommy didn't think the laugh sounded like Ms. Hussey, and it was definitely not Calder. Or Petra. Or Early. Or Gam.

That boot in the courtyard . . .

Once on the second floor, Tommy caught a glimpse of the guard and galloped in his direction, dragging Zoomy.

Inside the Dutch Room, the boys joined a silent group standing in front of a wall with two huge, empty frames on it. Mr. Steel paced behind them, his shoes clicking on the bumpy tiles.

Ms. Hussey turned and beckoned to the two boys. "Come closer," she said. "This is where Rembrandt's two paintings hung: *Storm on the Sea of Galilee* and *A Lady and Gentleman in Black.*"

Petra was fighting the urge to run. The empty frames felt shocking. *Like party clothes hanging on a wall after something bad happened to the person who wore them*, she thought.

Had someone *whispered* that to her?

It wasn't her kind of idea; it was more like Mrs. Farmer's. Petra had never been to a fancy party in her life. But sometimes an investigator just felt things . . .

She heard swallowing on all sides, the *ga-glump* sounds of people trying not to be emotional. Or was it a frightened sound?

Tommy looked slowly around the room. Did he imagine it, or were all of the portraits sad?

"It's like the others want to say something, but can't," he blurted.

Ms. Hussey touched his arm. "You're so right, Tommy. They *saw* what happened last week."

"If Mrs. Farmer was here, maybe *she* would get them to talk," Early said quietly. "Seems like she'd know how."

Tommy looked around wildly. "Don't say that. I mean, what if she hears you?"

"Hoo, hoo!" Calder breathed in his buddy's ear.

Zoomy, standing on Tommy's other side, smiled.

Petra tried to look brave. "I hope she does! We need her help."

"Come with me, Tommy and Zoomy," Ms. Hussey said. "This is where *The Concert* was. Propped on this table so that you could sit and look at it for as long as you wanted. The Flinck painting was behind it, on the opposite side. Both set up for dreaming, like Mrs. Farmer said in her writings. For making the art your own."

"Hey," Early piped up. "Here's a strange thought: The only person in this room who *didn't* see the theft was the man with his back turned, in the Vermeer."

Zoomy circled the table with the two empty frames. "I like Mrs. Farmer," he said suddenly. "She knows how to make people relax and enjoy, like I do when I'm lying in the grass and watching ants. And I'll bet she likes to laugh. Look at this chair, for relaxing in front of her best painting. Check out the lions on the arms, like in Mrs. Sharpe's house, and these two bendy people crouched on the top. Whoa, they're wearing nothing but beanbags on their heads!"

"How come you're talking about Mrs. Farmer like she's here?" Tommy asked just as Calder and the others crowded in to see the naked kneelers. Zoomy backed up, tumbled sideways, then disappeared. Arms grabbed at thin air and Tommy's sneaker flipped off as Calder stepped on the heel.

"Scaz!" Zoomy muttered. He sat on the floor for a moment tapping his chin, then pulled out his pocket notebook.

Tommy saw Zoomy write, -Jittery-splat.

"What's that mean?" Tommy asked.

"Nervous." Zoomy nodded. "Like all of us in this room."

"Not me," Mr. Steel said. "Hey!" he added, slapping his neck again. "If I didn't know better, I'd say something in this here place is poking me with a cold finger when I say the wrong thing."

"I believe it," Calder said.

"There's plenty of stories about Mrs. Farmer staying on as a ghost in her house." The guard lowered his voice as he led the way toward the next room. "Other guards say they've seen someone after hours, when they were supposedly alone in the building. A woman in a long dress peers out of a window or drifts past a doorway. Just a glimpse, but still: wouldn't want to be in here at night. Never have been, and don't plan to be."

"So since the theft, are there more guards around?" Early asked, hugging her clipboard. "I mean, just to be sure . . ."

"You have no idea, young lady." Mr. Steel stopped walking. "They have two who patrol the galleries all night and four posted outside, one at each corner, and they move around also. Not like the old days, oh my, no."

"Guess that's it for intruders," Calder said, stirring his pentominoes. He pulled out a P.

"Are they all men?" Early asked.

"Now, that's an odd thing to ask," Mr. Steel said, looking around him.

Suddenly everyone in the small group was quiet again, but it was the kind of quiet that was buzzing with things people wanted to say but couldn't.

"P for *player*," Calder said. "*Paranormal.*"

"She must be angry," Zoomy blurted. "When bunnies get into our garden and eat the best seedlings, my grandpa says he's mad as a broody chicken in a plundered henhouse."

"But I'm sure if Mrs. Farmer knew you guys were working on this terrible theft in her henhouse, she'd be pleased," Ms. Hussey said, glancing around at the kids, "Not broody." Pulling her turtleneck high on her neck as they left the Dutch Room behind, she muttered, "Much colder in there."

Calder, Petra, and Early peppered the guard with ghost questions as they moved down the hall toward the next gallery.

Early, turning her head for a last look at the empty frames, froze. Then she rubbed her eyes and hurried ahead, pushing her way into the middle of the group.

Score, Tommy thought, suddenly less worried about the unseen as Early squashed in between him and Petra.

Downstairs, Gam looked up from her paper and then out at the courtyard. "Mighty nice home here," she murmured. "No wonder you gotta get them things back."

A gentle breeze ruffled the ferns, and Gam sniffed appreciatively.

◻◻◻ Each room on the second and third floors had its own color scheme. Some were persimmon, some golden, some a watery silver, or blue like the sky. Each had a massive fireplace that had been brought back from an ancient castle or palace in Europe, and on either side of the hearths there were almost always a couple of chairs set up for a knee-to-knee chat.

Zoomy noticed that these seats were extra small and low. "Look, it's like they're kid-sized! And check out all the carvings and cushions; each one is different from the others. Maybe she wanted kids to feel welcome and then come back. I wish I could try one out. But don't worry — I won't!"

"Good point, Zoomy," Petra said. "In *The Truth About My Art*, it said Mrs. Farmer was heartbroken when her little son died, and she never got to be a mother to another child. Now I'm noticing that there's a ton of mother-and-child paintings. Peaceful ones. It's as if she wanted her little son to feel welcome in the house even if he was gone."

"Ooh, *that's* shivery," Tommy muttered.

❏ ❏ ❏ As one room followed another, Petra began to relax. Being in Sarah Chase Farmer's home after finding the red book felt magical — as if part of their investigation was happening inside one of Mrs. Farmer's parties. She had known how to mix coziness, elegance, and surprise. And she didn't put labels next to the art, as in most museums. If you wanted to know about an object — like who'd made it and when — you had to look it up on the big information cards that stood in a rack in the center of each room. That took some doing, as a diagram of each wall had to be deciphered by number. Plus the rooms were dimly lit, making the writing on the cards hard to see.

"Hey, can you turn up these lights?" Tommy asked at one point, noticing Zoomy was doing his best to check out a hunting scene on a tapestry.

Mr. Steel shook his head. "When she started the museum, Mrs. Farmer had only candles in these wall sconces. Then electricity came in, and she wanted the lights to stay as close to candlelight as possible. You're not even allowed to use the light on your cell phone. What you see is what you get."

Mr. Steel cleared his throat and looked around. "I'm sure her intent was for people to visit many times, from season to season. What you see on a winter afternoon is completely different from what pops out on a summer morning or a spring evening. Of course, for years now the museum has only had limited hours, so it can't work that way. Not easily. A pity."

"It's like Mrs. Farmer wanted you to see her things in a homey way," Early said. "To enjoy them and not worry about whether something was especially valuable. Maybe she wanted you to let the art speak for itself."

"Yeah, not think about how famous the artist was or stuff like that," Calder added. "Just see what he or she made."

"Exactly," Ms. Hussey said. "It's refreshing, don't you think? Nothing is more important than anything else. Or at least, that used to be true, before the theft."

"Seems like the thieves were a bit like Mrs. Farmer," Petra said. "They chose some of this and some of that."

"And some of it's worth a fortune, and some not as much," Early said. "It really is weird. Why wouldn't a thief just go for the big-ticket items?"

Ms. Hussey was studying a painting of a woman playing a lute. "You're right, Early," she said. "It's funny, isn't it, that they didn't take some of the other hugely valuable art instead. There's *Europa*, over on that wall, which many believe is the finest Titian in the United States, or the Michelangelo pen and ink. Or a Raphael, a Botticelli, a Fra Angelico, a Bellini . . ."

Petra wandered over to look at *Europa*. Tommy joined her.

"Scaz, she needs a new nightgown," he muttered as he witnessed the woman flying through the air on the back of a bull and losing most of her ripped clothing in the process.

"Guess nakedness was just part of life in those days," Petra said.

Tommy nodded. He felt he'd seen enough bodies today to last for a while.

Mr. Steel was pointing to a corner. "The brass eagle came off a flagpole that stood here. Not valuable compared to some of the other treasures that were taken," he mused. "Like you kids were saying, this is truly one of the oddest art heists in history. Maybe it was done by someone insane. *Ouch!*" He slapped his hand on the back of his neck. "I keep getting these freezing-cold sensations. Almost like a sting. Gotta see a doctor."

"I wonder *why* they chose that eagle? And why the Ku, the wine cup?" Calder said. "It's like they went from top to bottom in the museum, just grabbing whatever they felt like. But what art thief does that?"

"Yeah, it's definitely odd," Ms. Hussey said. "Most thefts are only one or two paintings or works of art, and the choices are predictable. This combination of famous art and everyday objects seems . . ."

"What?" Petra prompted.

"I was going to say 'personal,'" Ms. Hussey finished.

❏❑❏ "Oh, man!" Zoomy crowed. In another room, he'd found a long table covered with small boxes, some with fancy locks, inlaid shell, and chips of gems. "Danger boxes for priceless secrets! If I'd been the thief, no question I would've kept one of these. *Ha-chooo!*"

"Stop!" Tommy warned as Zoomy reached out to blot the sneeze.

Mr. Steel spun around and snapped, "No touching, young man!"

"Sorry, didn't mean to get spit on it. Guess I snorted some old dust," Zoomy explained, looking shaken.

"No harm done," Ms. Hussey said, shooting a cool glance at Mr. Steel. "These kids know what's what."

"Do they," he muttered. "Kids, yeah, always have to remind them to keep their mitts off the goods. *Holy* —" He grabbed his nose with one hand. "I could swear someone attacked me with ice tongs."

Whoa, there's that same silvery giggle, Tommy thought. *The one I heard downstairs. Or did I? No one else seems startled. Maybe it's just the trustees upstairs, and sound travels around here in funny currents.*

"Zip, Zoomy," he said, pulling his friend over to where Petra and Early were standing.

"Check out this leather book!" Petra exclaimed. "It's about three feet long and wide! Biggest one I've ever seen — and it's a notebook. Scaz, can you imagine having something so cool and huge to write in?"

"Awesome," Zoomy agreed. "Like turning into one of the Borrowers."

"And here's something for Goldman," Calder called out from across the room. He stood by an ancient stone bowl in front of one of the windows to the courtyard. Two stealthy cats, worn by decades of touching, crept up the sides. "He'd get a fresh-air workout plus a view in here. Round and round."

Even from across the room, Tommy could see that Goldman would die of terror if he spent even five minutes in that bowl.

"That's okay," he called. "But check this out, Calder."

Soon Tommy and Calder stood side by side, facing the wall where the Degas sketches had hung. "That square of yellow crime tape makes the emptiness worse," Tommy said.

"Yeah, like a puzzle frame with no pieces inside." Calder scratched his head with the M pentomino.

Petra joined them, adding, "No pieces seems pretty sad. Do you think we used to be faster at figuring out stuff?"

Tommy told them about the lions that might be a clue about lying — or a Mrs. Sharpe piece of trickiness. Petra listened with a respect that made him blush happily.

"That's awesome, Tommy," she said. "Maybe the solution is all about double meanings. Like the thief picked items that are somehow a clue to her or his identity. That, or the theft is disguised to look like what it's not."

"A flip, like the M pentomino could also be a W," Calder said. "Or the truth could look like a lie."

"That all sounds smart," Tommy said flatly. "But what the *scaz* are we talking about?"

"Something we don't understand and can't see," Petra said glumly.

"But we're thirteen now, and thirteen's gotta be a key," Calder said.

"A team of *five* thirteens," corrected Zoomy from behind them.

Early had been studying a nearby oil portrait of Sarah Chase Farmer that was hung high on a wall; the woman was young and faced the viewer in a flowing white dress, arms raised as though she'd just flung open the doors to her balcony in order to welcome the world.

"It's not just about *meanings*, you guys," Early said suddenly. "It's about *what she saw and heard*, which was a whole bunch of secrets! Secrets connected to the heist."

"Nice," Tommy said, sucking in his cheeks and offering a fist, which Early didn't see. His hand slid back into his pocket.

Early's tone drew Ms. Hussey and the others over.

Ms. Hussey sighed. "I love this portrait by Anders Zorn. It *is* horrifying to think that this painting of Mrs. Farmer witnessed the theft of those Degas pieces. When you think about how alive everything was to her, and —"

"Early's right!" Petra interrupted. "Maybe the stolen art will *speak to us* like it spoke to Mrs. Farmer."

"From wherever it is?" Zoomy asked.

"Why not?" Early threw out her arms, looking suddenly like the woman in the painting, minus the fancy dress.

Tommy couldn't believe he'd ever thought Early was shy and Zoomy came from another planet.

"I guess you five will find out," Ms. Hussey said, with a secretive gleam.

Her cell phone rang. "Yes, ten minutes," she said. As she slipped the phone back in her pocket, she announced, "The trustees will see us. Think of any questions you may have for them about the theft or the collection. Anything you feel is relevant."

Early whispered something to Petra, who nodded.

"Ms. Hussey, can we find the ladies' room first?" Petra asked.

"Ah, let's ask —"

Mr. Steel cleared his throat. "Sure thing. We'll make an exception. Follow that corridor around the corner, then three or four steps down and take a right. You'll see it before the small stairwell. Says 'Staff Only' on the door."

Shoulder to shoulder, the girls hurried away. Ms. Hussey left the three boys to look around for a few minutes without any girls nearby. They headed toward a panel covered with soldiers in armor.

She walked over to one of the French doors that opened onto the courtyard, and gazed up at the apartment where Mrs. Farmer had lived.

Was that Mrs. Sharpe shaking her finger at another old

lady? Seeing a number of faces in profile, Ms. Hussey could almost feel the fury in that room. Mrs. Sharpe had said to her once that the old are free, because they aren't afraid to die.

Did being free mean you could do or say anything you felt like? What if you hurt the people around you?

And was a ghost free?

Ms. Hussey shuddered, and wondered for the first time if she'd been right in helping Mrs. Sharpe to gather the five kids and invite them to tackle this hideous crime. Speaking of double meanings, the younger woman realized recently that her old friend had hidden some big truths from her, truths that almost felt like lies.

What else did Mrs. Sharpe know? And what else was she hiding?

□ □ □ The stairs opposite the bathroom curved upward in a slow spiral marked by a delicate brass rail. As the girls paused by the first step, a roar of anger gusted down.

Bam! Bam! Something pounded the floor. "You are over the top, Hersh! How can you say such a thing?" An old voice, a woman's, crackled and trembled with rage.

Now, a man, his voice hoarse and his words thick, hollered, "It's not like we didn't discuss it, Carolyn, and in front of William. No use pretending we didn't talk about an occurrence!"

"Not an *occurrence* — you make it sound like indigestion or litigation. It's more like an *event*. It's a reason for the world to pay attention to our crisis and —"

The third voice, a woman's, was cut across by a fourth, a man's, and all were creaky but bright with fury. "Let's face it. We've been idiotic, having taken so much time to discuss options. Like a bunch of children who all want their way. And once the discussion got out into the press, with all that embarrassing information about leaks and humidity and inadequate security, well — what did we expect? That all the art thieves in the world would stand back and wait for us to become impenetrable? We practically invited the heist."

There was a moment of silence, and then Mrs. Sharpe's voice. "Turning on each other will get us nowhere. Whatever mistakes have been made in the past, let's do our best to move ahead. For William, if not for each other.

"He invited each of us, years ago, to sit on this board and contribute our individual experience, feeling the input each one of us brought to the table might be of value. But we sit in his family's museum. It's *his*, in a way, even though every group of trustees should provide balance to the director. And he tried so hard to tell me something. I've asked you all to think of the *F* followed by *A*. He trusted us, and now we need to trust him — he was *desperate* to communicate something. I'm sure it had to do with the heist, as he did nothing but talk about what it might mean last week, if you remember. Let's use these brains of ours. Well?"

At that point, the voices all talked over one another in a gravelly garble, the sound of dry sticks being rubbed together. Petra and Early heard "favor," "fate," "faith," "fault," and "fake." Next came "face" and "facility," followed by "fatuous," "false," and "fair."

Bam! Bam! The first voice cut across this pileup of *F-A* words. "And we must include the thinking of others. The authorities are working on it, of course, but Louise knows some children who've come up with creative solutions that have actually *solved* major thefts in the past. You may have read about them in the news. They're local, and her young friend Isabel Hussey taught some of them. Louise believes that children can contribute valuable insight to a crime of this sort. She's invited the teacher and the five kids to meet us briefly this morning, for an information session."

Next came the dry *rumpa-rumph* sound of Mrs. Sharpe clearing her voice for emphasis, the sound she used with the kids when she wanted them to listen but not respond. "Thank you, Winnifred. I've also included my son, Eagle Devlin, who has been away for a couple of years now. Perhaps some of you will remember him; he runs a fine arts storage and handling business in New York. He grew up in an orphanage in Chicago, and Leland and I adopted him at eighteen, after meeting him here, at the Farmer. He arrived late today for business reasons, but has probably joined the group downstairs by now. Shall we call them up?"

Petra and Early made *whaa?* faces at each other just as they heard the voices of the others coming closer. Mrs. Sharpe had a *son?* The girls ducked out of the stairwell and faced the galleries.

Around the corner came the guard, followed by Ms. Hussey and — "Huh?" Petra said aloud.

Here was the man from Powell's, the one who had been reading Mother Goose to Jubie. Ms. Hussey's face was grim.

"We meet again. Just call me Eagle," the man said to the girls with a twinkle.

Mr. Steel knocked loudly on the wall at the base of the stairs. "Hel-lo!" he called. "Coming up!"

As the silent group of seven followed Mr. Steel up the

narrow staircase, Tommy had a flash of *yikes, we're meeting in her apartment, is that okay?* Remembering the small chairs by the fireplaces, he relaxed. *Mrs. Farmer likes kids. She'll be on our side.*

Moments later, they were seated in the boardroom, a bright space with a huge mahogany table and a dozen upholstered chairs. Oriental carpets, lacy curtains, and cut flowers made it look oddly like Mrs. Sharpe's house. The six old people, now lined up on one side of the table, were resettling coats and scarves. The five kids and two adults squeezed in opposite the trustees after Eagle popped around a corner and returned with an extra chair.

He knows his way around her place, Tommy realized. *Wait, why am I thinking about Mrs. Farmer like she's here and knows what we're up to?* He sat up straighter in his chair, as if to make his thoughts line up with the real world.

Mrs. Sharpe made the introductions. The trustees barely smiled. *It's a wall of wrinkles and wispy hair*, Tommy thought. *Kind of like a zombie movie.*

Petra had bravely put up her hand and now asked a question.

"Is there a museum copy of *The Truth About Art* I could borrow? Maybe Mrs. Farmer's ideas can help, even though, you know, it's from so long ago."

"Published after her death, per her wishes." Monument Cracken nodded and ran a bony hand along the silver head of his cane. "Not many copies around. You may borrow mine, if you handle it with utmost care." Petra followed his eyes to her fingernails. Luckily they were short and clean. "Come to my house on Blackstone Avenue, tomorrow at 2:00 P.M." His voice shook slightly as he spoke, as if someone were jiggling his chair.

What if she had something else to do? Tommy wondered. *These people are used to giving orders.*

Petra babbled, "Very kind," and was cut off by an icy croak:

"Face-off — that's what we've had around here!"

"Now, *Hurl*ey," Ms. Crunch said, sounding as if she wanted to throw his name at him.

"Might as well be honest about it. Not enough truthful disclosure since all this happened. The fact is, we've been tearing each other to pieces over whether to move the museum or not," the old man barked, looking pleased with himself. "Like a bunch of hungry jackals." He licked his lips, which were pale.

More like the skin of an onion than flesh, Tommy noted.

"Excuse us, children. Passionate discussion," Winnifred Whacker sniffed, jingling a charm bracelet the size of a jailer's handcuffs.

"You can say that again," Carolyn Crunch muttered, fingering the loops of pearls around her neck.

Early raised her hand. "Um, do you have any thoughts to share with us about why that particular group of thirteen things was taken?"

Immediately there was a buzz of "Racehorses, one of my favorite sketches," "Always loved that Flinck, so peaceful," "The Manet, so much the story of writers everywhere," "That Ku, so rare," and "My Lord, who wouldn't want *The Concert?*"

"She's made a valuable point," Ms. Hussey said politely. "It's almost as if the thief picked things that all of you especially love."

Bam! Bam! A fist thumped on the table. "Outrageous!" Hershel Hurts's voice was quivering with emotion. "What are you suggesting, young woman?"

"Now, Hersh," Mrs. Sharpe said. "Behave yourself. We're all here to question and comment, aren't we?"

At that point, Eagle Devlin leaned forward and said, "Sometimes the most obvious solutions offer the best answers. I mean, a fact is a fact. All of you had keys to the place. Nothing was broken on entering."

Zoomy leaned over his notebook and wrote, *-trustees had keys.*

"Oh!" Carolyn Crunch gasped, having seen Zoomy's entry. "You'll be suggesting *we* did the robbery next!

Calder wasn't about to make that suggestion — but he noticed that Carolyn Crunch appeared to be the only trustee who was truly shocked by the idea.

"But that would hardly be logical, would it?" Eagle said smoothly. "Why would a board of devoted trustees endanger the art they love so much?"

The lineup of old folks shifted uncomfortably in their chairs — this was more a challenge than a question. Ms. Hussey glanced at Eagle with the first glint of friendliness.

"Thank you," she murmured.

"What if someone turns?" he half whispered with the suggestion of a smile.

Petra stiffened. Had he been listening to their meeting in Powell's? And where *was* the red book?

"What was that, Eagle? Speak up," Mrs. Sharpe said.

"Just remembering Sarah Chase Farmer's feeling that the people in her art came alive," he said. "Talking about Vermeer's man."

"Indeed," Monument Cracken said. "And your point?"

"That it might be true," he said simply. "And if so, the art may tell us what it knows."

"Maybe if we ask it for help," Early blurted. "I've done that before — I mean, with a different kind of art. Not stolen. I mean, not by me, not on purpose — words, not stones —" She broke off, staring at a pileup of diamond bracelets on Carolyn Crunch's arm with such intensity that the woman slid her arm out of sight and then pushed her chair several inches away from Early's.

The room was dead silent for a moment. Petra noticed the old people glancing at one another as if to say, *Are these kids dreadful or what?*

Mrs. Sharpe cleared her throat. "Never underestimate this group of five. They have a way of — well, uncovering, identifying, and then *utilizing* important truths. And in a *prime crime —*" Mrs. Sharpe sat back, looking for the right word.

"You need to see what fits," Calder finished for her, plunging a hand into his pentominoes pocket.

"Harrumph," Hurley Stabbler said, as if he wanted to laugh. "Watch your jewels, ladies." Monument Cracken and Hershel Hurts smiled meanly, and Winnifred Whacker and Carolyn Crunch hunched coats around their necks and pulled gloves over their hands.

Mrs. Sharpe's voice now had a hard edge that felt razor-thin. "And in a prime crime," she finished slowly, *"any of us could fit."*

☐☐☐ As the group of five kids and two adults — minus Gam, who went by truck — walked awkwardly back toward Hyde Park, Ms. Hussey said coolly, "You don't have to come with us, Mr. Devlin."

"Please — call me Eagle. And I'd like to," he said in the same tone.

Calder pulled a pentomino out of his pocket. "N for *near. Nowhere. Never.*"

Petra, next to Calder, said quietly, "Yeah. That's us and the trustees, the stolen art, and William Chase maybe not speaking again. Let's hope the last one is wrong. We *need* him to finish his *F-A* word."

Tommy, just behind Calder, said, "N for *night.*"

He was remembering a horrible nighttime adventure the three of them had had while they were working to save the Robie House a couple of years ago. He also thought about whoever had robbed the Farmer Museum in the middle of the night, sneaking through those huge, dark rooms filled with people watching from the walls. And then there was old Mr. Chase. Had something happened to him in the middle of the night, a fright that made him have that stroke? Maybe a person whose initials were F. A. had crept into his bedroom, the old man sat up, his face twisted with horror and —

Tommy jumped as Zoomy blurted, "Seems like most bad things happen in the dark. Like when I heard footsteps near the shed, and when my grandpa's store burned down."

Tommy glanced at his new friend. "Yeah," he muttered. He'd ask about it another time, when the grown-ups weren't around.

"N for *nightmare*," Early said, catching up to Calder.

"N for *negligent*," Eagle added.

Nice voice, Tommy thought. *Hope mine ends up that low. Hey, speaking of voices, Ms. Hussey's awful quiet. Usually she'd be all excited after a visit like this. Seems like Mr. Devlin makes her unhappy. Or is it worried?*

He was so busy turning that over in his mind that he forgot to warn Zoomy about a crater in the sidewalk.

Tommy grabbed for Zoomy's arm as he staggered sideways, crashed into a tree, and then boomeranged off Mr. Devlin's foot. That was when everyone noticed that the man had snakeskin cowboy boots on, boots that didn't look like they were made for Hyde Park. Boots a boy could slide off.

As Zoomy straightened his glasses, he bent over to see what he'd stepped on. "Oh, sorry," he said. "My grandpa would say those were Sunday Best."

Mr. Devlin laughed. "Just slippery," he said.

"Snakeskin." Zoomy nodded. "I once found a snake in our garden."

"Goes with Medusa," Early said. "I mean, the snakes on her head."

"Like if you didn't look out, my boots could turn you to stone?" the man asked. "I've always liked the idea that eagles can catch snakes," he said cheerfully.

"Birds of prey," Ms. Hussey muttered. "So why hasn't Mrs. Sharpe ever told me about you?"

"That's hard to say," he replied. He didn't seem hurt by the question, but he also didn't answer it.

There was an uncomfortable silence while Zoomy retied his shoe. It was then that Petra noticed two people with black leather jackets about half a block back. One, a woman, stopped and looked the other way. The other seemed to be digging in his pockets.

Petra tapped Early on the arm as soon as they were walking again.

"Seems like those jackets *are* everywhere these days," Petra whispered. "But these guys look more like students than anyone scary. Messy hair and high-top sneakers."

"Yeah." Early frowned. "And not the same people as the ones I saw yesterday."

Tommy apologized to Zoomy for not spotting the sidewalk tripper, then thought, *Ms. Hussey is right. Who is this Eagle Devlin guy and why haven't any of us heard about him before? He seems like an okay guy, but not someone to mess with. But then, Ms. Hussey isn't someone to mess with, either.*

He snuck a sideways look at Mr. Devlin's feet as they all started walking again. The snakeskin made him think of the tiling on the floor of the Farmer Museum — those large, uneven sections. That meant a very large snake.

Like in a nightmare, he thought to himself; like the difference between cats and lions, or real blackbirds and the kind that snapped off your nose.

Ever since Mr. Devlin had turned up, Mother Goose rhymes followed.

Rhymes even fit primes, Tommy thought. *It's almost like those Goose rhymes are made to work with whatever is going on, like a shadow attached to something alive.*

Tommy's shivered. Would they also fit with something dead, or left behind — like a ghost? What if Mrs. Farmer was right, and art was alive? And if the art was alive . . . had it been listening to them today?

Tommy thought of the man crushed beneath the lion in the courtyard, his mouth open in a silent scream.

☐ ☐ ☐ Eagle's presence made everyone quiet — the kind of quiet that feels loud. The kids breathed a sigh of relief when they got to Mrs. Sharpe's block.

"My place for lunch?" Tommy asked the other four. "My mom's at work. She won't mind."

Ms. Hussey cleared her throat. "Never announce an empty home," she said, her voice clipped. "Well, I'm off to do some work in my classroom."

"My mother's having lunch with the other trustees today," Mr. Devlin said. "Won't you come for lunch, Isabel? And oh! Let me introduce all of you to my cat, Rat-a-tat. He's visiting, too, since I couldn't leave him behind in New York."

Isabel, Petra thought. *I'll bet she doesn't like him calling her that.*

A cat that looked more like a small lion with a bushy tail rushed over, meowing loudly. "Thought I'd forgotten about you?" Mr. Devlin asked, and stooped to rub his ears.

"Awesome name," Tommy said.

"Gangstery," Calder added.

Both girls reached to pat Rat-a-tat, but he hurried toward Mrs. Sharpe's front door. Once there, he reared up on his hind legs and rested huge, hairy paws on the wood. Zoomy followed and knelt down, his nose inches away from the cat's ruff.

"Hungry boy," Mr. Devlin said. "Just like me."

Tommy wondered, *Is that a warning? Like one of them might bite?* The cat, ignoring Zoomy, looked back and blinked his green eyes pleasantly.

"Well?" The man blinked at Ms. Hussey, as if copying his cat. "Ratty and I request the pleasure of your company."

Tommy was backing up now. "Guess we're off. Come on, Zoomy. Later." He wasn't sure what else to say with Mr. Devlin there. He also didn't know whether he should be inviting Ms. Hussey over to eat with them. She never went to their houses, but . . . there was always a first. Did she need an excuse to say no? But if they invited Ms. Hussey, it would be rude not to include Mr. Devlin. Tommy shuffled his feet, kicking at a pebble.

"I'll call you guys later," Ms. Hussey said, her voice still formal but a bit less tight. "I have some ideas for this investigation."

The kids left with a wave and no one looked back, even though they all wanted to. Would Ms. Hussey go inside the house with this guy, and should they be worried?

Abruptly Zoomy announced, "There's a collar under all that fur, and it has some kind of communication switch on it. I've seen them before. I think it's the kind that can either record or track, so someone can find you. Does a bunch of things."

"So maybe Mr. Devlin's a spy! And we caught him," Calder announced.

"Thanks to sneaky you," Tommy said to Zoomy, who held up a fist for bumps.

"Or maybe Mr. Devlin works for Ratty," Early said.

"And speaks cat." Zoomy grinned.

"Speaking of spies," Petra said, "shouldn't we have some private way we can communicate around grown-ups? You know, like a Pig Latin that would let us say stuff and not be understood."

They walked the rest of the way to Tommy's happily trying out codes and forgot, for a moment, all about cats and art and difficult adults.

A shiny black car with a driver slid slowly down the block behind the five. As they ducked in the back door of the Robie House, an old hand covered with rings pointed in their direction. Another old hand, also in the backseat, waved through the air as if to say, *How could you think of such a thing? Not* that!

The hands flew to left and right, chopping the air as the car sped off.

❑ ❑ ❑ "Whinigo winigants binigalinigo — yipes! — ninigeinigy sinigandwinigi — whoa! — chiniges finigor linigunch?" Tommy asked, unlocking his door. "Man, I sound brainy," he panted. "And talking that way takes all day."

"Inigi dinigo!" Zoomy shouted.

"This would look plenty confusing if we wrote it down, but if we can speed up and say it fast, it'll be close to uncrackable." Petra practically skipped into Tommy's apartment.

"Yeah, it's awesome even when we're beginners," Early said. "If we practice and get smoother, we'll be chinigampinigi — wait — inigon spinigiiniges!"

"Not to leave out Ms. Hussey, just the police or Mr. Devlin or the trustees. Whinigen winige ninigeiniged tinigo kinigeinigep iniga sinigecriniget. Oooh, I love it!" Petra purred, plopping down next to Goldman. "Now we're talkin', we could take this iniganinigywhinigerinige."

"And it even works with pinigentinigominigin — oh, man! this'll take me all week — inigoiniges. Scinigaz!" Calder crowed. "That word's gotta be longer than the alphabet."

"Okay, it seems like we've gotten through some firsts today. How about linigunch?" Tommy asked. He brought a package of baloney, a jar of mayonnaise, bread, chips, pickles, and butter knives on the table. "Help yourselves. And Zoomy and Early: We three always had some kind of trinigeinigat when we needed a pat on the back during other adventures. Like, blue M&M'S, red gummy fish, or chocolate. Anyone got an idea for what the five of us can use?"

"I do!" Zoomy said immediately, his mouth already full. "Beans! Dilly beans. Gam's always got a big jar in the truck. Won't cost us a penny."

"But don't those make you finigart?" Petra said.

Calder laughed and a piece of baloney shot out of his mouth and into Goldman's bowl.

"Scaz, you knucklehead!" Tommy shouted. He reached for the runaway baloney just as Goldman swallowed it. "Now it'll be all your fault if he turns into a carnivore. He may start trying to eat my fingers! He may jump out of his bowl and launch an attack while I'm asleep!"

Goldman burped and a large bubble rose to the surface.

"Hey, that gives me an idea," Calder said. "I wonder if the trustees were really fighting? Maybe they were just *feeding* us that idea. Like it was all *baloney*, ha."

"But Early and I heard them fighting before you guys got there," Petra pointed out. "And they're on two sides of the moving question, so of course their fight is real."

"But they all want the art found," Zoomy said.

"Not if one of them has a reason to feel guilty," Early said slowly. "Maybe they're more together on all this than they want us to know. We overheard someone mention an 'event' they'd all talked about or planned. Maybe one of them did something stupid, like lend their museum key to a person who shouldn't have been trusted, and now they're covering it up. At least, in public."

"But Mrs. Sharpe — *she* wouldn't have anything to do with stealing the art!" Petra protested. "I'm sure she wouldn't. And besides, she wouldn't fool Ms. Hussey, would she?"

"I don't think Ms. Hussey knew that Eagle Devlin even existed before he showed up this week," Early said. "That means Mrs. Sharpe never mentioned him."

Petra still felt as though she needed to defend Mrs. Sharpe. "So it's not like she lied, but she definitely kept a big secret."

"Maybe Mrs. Sharpe is protecting her son," Calder said. "Even if she's not sure she needs to. Or maybe it's *Ms. Hussey* she's been protecting, and she didn't want her to meet or even know about that Devlin guy!"

"Yeah," Zoomy said. "Maybe he's trouble."

"It feels like all of those adults with us in the room today, all eight, were hiding things," Calder said. "Even if they didn't want to, like Ms. Hussey. She was pretty weird this morning. Not so open."

"You mean, like they know stuff they haven't shared with the police." Early put down her half-eaten sandwich. "And maybe the guys in black jackets are undercover."

"I hope they're on our side," Tommy said. "Because they seem to be around wherever we are. It's like someone told them to keep an eye on us."

Early looked worried. "If that's true, how do we figure out if they're good guys? I mean, who do we know is a hundred percent on our side? I guess Ms. Hussey is, but she's also on Mrs. Sharpe's side."

"Goldman," Tommy said. "And Sarah Chase Farmer, if you believe in ghosts." Tommy braced himself for questions, but no one asked.

"Good thing we can trust each other up close, with all these deeps," Zoomy said.

"What *are* 'deeps'?" Calder asked.

"Everything that's past the end of your arm. Everything that's blurry," Zoomy replied comfortably. "Like deep water."

"I like that," Early murmured, eating again.

"Me, too," Petra said. "Kind of perfect for right now."

Goldman nodded and dove for his deeps as Tommy glanced out the window, wondering how Zoomy could both see less and catch more. Maybe deeps could be both bad and good, like so much else that was going on.

Tommy thought suddenly about that silvery laugh in the Farmer. There had been five kids and ten adults . . . and a whole lot of deeps.

Maybe there'd been more people out of sight — hidden in the deeps — just as there might have been in Powell's.

"It's hard to know what you can't see — like, who's there but not visible and who's invisible but still there," Calder said suddenly, and Tommy elbowed him.

"Hey, you stole that from my head," Tommy blurted. This wasn't true, but Tommy suddenly felt like Calder was leaving him behind.

"I think we're all thinking about the same stuff," Early said, and the way she said it made Tommy feel less alone.

He tried to sort things out, but these deeps made everything feel distorted. And they changed the rules. If a boot could appear, icy fingers tweak, or a giggle come from nowhere, how could the five decide what was real and what wasn't?

For some reason, Tommy didn't dare say this aloud. Whoever else was in the deeps could probably see — and hear — a lot more than they could.

"Scaz," he moaned. "How can you tell who's in the deeps?"

"I can't," Zoomy said comfortably. "But sometimes I just know."

"Got it," Tommy said. He glanced around anxiously, glad they were in his Robie House apartment and not in the Farmer.

❑❑❑ After lunch, Early and Petra each headed home. Tommy and Calder walked Zoomy back to the guesthouse he and Gam were staying in. On the way, they'd planned to check on Mrs. Sharpe's house and make sure Ms. Hussey wasn't in trouble with Mr. Devlin.

"We'll listen for screams from inside," Calder had joked. Now they stood on the sidewalk in front of Mrs. Sharpe's door.

Tommy thought suddenly of the stone man trapped beneath the lion, but all he said was "Hey, ever thought about how violent all these last names sound when you line them up? Chase, Crunch, Hurts, Cracken, Whacker, Stabbler, Sharpe . . . and now Devlin. Like you've got chasing, breaking, hurting, hitting, stabbing, and now deviling!"

The three laughed, but it didn't feel too funny.

"Ms. Hussey won't like us checking on her," Calder said abruptly. He pulled out the V. "V for *vexed*."

"*Victim*," Tommy said.

"*Vinigerminigeiniger*," Zoomy said.

Tommy smiled. "*That's* a winner! The great man's name is related to vinegar."

Zoomy grinned happily. "How rude!"

Meeow! Ratty popped out of a bush and rubbed himself back and forth on Zoomy's legs.

The boys stopped laughing. Zoomy bent over and whispered, "Spies!" into the collar.

Tommy grabbed Zoomy on one side and Calder on the other. The three rushed down the street and around the corner, voices cracking under the strain of the moment, laughing again once they were safely away. Ratty sat calmly on the porch and watched them go. He hopped up as Mrs. Sharpe's door opened.

Ms. Hussey stooped to pat him. "Where're the kids? I thought I heard them," she said, rubbing his ears. "You're the pussycat who came to visit the queen!"

"Which would make them the mice under the chair," a man's voice said behind her.

If the boys had heard, they might have stopped laughing.

❏ ❏ ❏ Monument Cracken's house was forbidding. A Victorian hodgepodge of turrets and curved rooms, it was painted a bloody crimson with black trim. Petra looked up at the windows, which were shuttered. Why would anyone want such spooky paint on a house? She reached for the knocker, which was a brass hand with an old-fashioned ring on one finger. The ring had a bumblebee imprinted on it, as if for stamping letters. A snake bracelet encircled the wrist.

Bam! Bam! The sound was deafening. Petra stepped back and smoothed her hair. Then she ran her tongue over her front teeth, just in case there was any leftover lunch.

The man who opened the door was much younger and taller than Mr. Cracken, and wore a penguin uniform. Nodding stiffly to Petra, he handed her a sealed mailing envelope.

"Please return this in the condition in which it was lent," he intoned. "Mr. Cracken is allowing you twenty-four hours."

"Thanks so much," Petra said, staring behind him into the hallway. She then added, as if stalling for time, "So . . . I should be back here tomorrow, same time?"

The man nodded again and seemed to slide backward on ice as the door clicked shut.

Hugging the package, Petra stood for a moment on the porch, shocked by what she'd seen.

Behind the Penguin, five or six expertly wrapped, slender rectangles leaned against the wall, rectangles of various sizes that could have held the Manet, the Vermeer . . . certainly any number of the missing thirteen. But why would Monument Cracken have the art hidden — and not exactly hidden! — in his house? And if not — would an old man like that be buying expensive art at his age? What had she seen?

She hurried toward Early's apartment. She'd promised to share. On the way, she made herself think calmly about Mrs. Farmer's family of art and her kind wishes for the rest of the world.

Squeezing the book tighter, Petra whispered, "We'll find your missing family, we will. And maybe the man in *The Concert* will turn and help us."

Just then a group of children ran by, and one shouted, "Your turn! Your turn! Take your turn!"

Petra frowned. What *was* this? Why were things echoing each other in a nonsensical way, sort of like the snakeskin boots fitting with the snakes around Medusa's head? Or Mr. Devlin mimicking Ratty's expression? Or the bee and the snake on the doorknocker?

It felt as though the line between what mattered and what didn't was getting blurrier with each step.

❏ ❏ ❏ Early's mom, Summer, welcomed Petra at the door. Jubie jumped up and down waving a drawing he'd made of a garbage truck dropping things off the back. "It's doin' poo! We got new markers, too! Just for us," Jubie shouted.

Their apartment was one room, as Early had warned her,

and spotless. Petra saw almost no furniture aside from a table, but there were bright bedspreads, mats, and pillows along each wall. Lamps balanced on milk crates shed inviting pools of light in the darker corners. Shoes sat two by two by the door, largest to smallest. Four cloth napkins, each with its own design, were neatly rolled and held with kid-made pipe cleaner rings. Even the spices in a kitchen area, organized by color on a shelf next to the stove, looked orderly.

Petra sighed, untying her sneakers. "You're so lucky. Everything's so inviting, and you only have one little, ah, assistant around. I'd trade any day!"

When Summer brought the girls a huge bowl of popcorn, Petra said happily, "How did you know? I'm in heaven. Never leaving." She noticed that Early's hair was loose and fell in a puff of curls around her face. "Hey, our hair looks kinda the same now," she pointed out.

Early smiled until Jubie leaned close and whispered, "Yum yum popcorn sistahs!" and almost fell into the bowl.

"We're going out, young man," Summer announced, whisking Jubie into his jacket. "And I've made you your own bag of popcorn, see? And I've made one for Dash, who will be home in a while. Back soon, girls."

"There's drawbacks to living in one room, let me tell you," Early said as the front door closed. "Jubie could make a house the size of Mrs. Sharpe's feel like a peanut shell. I think he'd even make the Farmer feel small."

Petra opened the envelope Mr. Cracken's butler had handed to her. "Ooh, this copy's in great shape," she purred. "Yikes, the popcorn! I bet he'd call the police if we got even one grease spot on it."

They put the book to one side and sat for several minutes eating and talking. Early told Petra more about what had happened to their family, and how hard she'd had to work to scare away "the ghosts of bad guys," as she put it. She also shared the word and quote notebooks that the Pearl family had kept for years. Petra was thrilled and told Early about her own notebook, her dreams of becoming a writer, and how difficult it was to get any peaceful thinking done in her home.

"My dad says what burns is what turns," Early said. When Petra looked worried, she added, "He only means that what's hard can send you to new places in life, you know?"

"Yeah, it's just . . . the *turning* thing reminds me of 'What if he turns?' Mrs. Farmer's question about the Vermeer man. It seems like I keep hearing that phrase."

"Maybe that's good. It means he's come alive!" Early crowed, and made a scary Frankenstein face.

Petra rolled her eyes. "Yeah, and it'll be your job to get him to call us and tell us where his painting is — and who stole it!" She went on to tell Early about the oddly perfect rectangular packages in Monument Cracken's hallway.

"But why would they be there — except that it's so unlikely, it's safe," Early mused.

"And if I saw other paintings — why?" Petra looked unhappy. "He doesn't seem like the kind of guy to be buying fancy art right now, you know?"

"I'll come with you tomorrow when you return the book," Early offered. "Another pair of eyes."

"Great," Petra said, her mouth full. Sharing worries was always a relief. "Hey, your mom makes such good popcorn — I can't believe I've almost demolished the whole bowl. Whoa, look: Some of these pieces have *faces*, like a nose and two eyes! Here's one that even has a mouth. Maybe I'm next."

"No way! I'm not meeting that penguin guy tomorrow with a piece of popcorn standing next to me."

Petra laughed, and helped to chase runaway kernels and wash and dry the bowl. They settled side by side against the wall, the small red book open between them.

"So, here's the part we read in Powell's, about art being like family to her," Petra said. "I notice she writes in short bursts, like these are things she's thought about for ages and then boiled down to just a few words. Listen to this:

"Most great art begins with the human face. It can make the plain beautiful and the undistinguished immortal."

"Mmm, that's so true," Early murmured. "I'll bet if you were in line with the Mona Lisa lady in a grocery store, you'd never think she was unforgettable. Oh, good, more on faces.

"From birth, we work to decode the human face. Art is built on that truth."

Petra nodded. These days, that felt miserably true. She struggled each morning to decode her own face — in the bathroom mirror. "Here's another," she said to Early, pointing at the page.

"Art speaks through the language of the human face. Imagine what would be left of art if we erased all faces!"

Early whistled. "What a nightmare! I don't know about Zoomy, but if you're used to seeing faces, imagine how lonely and confused you'd feel without eyes, noses, and mouths to show what's going on. You'd be lost."

Petra nodded. "And art would feel pretty empty."

Early read on:

"A face captured in art, one that resonates, can remind you of yourself. There is magic in recognizing the face behind a face, in seeing that art can reflect with greater accuracy than any mirror.

"The right art, when you find it, will dovetail with your soul."

"Oooh," Petra said. "I have to let that sink in for a minute."

Early was already grabbing for the dictionary. "*Dovetail* . . . It's such a cool idea, that art can interlock with your true self."

"It's almost," Petra said in a dreamy voice, "as if Vermeer's world and the expressions on the people he painted make me feel more at home in my own face; or like they make me feel as though one day I might be just as . . . well, as serene and mysterious, you know? As complete."

Early nodded. "Like you'd have a right to be who you are — whatever that is — and everything would work out fine."

"You've got it," Petra said happily. "An understanding world." She glanced shyly at Early.

Her friend nodded and pointed to the page. "Listen," she said.

"If you ask a person on the street which piece of museum art they remember best — or would like to own — it is almost always one with a person in it. People feel close when they understand each other. Anyone who thinks the living and the dead aren't connected through art is a fool."

"Whoa, I love how this fits," Petra said. "And we're surrounded by patterns! Faces in popcorn . . . faces in art . . ."

Early was already writing furiously in the family Quote Book. She paused. "I wonder why more people don't know about this book? It's a game changer for anyone who looks at art."

"Maybe Mrs. Farmer thought she'd be made fun of," Petra suggested. Her phone rang. "Ms. Hussey?" she said, then listened for a moment. "I can do it, and I'll spread the word. Tomorrow morning at eleven. Really? *Really?* That's weird."

After she hung up, she looked at Early, her face suddenly frightened. "I'm not sure I like this. Ms. Hussey said she was just thinking about all the faces in the stolen art, and about how the pieces might be hidden *behind* other art, in public places. You know, like the last place that would be likely for most thieves. She wants to go on a trip downtown with all of us tomorrow, on Monday. But Early, can you believe she called just as we were reading this part about faces in art?"

Early sat up straight. "She's been talking to someone who's read this book. Like Eagle. After all, he's the one who heard us reading it in Powell's the other day — maybe this is proof that he did steal it!"

"We've gotta warn her," Petra said. "There may be a very good reason that Mrs. Sharpe never told Ms. Hussey about him."

"Yeah, like he's the mystery man in *The Concert*," Early said. "The only one without a face."

"The one who turned," Petra said softly.

🔲 🔲 🔲 "We'll knock. SHUT UP! Oh sorry, Early, I didn't mean you!"

Early grinned into her cell phone. "I get it. You mean, go to the spooky house before you're expected?"

"I knew you'd understand," Petra said happily. "We'll show up to drop off the red book on our way to the train station this morning — and I'm thinking that arriving unannounced might be good."

"You're on," Early said. An hour later, the two girls had met on a corner near Powell's. They walked north on Blackstone Avenue, Petra clutching the small package.

"I see what you mean about this place," Early said quietly as they approached. "If you wanted your house to look unfriendly, you couldn't do a better job."

They were still across the street when a limousine pulled up in front. The driver stepped out and flung open the back door. Just then, the Penguin opened Mr. Cracken's front door and hurried down the steps to help carry *three more* carefully wrapped packages into the front hall.

"Scaz," breathed Early. "What're we seeing?"

"Keep walking, as if we're just going by," Petra hissed. "It's too late to hide."

"No, because we have to return the book!" Early whispered. She pulled Petra's arm and they half sank, half fell between two parked cars. From where they landed, they saw a number of skinny ankles and canes follow the packages out of the back seat.

"I'll pretend I have a bathroom emergency!" Early said, and before her friend could respond, she popped upright, dragging Petra after her.

"Lovely," Petra mumbled as they clumped up the porch steps behind Winnifred Whacker and Hershel Hurts. The two old people didn't seem to have heard them, but the Penguin pointed to the girls in horror. The two in front turned slowly around.

"Had to return the book early — our teacher is taking us downtown today," Petra blurted.

The Penguin held out his hand and then snapped his fingers when the girls didn't move. Neither Ms. Whacker nor Mr. Hurts moved either, which meant everyone was stuck.

This gave Early time to squeeze around Ms. Whacker, who looked ready to scream. "I have, um, a bathroom emergency," Early said, as if mortified. "Forgive me, but nature calls."

The Penguin frowned, rolled his eyes, but stepped back, and before Petra knew it, Early had vanished into the gloom inside. Still holding the doorknob, the Penguin turned to honk directions, his tone making clear that this was an imposition.

Meanwhile, the two old folks examined Petra as if she had just escaped from the zoo. Painfully aware that she had a ragged hole in the toe of one sneaker, she froze. Ms. Whacker wore pointy high heels with artsy swirls all over them, as if someone had taken an Impressionist painting, chopped it in half, and wrapped it around her feet.

As the two turned away and stepped slowly through the open door, Petra knew she had to do as Early had, and simply assume she could enter. Having forgotten about the book, the Penguin began to close the door just as she slid one foot into the hall.

"Oh, I'll wait in the entryway here, that's fine!" Petra mumbled, stepping inside as if he hadn't just tried to shut her out.

"Don't move," the butler hissed and spun on his heel, gliding after Ms. Whacker and Mr. Hurts into another room.

Her heart pounding in her throat, Petra glanced wildly around. The packages that had leaned against the wall yesterday were gone, but the three that had just been unloaded stood in their place. There *was* one way to find out whether these were priceless . . .

Just as Early stepped out of a door at the end of the hall, the sound of the toilet flushing behind her, the Penguin hurried back toward the girls and Petra pretended to stumble toward the rectangles leaning against the wall.

"Whoa," she gasped, as she lunged toward the largest one, one arm waving as if to catch herself. The Penguin dropped the two coats he'd been carrying and reached out to grab Petra, who then really *did* lose her balance. Early, nearby, got her foot ground beneath one of the Penguin's fancy flippers, and the three tumbled into a ghastly, noisy pile. One of the packages leaning against the wall tilted slowly toward them, coming to rest on the Penguin's head.

It was Monument Cracken who lifted the rectangle off the pile and, without asking whether anyone was hurt, tucked it under his arm. He then turned toward Petra. "And the book?" was all he said, his voice sounding as if it had never been young.

Speechless, Petra handed it over.

"Thanks so much, Mr. Cracken," she croaked as she struggled to her feet. "It's a treasure, so filled with wisdom and wonderful ideas about —" Mr. Cracken had already turned away and was stumping back into the next room. The door closed with a polished thud, ending her sentence.

"There you have it," the Penguin said, and as he leaned over to straighten the pleats on his trousers, a large, gleaming knife slid from his pocket and clattered to the floor. The blade bounced open in a flash of light.

"Out!" he said, the front door now open.

"Thanks so much for —" Early began as the door whumped shut behind them.

"They're not big on manners around here." Petra giggled as the girls rushed down the steps, talking over each other and comparing notes on what they'd just seen.

If they hadn't been so busy, they would have noticed a man in a familiar black jacket and hat stepping quickly into Powell's at the end of the block. Tucked beneath one arm was a package that looked exactly like the three they'd just left.

The girls never knew.

☐ ☐ ☐ On the way downtown with Ms. Hussey and the three boys, Early and Petra shared the news.

"Early was the brave one," Petra said generously.

"I wasn't!" Early said, glowing with pleasure. "I was hiding in the bathroom listening through the door while you had to fight your way past the dragons."

"But you started it," Petra said.

"I've learned not to hesitate when you see an opening at the right time," Early said. "For better or worse."

"I'm glad we didn't get stabbed by that knife in the pileup," Petra added.

Tommy and Calder were looking from girl to girl with interest.

"Sounds like a switchblade," Tommy said in his deepest voice.

"So what were those folks hiding?" Zoomy asked.

"These are wealthy people who probably buy lots of new things, even at their ages," Ms. Hussey said. "Maybe it *was* art, but not the art we're looking for."

Calder had the X pentomino in his hand. "Why would *any* of them be shopping for art right now? It's a terrible time for both the museum and Mr. Chase."

Ms. Hussey looked troubled. "Mrs. Sharpe was convinced we should head down here. I wonder . . ." She seemed to shake off the idea. "Well. I suppose there are many things we'll never know about a bunch of old, rich folks." She paused for a moment. "I didn't mean Mrs. Sharpe."

You sure? Tommy thought and sucked in his cheeks.

Once off at the last stop, the Millennium Park station, Ms. Hussey marched the five kids right into the closest Subway shop. They split three foot-long sandwiches and drank lots of water.

"Teenagers need fortification," she announced, pulling money out of her back pocket. "Mrs. Sharpe insisted we have some expense money, no worries." Ms. Hussey had a way of turning the world into a place that was waiting for what kids had to offer.

"Ms. Hussey," Petra said, then hesitated. "Um, you know, Early and I read lots from *The Truth About My Art* yesterday. It's great, and we shared with the boys last night, by phone. It has a ton about faces in art . . ."

"Oh! Funny thing," Ms. Hussey said, folding her paper napkin into smaller and smaller rectangles. "I guess. Right."

"Have you read it?" Early asked.

"Not exactly, but I listened to some inspiring parts. I knew you guys would love it, and I asked — oh, never mind, you did find a copy! Doesn't Sarah Chase Farmer seem like a friend?"

"Did Mr. Devlin say it was his?" Tommy asked abruptly.

"Eagle didn't say and I didn't ask," Ms. Hussey said slowly. "What are you getting at?"

Eagle, Tommy thought. *Heard that! No more Mr. Devlin.* Tommy looked around for backup.

"We're wondering if Mrs. Sharpe didn't tell you about Devlin — I mean, whatever, Mr. Eagle —" Calder broke off.

"I think he'd want you to call him Eagle," Ms. Hussey's tone was neutral.

"— because she wasn't sure what Eagle was up to," Calder blundered on. "What if Mrs. Sharpe didn't want you to meet him? And you know, the copy of Mrs. Farmer's book was on the shelf at Powell's one minute, seconds after we met Eagle Devlin, and then it was gone."

"Why don't you guys like him?" Ms. Hussey asked.

"It's not that." Petra shifted uncomfortably. "We don't know him. And he seems to be familiar with stuff that fits too well with the heist. Like he's been investigating it on his own. We were worried about you."

"Hark, hark, the dogs do bark," Ms. Hussey laughed just as her phone rang.

The kids watched her face light up — even Zoomy, who leaned in close. "Oh, wonderful," she said to whoever was on the other end of the phone. "Yes, I hope so. Downtown with the kids. I'll tell them."

She ended the call and announced, "The news from Mrs. Sharpe is that Mr. Chase is sometimes awake but not responding to any conversation. They say he may recover all of his speech with time." Ms. Hussey looked thoughtful for a moment and then smiled at the group. "She's glad we're here."

Tommy had to struggle to imagine Mrs. Sharpe looking glad.

Once outside and into the park, they wandered. It was lunchtime, but the sun was already on its way into afternoon.

"Wish we were seeing all of this in full summer, when the water is on," Ms. Hussey said. "But we can imagine. I know we're not going to find the stolen artworks peeking out from behind a face in the middle of a park, but I'm hoping some detail will get our minds racing in the right direction."

Human faces aren't the only things we try to decode, Petra thought.

Tommy couldn't help but be nagged by an opposite thought: Was Ms. Hussey taking them away from the real investigation for some reason? Had Mrs. Sharpe or Eagle Devlin put her up to it? But that made no sense — didn't Mrs. Sharpe want them to find the paintings?

As if reading Tommy's mind, Calder then said, "Ms. Hussey, can you call Mrs. Sharpe back? Just to be sure she isn't on her way to Mr. Cracken's house right now? I mean, what if she got lured there and it really *is* the stolen art and — well, the police come and she goes to jail forever? Besides, there's that Penguin guy with a knife."

Ms. Hussey stopped moving and faced the five, a quick grin fading as she thought about what he'd said. "I guess I could call back," she said slowly. "There're so many confusing pieces here."

They stood in a small circle as she turned away, the phone to her ear. "It's me again. Just a quick question: Will anyone be joining the other trustees at Monument Cracken's house? Early and Petra were just there."

Zoomy suddenly leaned closer to Ms. Hussey's back.

"Oh, I see," she said. "Of course. Well, don't overdo it." As she shut her phone, she avoided the kids' eyes.

"The trustees are apparently showing each other pieces of their individual collections and getting advice," she said unhappily and walked toward a bench and sat down.

The kids followed, wanting now to reassure her. "If I were a thief," Petra said, "I'd hide art in the most unlikely place possible, and that would be a place like *this*, like Millennium Park, a public space that's filled with huge, hollow structures that happen to be art as well."

"Right! A place that no one would look because everybody's already looking." Early nodded. "And those old folks can't be out investigating with their fancy shoes and canes, so better us than them."

"Oh!" Ms. Hussey said, looking faint. "The thought of Mr. Cracken's house! What if, as you said, the trustees are being used in a police sting of some kind, and have no idea . . ."

"Unlikely they wouldn't see the game, but it's a definite maybe," Tommy muttered.

"What if Mr. Cracken invited them all over so they could get friendly again? After all that fighting, you know?" Zoomy suggested.

"But why all the wrapped packages?" Petra blurted. "It doesn't make sense. Unless each of the trustees was responsible for one or two of the stolen pieces and — oh, forget it."

Ms. Hussey shrugged, stood, and brushed off the front of her jacket as if brushing off her fears.

"Maybe it was show-and-tell time," she suggested, her voice taking on some of its old I'm-in-charge-now confidence. "I think this is a case of moving ahead with our faces investigation, following Mrs. Farmer's lead and not worrying while we're down here. There are both so many pieces and so many players in this picture — you remember the sheet you guys were given in the Farmer — that it's easy to misinterpret things. And hard for anyone to juggle such a varied group of missing objects with such a variety of people. But our — I mean, *my* — idea, after all, is so logical, the idea of hiding art in the open, where no one would think to look — and hiding faces behind faces."

Our? Tommy thought. Our *meaning who else?*

As if reading his mind, Zoomy gave him a funny look.

Although the five all had uncomfortable questions, they wanted to believe Ms. Hussey. After all, who could tell what step might become a clue, or what clue lead to what step?

She walked them to the middle of the Crown Fountain.

"I've never been here before," Zoomy said. "Someone tell me about the deeps."

Ms. Hussey's expression softened. "You'd love it. In warm weather, a video of a face appears on the wall at either end. There are hundreds of different faces, all belonging to everyday Chicagoans. Every ten minutes, there's a new one. Meanwhile, these tall, rectangular structures pour water down their sides, and there's a shallow pool between the two. Shoes come off in summer, and everyone becomes a kid — tiptoeing, splashing, rolling, leaping, running. It's a place where water allows people to forget what they look like." Ms. Hussey paused. "Cool, huh?"

"Tell Zoomy what happens with the faces," Calder said.

"Well, each face was filmed slowly puckering her or his mouth, and then presto! At a certain point, a powerful stream of water shoots out from each one at the same exact time. The faces are like giant, living gargoyles, spitting water both toward each other and onto everyone beneath. These people's expressions aren't frightening, though; they're not like those scary stone gargoyles on old buildings. They're relaxed. Unselfconscious. This is interactive art, different every time because of the changing videos, the come-and-go of people playing in the fountain, and the shifts in the light and the weather. The artist is Jaume Plensa, from Spain."

Petra, Calder, Tommy, and Early all agreed that you could spend a long time there without becoming bored; as Ms.

Hussey said, the changing images and the visitors around them created an endless flow of pieces and players. Zoomy said he wanted to come back in August and bring his grandpa, who he said hated sand but loved spitting water. He'd understand this art.

Then Ms. Hussey pointed out that you could certainly hide climate-controlled storage boxes somewhere inside these giant towers, or in the operating rooms beneath them, the places for water pipes and computerized controls; there had to be more than enough dry space.

As they walked away from the Crown Fountain toward some of the other sculptures, Petra thought about all those combinations that made up the art in the summer, and the blank, sleeping walls as they looked now. *Blank spaces.* Suddenly the sadness of the missing art in the Farmer, art that couldn't just reappear with the warm weather, came back in a rush. The pieces that were still there offered joy, of course, but the gaps created by what was missing felt so horribly wrong. Each day added weight to the crime.

The faces in the fountain belonged to living people, but the faces in the Farmer — well, Petra thought, if they were truly family to many, they were now missing family.

The word *murder* drifted into Petra's mind. No! She tried to get rid of the thought. *These pieces are waiting*, she told herself, *and still hold a mirror to so many dreams* . . .

"This one is nothing *but* faces!" Early exclaimed as they reached the Bean.

And nothing but a mirror, thought Petra with a little shock of recognition. *As if it's literally doing what Mrs. Farmer knew art could do.*

"Birds of a feather." Ms. Hussey smiled.

"Birds of a feather flock together," said Calder. "Don't *you* start with the Mother Goose stuff, Ms. Hussey! Please!"

His old teacher laughed and frowned, as if wondering herself why she'd said that.

A giant, lima bean–shaped sculpture made from mirrored steel, the Bean pulled everyone closer, inviting them to touch, circle, and walk through the arch in its center. Once inside, looking up, the world became a swirl of reflections, symmetrical but not, because of the people flowing beneath. A dash of red, a snatch of blue: *Here you are! And here! And here!* it whispered, teasing all who tried to puzzle out its magic.

Ms. Hussey watched as Early and Petra walked straight toward the curved surface and placed their hands against it. Twenty fingers suddenly became forty, palm to palm.

"No secrets," Petra said happily. *I'll just enjoy this moment*, she told herself.

"Or *all* secrets," Early added. "Like there are so many crazy ways to see yourself in this world that you don't know which one is real. If there *is* one."

"Right," Petra said, glancing happily at her new friend.

"Hey," Early said, "let's see how far away we can get before we disappear." She and Petra backed up as the three boys vanished under the arch.

It was dizzying either way. Stepping back from the Bean, it became half crowd and ground, half sky and clouds. An elliptical landscape soared up and down and side to side as if the world had shrunk, come loose, and was rolling around itself — as if everyone was on it but off it. The girls noticed that people forgot to be normal and did crazy things near the sculpture: dancing in place, lying down and waving their feet in the air, looking over one shoulder, snapping pictures from all angles. Some just stood and stared with their mouths open. Others circled it, grinned, walked closer, then farther away, and even tried everything over again, as if repetition would help them to understand what they saw.

"Its real name is *Cloud Gate*," Ms. Hussey said. "It's by a British artist, Anish Kapoor. His work is often about the Hindu ideas of transformation, of nature and humanity working together, and the play of *here* and *what if*. You can sure feel that in this piece. At dusk, I love the way the Bean lets you follow the colors of the sky better than you can with the naked eye. Kind of like someone is painting them on that huge, curved surface. Like that subtle shift of light becomes art, which makes it easier to see. And then *bang!* electricity takes over the city, and the sculpture becomes dazzling all over again. That's when people vanish into the Bean's mirror. But during the day the crowds are everything, as if you can suddenly watch busy lives, good plus bad, standing out against the earth."

"I think Mrs. Farmer would get it, even though it's so modern," Early said.

"Yup," Petra agreed. "Like all great art, it makes you notice life."

"Now, *that's* a thought." Ms. Hussey released her hair then swirled it back into a bun, always a sign that she was working on an idea.

Tommy came running over. "Hey! Zoomy's gone!" he panted.

Ms. Hussey and the girls dashed into the arch only to find themselves stuck in a dense crowd of kids all talking, laughing, and turning slowly in circles. Calder's head popped out in the middle, but Zoomy was nowhere to be seen.

Suddenly the group surged on and Zoomy appeared, squatting and chin-tapping in a corner.

The kids leaned over him. "Zoomy, man! Sorry I lost you!" Tommy said breathlessly.

"Got your notebook?" Ms. Hussey asked.

Zoomy nodded, pulled it out, and wrote, *-confusing bean.* He stood up and hit his head. "Ow! Think there're any doors in this thing?" he asked. "I was looking for a way to get inside, and suddenly you guys were gone and it seemed like the wall was squashing me."

"Hey, good work on the door idea!" Calder said. He had the T pentomino out of his pocket. "T for *turn. Tricky. Try.*"

"Try, tricky, turn," Tommy added.

"Let's stop being tricky and go sit down over there for a moment," Ms. Hussey said, pointing to a long table with benches. They did. Somehow, the Bean took a lot of energy.

They watched for a while in silence as one group of people after another turned a corner in the park, saw the Bean, and flowed toward it as if pulled by a huge magnet. All languages drifted through the air.

When the sun hit the Bean at certain moments, it blinded. When clouds moved overhead, it seemed to rock like a boat, but one that was upside down.

Calder, in that quiet moment, thought suddenly about the desperate faces on Rembrandt's bean-shaped ship and felt discouraged. Ms. Hussey had made a good point — there were so many priceless objects involved and this was such a confusing puzzle. Why were the five of them even down here? Was it just to get them out of the way? And did Mrs. Sharpe *really* believe that a bunch of thirteen-year-olds could help to decipher what was going on? Was their group of five *really* that smart?

Tommy, next to him, was wondering why they hadn't researched Crown Fountain and the Bean *before* coming here. If the stolen art was hidden inside either one, you'd never see it from the outside. Was Ms. Hussey so used to being around sixth graders that she'd forgotten they were eighth graders now, and could handle a lot more?

"Maybe we can learn about how the art could have gotten inside either the Bean or the Crown if we go online,"

Tommy said. "I mean, it's fun looking at these sculptures, but what good does that do?"

Ms. Hussey shot him a look, as if to say, *Are you complaining?*

She and the kids had already touched every inch of exposed surface on the Bean that they could reach, trailing their fingers across the reflections. There didn't seem to be a seam or even a line anywhere. No way to get inside.

"Fine," Ms. Hussey said, pulling out her phone, and looked up the story of the Bean. "It is indeed hollow and took a long time, two years, to finish," she reported. "It was completed in 2006. It weighs one hundred and ten tons and stands thirty-three feet high. It's made from one hundred and sixty-eight stainless steel plates welded together, and Kapoor was inspired by the movements of a drop of liquid mercury." She looked up. "Have you kids ever seen mercury? It's a poisonous element, but a drop is similar to a near-weightless, elastic, silver marble. It's treacherous, beautiful — and keeps changing shape."

Just like this mystery, Early thought. *Treacherous. We five should watch out. That butler today had an awfully big knife and it caught the light just like the Bean.*

"What's the story on the big fountain? Any details on where to hide loot in there?" Zoomy asked.

"Hold on." Ms. Hussey tapped and scrolled. "Hmm, open to the public in 2004, the two towers are fifty feet high and made from glass brick. They bracket a black granite reflecting pool . . . light-emitting diodes — LEDs — show digital videos of 960 faces . . . each appears for the same number of minutes . . ." She closed her phone. "What a place to hide art that everyone is searching for, inside art that is looked at by hundreds, sometimes thousands, every day!"

"Yeah, art under art," Petra mused. "Like it's invisible —"

"— but almost in plain sight!" Early finished, and the girls high-fived.

Calder and Tommy looked at each other and shrugged.

"You'd have to be a super-sneaky type to make friends with the maintenance crew and get them to store a humongous box for you," Tommy added. "Why would they ever agree to do that?" *Sometimes girls get so carried away with word jabber that they say impossible stuff,* he thought to himself.

"But it's true that people sometimes don't notice what they're looking at," Zoomy said. "Like my gam says: Their eyes are always in a hurry and about to move on to something else."

Petra turned back to look at the Bean before they left. In the upper curve, far above her head, she thought she saw two black jackets. By the time she'd pointed them out, they were gone in the crowd.

"I think you guys have Eagle and his clothing on the brain," Ms. Hussey joked. "Kind of like the *Where's Waldo?* pictures — if you spend too much time looking at them, you start imagining things everywhere."

"Shouldn't we be?" Tommy asked.

Zoomy nodded.

"Don't be rats, you guys," Ms. Hussey said, her voice cool and crisp. "Or cats," she muttered. A moment later, they were all walking toward the train, Ms. Hussey in the lead, and she seemed normal again.

Grown-ups sure can say weird things sometimes, Tommy thought. *Even the best. What did I do? Just being a detective.*

As if reading his mind, Early said softly, "Jack be nimble, Jack be quick, Jack jump over the candlestick." She glanced at Tommy, who was now staring at her. "If Eagle is Jack, he's nimble. Oops, here we go with Mother Goose again."

"Guess Jack is trying not to get a burned behind," Tommy said.

"Why would Eagle be following us today?" Early was frowning.

Zoomy faced the group. "Come closer, you guys," he said softly.

"Ms. Hussey was talking to a man on the phone earlier today," Zoomy whispered. "I could hear."

"Really?" Petra squeaked. "But she's always so honest with us!"

"She didn't exactly lie," Early said quietly.

Half a block behind the group, a man in a black leather jacket wove in and out of the crowd.

▯▯▯ Once off the train in Hyde Park, the five kids stopped with Ms. Hussey at Powell's Books. Petra wanted to point out where Mrs. Farmer's book had been on the shelf, and where Eagle had been sitting with Jubie while four of the five talked. She wanted to show Ms. Hussey that they weren't suspicious without reason.

"Perfect timing!" Mr. Watch called out. "Mrs. Sharpe's son just dropped off an envelope of copies of the text in Sarah Chase Farmer's book, one for each of you kids. Said he ran across a copy. He explained that you're doing research on the theft and might each need to have your own."

Five mouths made a row of Os, and Ms. Hussey grinned. "You were saying?" she asked the kids.

"Did that copy I was looking at ever end up back on the right shelf?" Petra asked Mr. Watch.

"Oh, hmm." He snapped his suspenders. "I think it did. Sometimes people reshelve books improperly, return for another look, and then assume the worst." He gave Petra an unfriendly wink.

"Huh," Petra said. Was he implying *she* had lost the book? Insulted, she hesitated for a moment, glanced at Ms. Hussey, then decided she'd said enough.

If Eagle had "borrowed" the book in order to help the kids, was that okay? And why hadn't he just *bought* it from

Mr. Watch? A grown-up with a business could certainly afford to pay for a book like that.

On the way out, Petra glanced back at Mr. Watch, who turned away and picked up the phone.

▯ ▢ ▯ After their stop at Powell's, Zoomy made the group step into his guesthouse, where each ate a dilly bean.

Ms. Hussey, hugging the packet of copies of *The Truth About My Art*, was suddenly in a great mood. "Mmm, they're crispy, sweet, and salty all together," she said. "What a productive couple of days we've had," she purred.

"That's good," Gam said.

More filled with confusing deeps than anything else, Tommy thought.

Before Ms. Hussey went her own way, she distributed the copies of Sarah Farmer's book. Minutes later, before the five separated that afternoon, they agreed to try an experiment. Mostly, it was Petra and Early's idea. The girls, talking intently together, had dropped behind the group after they'd all left Powell's.

The plan was this: Each of them would read through *The Truth* that evening and the next. Then, before going to sleep on Tuesday, they'd each look through the pictures of the stolen art. Each would pick one item, the one they'd most like to keep forever, and ask it to communicate. Or, as Early put it, "to talk and tell us what's up," perhaps in their dreams.

"And it's a full moon," Petra finished.

"What if the art starts howling?" Tommy asked. Calder jabbed him, and Zoomy laughed.

"Maybe the Rembrandt boat will sink and the wine goblet will say *gobble gobble*," Calder said.

The other two boys snickered. The five, divided at that moment into a three and a two, didn't see a black limousine sliding along the block behind them, a familiar face in the front seat.

⬚⬚⬚ While the five kids looked forward to their experiment, an elderly man, alone in his hospital room, drifted in and out of consciousness.

Unable to apologize or communicate during the past couple of days, he found himself imprisoned in silence. Faces cycled through his mind, the living mixed with the dead. He remembered holding Sarah Chase Farmer's hand as a boy, as she walked him through her museum and home. She had asked him which piece of art he loved the most; which painting made him believe the people or places inside it were alive, a world with moving air, rustlings, whispers, and secrets?

He had picked *The Concert* that day. It felt cozy to him, as though a small boy could crouch by the table in the foreground and hide forever, watching the woman who played the harpsichord. His mother had died the year before, swept away by a frightening illness. She had played the piano every morning of his life, or so it seemed, in the sitting room of their giant house. He'd always been allowed to bring books or a toy and stay nearby as long as he was quiet. Sometimes he simply lay on the floor, watching the sunshine catch on a curl of his mother's hair or her earring, the music pouring and puddling around him. These sunshine concerts had the comfort of a warm bath, a time when no one expected him to be anything but himself. When he looked at that Vermeer painting, the woman at the harpsichord always seemed to know he was there. The boy shared that with his great-aunt.

Mrs. Farmer had hugged him and said, "And one day, you'll never have to be apart."

He had said, "When I die?" and she had shaken her head and laughed, a jingly sound. "No, no! When this museum is yours to treasure and share, and all of these people will welcome you to the world each morning."

He never forgot her words, although they had dulled with time. She had willed the museum to him, in a trust, overstepping many others in the Chase family — and yet he had never moved to her cozy apartment on the fourth floor, even though he hadn't married. He had lived a lonely, pennypinching life in a big house with not enough sunshine in it and no children. He hadn't treasured and shared, not enough. By waiting too long to pour his money and his heart into that magical place, he'd let down his great-aunt, art lovers everywhere, and the woman playing the harpsichord. Plus, he'd done something unforgivable that would have made his family hate him. Regrets swarmed and hovered, flapped their wings and meowed, and he felt heavy — oh, so heavy! — with long-held hopes, sadness, and broken dreams.

He was aware now of a hugely round and bright moon. *What?* Across this moon flew an old woman on the back of a goose — perhaps his great-aunt Sarah. She held a baby in her arms. For some reason, the sight filled the old man with peace.

It was then that he suffered another sharp sting, one that mercifully carried him off.

☐☐☐ The news of William Swift Chase's death traveled fast the next day. On the phone with Tommy, Calder pointed out that with William Chase gone, the number of pieces and number of players were the same: thirteen to thirteen.

After she heard the news, Petra pictured the majestic hulk of the Farmer Museum and wondered if the soul of Sarah Chase Farmer was especially sad. Were the rooms of treasures — the carved chairs and danger boxes, the paintings, the many dancing people and stone lions, the tapestries and old china — mourning Mr. Chase? Was Medusa still looking cheerful in the middle of the courtyard?

It was a dark thought, not in the least bit comforting.

Early shivered, glad the five of them weren't in the museum when the news broke. She could still picture what might have been a sleeve, and then a skirt whisking around the corner of the Dutch Room as they'd walked away. Would

Mrs. Farmer be feeling frustrated? Grief stricken? Or both? Sometimes upset adults lashed out at kids, and upset spirits might do the same.

Gam read lots of *The Truth* aloud to Zoomy that night while he scanned page after page of the art, deciding which piece he'd want to keep. Early, Calder, Tommy, and Petra each read their copies of the book, then soaked up the thirteen images, turning them around and around in their minds before going to sleep.

❏ ❏ ❏ It's said that a full moon coaxes the human heart and brain closer together, just as it pulls the tides in the ocean. Some stumble and some catch their balance; some are pulled toward death and some toward life. That night, the moon traveled in and out of bedroom after bedroom in Hyde Park, as if hunting. When a certain five kids were touched by that cold, bright light, each startled awake — awake and feeling as though they'd never sleep again, not until they'd taken what was offered.

❏ ❏ ❏ Zoomy was the first to sit upright in bed. He looked into the face of a man with a dark top hat and coat. His eyes were bright and steady, his mouth absorbed beneath a small, cheerful mustache. His surroundings were blurry — perhaps his world also held deeps. The man gripped a pencil in his right hand and covered what he was writing with his left, as if surprised that Zoomy had found him. As if he didn't want him to read what he was writing, not yet. *You'll understand this message*, he seemed to say. *You will! Just keep watching. And when the moment comes . . .*

Zoomy dropped off to sleep, muttering, "I will, I will," somehow filled with the certainty that he, although legally blind and sometimes jittery-splat, wouldn't disappoint.

❏ ❏ ❏ Early, lying on her sleeping mat in the Pearl apartment, listened to her parents snore and Jubie stir restlessly nearby. The moon was the roundest moon she thought she'd ever seen, as round as a marble or a coin or a golf ball. As Early stared up at it, the moon flattened into a collar, a disc-shaped collar around the neck of a woman with pearls in her hair and lace at her wrists. A ring gleamed on one finger. The woman waited, a smile playing around her mouth, not in the least bit impatient. A man stood nearby and looked directly at Early with a quizzical, pleased expression. *Well, come in*, he seemed to say. *Have a seat here, on this chair with the red cushion. They will arrive soon and will be so happy to see you.*

Early stepped in, feeling oddly calm. Somehow she knew she would shine. She'd fill this room with her own truth, whatever it might be, and everyone in it would thank her for it.

❏ ❏ ❏ Calder startled awake and grabbed for the wooden bedpost. He was blinded by light, by a feeling of not being able to catch his breath. He knelt by a mast, holding on for dear life as the boat beneath him shuddered and pitched and rolled, the cold slap of salt spray mixed with the screams of men. The waters around him were dark and furious, and suddenly he knew how little anything mattered — even his pentominoes — in the face of such power. As he lost his grip, rolling along the bottom of the boat, he shouted, "But I want to live! I do! I wasn't meant to be here!"

His father opened his door. "Everything okay in here? Bad dream?"

Untangling himself from a snarl of covers, Calder nodded. Then he said something his father repeated to him the next morning:

"They need help! All thirteen of them!"

□ □ □ Having read and reread Mrs. Farmer's thoughts about the Flinck painting, Tommy felt thrilled that Chicago starred in that landscape. She'd said it reminded her "of the treasures this city offers. We have the river, the grand lake, and much parkland for all to experience. We have paths and bridges to lead us forward. We have captured the essentials for human joy. In this painting I also see both our history and hopes for the future, as the obelisk resembles the one from the great 1893 Chicago World's Fair." It was a cool idea, the thought that a painting from well over three hundred and fifty years ago could also be about Tommy's world, as if the painter knew how much glory was still to come.

He didn't remember falling asleep, but woke suddenly to see the road in the painting stretching ahead. The dirt was cool and smooth under his bare feet, the people under a giant tree — the woman on a donkey and the man standing next to her — were enjoying the day. And was that a door in the tree, an open door? The air was warm, the river nearby was burbling, there were flowers and birds, and he felt as though a million treasures were waiting to be found.

But the Farmer thirteen! They were waiting, too . . . and now he was *inside* one of the stolen paintings. Were there fresh clues to be found? And if so, where should he look? Perhaps the door in the tree, a door opening into darkness.

◻◻◻ Petra gazed so long and hard at her copy of *The Concert* that the singing woman moved her raised hand. She did! It opened farther, the fingers uncurling as if to release a flood of notes. Suddenly Petra was standing by the X shape on the tiled floor, invisible in a swirl of classical melody and creamy light. She felt herself being pulled forward by the path of three Xs that ended beneath the man's chair. She wanted to reach out a hand to brace herself on the table to her left, but couldn't.

And the woman playing the harpsichord — there she was! It was the Lady from *A Lady Writing*, Vermeer's great 1665 painting. Petra studied the lemony ribbon in her hair, the pearl dangling from her ear, her sleeve bright with light, and the heavy folds of satin in her skirt — and the rectangle of red on the back of the man's chair, which seemed to say, *Stop! Turn back!*

Then, as if it were the most natural thing in the world, the woman at the harpsichord turned her head and nodded to Petra. She was a young Mrs. Sharpe, and she whispered, *For art, this building — this comfort*, as if Petra would understand.

☐ ☐ ☐ Perhaps because William Swift Chase's death was followed by that night of full-moon dreams, the rhythm of the investigation changed. The five kids awoke Wednesday linked by a feeling of urgency. The art was out there that very morning, perhaps in danger, waiting for the right thing to happen. Each piece had seemed to reach out to the kid who chose it, pulling them closer to the crime. Their responsibilities, even as thirteen-year-old dreamers, had been clear.

The six remaining trustees were dizzy with publicity and worry, worry and guilt, guilt and anger — anger that they vented at reporters and newspeople. One mean question nipped at another, circling round and round. How could their old friend have died like this, leaving them to cope with such a mess? And to add insult to injury, he'd left a trust, to be activated "immediately, at the event of my passing, and at the discretion of the trustees" that allowed for the near-complete restoration of the museum building, although it wouldn't cover many other issues, such as staffing, programs for all ages, and transportation needs.

Why hadn't he shared that money as the building ran slowly downhill, year after year? Why had the seven of them fought so bitterly about what should happen to this exquisite collection of art when, all along, he'd known he could intervene? Had he been hoping to use the threat of a move to jolt Chicago donors awake and raise the remaining millions that would allow for art restoration, plenty of parking, increased numbers of guards and curators, education outreach, and international connections? Or had he been genuinely unsure of what was right for the art?

He'd always insisted that he wanted the art to stay in Chicago, where it belonged, but explained that the trust didn't have the means to carry out even a fraction of what was needed, not unless they hired a professional fund-raising team. No one had felt that using dwindling funds in that way would be either responsible or effective.

Mrs. Sharpe had known she would be his executor — the person in charge of making sure that what he ordered in his will was carried out. She hadn't, however, guessed what she'd have to do. After opening the trust envelope and reading the document aloud in the presence of the other trustees on Tuesday, she had found another, smaller envelope with her name on it. *Private* was printed in the upper left hand corner. She'd opened the letter quietly, as the others talked. Her mouth had opened in a slow O, a highly uncharacteristic gesture.

"Well?" Monument Cracken had barked, followed by a "Well?" from Winnifred.

"I'm not at liberty to share this," Mrs. Sharpe had said abruptly. "Not yet. I have to think about it."

☐ ☐ ☐ On Wednesday morning, Ms. Hussey contacted the five kids with more news: Mrs. Sharpe had felt unwell during the night. Not wanting any of the reporters to get wind of another possible trustee emergency, she'd refused to go to the hospital, insisting that rest at home would help. She had, however, invited the kids to set up a meeting room in the attic of her house, and asked Ms. Hussey to welcome them. In addition, she'd invited the other trustees to come to the house for tea that afternoon.

"It sounds like a madhouse," Ms. Hussey told Tommy when she called. "But that's what she wants. Maybe having your own workspace, away from each other's homes, will be good. How about it?"

The five met in front of Mrs. Sharpe's house at eleven o'clock. A young man in a black jacket lounged on a garden wall across the street, picking intently at a fingernail. Another paced back and forth at the end of the block.

After all that had happened in the last twenty-four hours, the five paid no more attention to these guys than they might have to a couple of crows, which was probably a mistake.

CHAPTER FIFTEEN   CLOBBERING THE PIE

❑❑❑ Ms. Hussey welcomed the kids inside. "Well. What a night we've all had," she said, as if she, too, was still sorting through dreams.

Mrs. Sharpe's living room, in the clear light of morning, looked both elegant and inviting. Without her in it, the kids were free to marvel. Flowery patterns hugged sofas and chairs; geometry and a wild array of colors marched underfoot; lace led the windows in a dance of bows and ribbons. Fuzzy velvet, inlaid wood, wallpaper with a drape of vines, and around it all, art. There were small Dutch oil paintings and watercolors, some filled with scenes of everyday life. One boasted a plate of slippery oysters next to fruit and a half-spilled goblet of wine, the crystal so sparkly that the mess didn't seem to matter. Across the room, a cabinet with a rounded glass front held stacks of porcelain plates and teacups, a silver teapot, and candlesticks.

A sideways glance told Tommy that the lemonade spilled the other day had soaked in nicely, leaving no mark. He saw Early's mouth open slightly as she turned first one way and then the other. Tommy noticed small statues he didn't remember from before. A naked woman was drying her foot, her bottom to the wall . . . and then on a table next to the window, standing upright, a nude man! Tommy knew this was normal for art, but the very idea of having no clothes was awkward away from a museum, especially around the two girls.

Zoomy ran his fingers over the lions on Mrs. Sharpe's chairs as Petra squinted at a thick manuscript-like pile on a side table. Had she read it wrong, or was the title *What If He Turns?* Ms. Hussey swooped over and covered the fat stack of paper with an art book. Calder had stopped across the room in front of a reproduction of *The Geographer*, a Vermeer painting that he'd always liked. "Look at this hair," he called. "Could he be the same man? The one with his back turned?"

Startled, Petra blurted, "Hey, I just read about him," and seconds later Mrs. Sharpe appeared at the top of the stairs.

She wore a long white robe with a matching shawl draped around her head and shoulders. *She looks like an old prize-fighter*, Tommy thought. *Or maybe she's practicing to be a mummy.* The wall supported her on one side and a walking stick on the other. The cane was dark wood, topped by a gold animal head. *Another lion*, Tommy noted. He'd have to remember to tell Zoomy, who couldn't see that far. It *was* weird that Mrs. Sharpe and Mrs. Farmer both went in for big cats and art — what else did they share? If Mrs. Sharpe admired Mrs. Farmer and the way she'd lived, were there any other leads in this place? And did all the lions point to something treacherous? After all, a big cat was rarely loyal to those who fed it.

"Your conference room is upstairs," Mrs. Sharpe said, her tone more of a snarl than a welcome. "You'll find research materials for reference." She stepped backward into a doorway, and there was a sharp click and the grinding sound of — what? A lock?

As they started upstairs, they heard a remote thump from below. "Oh, that must be Eagle," Ms. Hussey said lightly. "Mrs. Sharpe recently had a dehumidifier installed in the basement, and it's been acting up."

What a home, Tommy thought to himself. Hidden grownups and closed doors everywhere. What did Ms. Hussey see in the old lady, anyway?

Just then Tommy tripped on the edge of a thick rug in the second floor hallway, and he and Zoomy smacked into a wall. The four of them heard a meow from behind a door down the hall, as if Rat-a-tat had just realized they were in the house.

"Ambush," Zoomy said. "Rugs. Hard to walk on fat ones like this."

"Yeah," Tommy said. "Who needs extra trippers in life?"

"Okay, boys," Ms. Hussey said in her that's-enough voice, opening a small door at the end of the hall. "Up you go." All peered up a narrow stairwell with a latch door at the top. As they started up the stairs single file, Calder in the lead, the five were forced to duck; the ceiling slanted, turning the stairwell into a tunnel.

"Jeez, I feel like Alice in Wonderland," Calder muttered.

"You look like her, too," Tommy called up.

So as not to hit his head, Zoomy went on both hands and feet. Early followed.

Petra was the last to climb the stairs; the thought of the boys tracking her progress from behind was not appealing. When she stepped into the attic, she gasped.

Large windows bracketed a room creased by oddly angled eaves. Morning light flooded the corners, picking out knot-holes on the floor and wallpaper covered with a romp of scallop shells and moon snails, their spirals and fan-shapes somehow cheerful. An old church pew, chairs that were missing a rung or a spindle, and several short stools surrounded an oval table with a ton of legs beneath it. In the middle of the table was a cardboard box neatly labeled FARMER SNAPS, a pile of old art books, a jar of pencils, and a stack of lined legal pads. Worn cushions and quilts peeked from a huge wooden box in the corner, and paperback mysteries and a few old-time games like Monopoly and Yahtzee lined the only vertical wall.

"Thought you'd like it," Ms. Hussey said happily. "Eagle and I tidied it for you — and oh! I guess he added the box of loose museum photographs, from a cupboard in Mr. Chase's house. Mrs. Sharpe sent him over with some of the trustees, and suggested he bring these back for you to look through."

Zoomy walked right to the table, patted the sides of the box, and sat down. *Just keep watching*, he remembered from his dream. Abruptly he bent closer, sniffing the lid.

"Fresh marker," he said. "Someone just did this, I can smell it."

Ms. Hussey, who had her hand on the door, turned back toward the group, looking confused. "But he's been downstairs —" she blurted, then stopped.

"I'll be back with a snack," she finished abruptly, whisking out the door and shutting it behind her.

❒ ❒ ❒ "Okay, let's clobber the pie, as my grandpa says," Zoomy ordered, sitting down at the table and pulling the box toward himself.

"Hold on!" Early said. The others looked at her in surprise. "We should be organized about this. I liked the way Mr. Devlin — I mean, Eagle — gave us that neat Pieces and Players sheet in the museum, and then the five copies of *The Truth*. It seems like it kind of lined up our brains. How about if we share the dreams before we open the box? Who wants to take notes?"

"You," Tommy said promptly.

Calder grunted, and Zoomy nodded.

"Every detail," Petra ordered, "and then we'll make a list of who was getting a message from what piece. Next, clues or patterns."

Tommy saluted. "Aye-aye, General."

Petra stuck out her tongue and Zoomy pulled a sandwich bag filled with dilly beans out of his jacket pocket and plopped it down next to the box. "No treats until we've gotten our homework done," he said. "And that includes Ms. Hussey's snack, hodilly-hum."

"This sure is a bossy morning," Calder muttered.

"So?" Petra snapped. "Who wants to be like the trustees, rattling their jewelry and wobbling their skin at each other and getting nowhere?"

"Right," Early said. She pulled one of the legal pads over and got to work.

Minutes later, her Dream List looked like this:

—Zoomy: Manet's *Chez Tortoni*. This man is writing something that he knows Zoomy will understand one day, something that might be secret.

—Early: Rembrandt's *A Lady and Gentleman in Black*. A chair waits for her in their peaceful home, and they want to hear what she will share. She has no idea what that is, but feels welcome and not threatened.

—Calder: Rembrandt's *The Storm on the Sea of Galilee*. He's on the boat, caught in that terrible storm, and realizes that nothing matters but staying alive. Feels he's got to save the thirteen, but which ones — pieces of art, or others who're onboard? Note: Counting the figure that looks like Rembrandt, there are fourteen, not thirteen.

—Tommy: Flinck's _Landscape with an Obelisk_. He is happy that Mrs. Farmer saw Chicago in this painting. Suddenly he's inside it and knows he'll be finding treasures, perhaps inside what looks like a door in an old tree.

—Petra: _The Concert_. She stands in the room and at first no one sees her. The woman singing uncurls the fingers of her hand. Petra sees three Xs that pull her into the painting, on a path that ends beneath the man's chair. There's a message from the Lady at the harpsichord. She nods to Petra, looking like a young Mrs. Sharpe: "For art, this building. This comfort."

Early read the list aloud then added, "Seems like everyone had a pretty good time but Calder."

"Who could have fun in _that_ boat?" he squeaked.

"Why'd you choose it?" Tommy asked. "Seriously."

"It was like they _made_ me pay attention to them — the people who didn't want to go under, you know?"

The others nodded. "Yeah," Tommy said. "I kind of felt like my painting picked me, too."

There was silence for a beat as everyone thought about that.

"Maybe each one of us got the painting that told us we can _do_ this," Petra said.

Early tapped her pencil on the pad for a moment, then wrote:

— understanding a secret
— waiting
— fear of death
— treasures in Chicago
— art, building, comfort

"So maybe this is all one big message, but in five parts," Early suggested.

"Thirteen words." Calder nodded.

"Brought to us by the moon," Petra added.

Calder stirred his pentominoes and held up the X. "Of course — here it is. The most difficult piece to fit in any rectangle, and the Farmer Museum is a rectangle . . ."

"There were three Xs on those napkins that Ms. Hussey gave us at that first meeting," Tommy said. "Like a symbol of something, and they had a snarling lion on either side."

"I've been noticing a bunch of crazy echoes around me, sort of like coincidence but not random enough," Petra said. "Like when I saw a manuscript with the title *What If He Turns?* on a table in the living room just now, and Calder immediately said something about the man in *The Geographer* looking like the man whose back was turned in *The Concert*. I know he didn't see what I saw. Or like the Xs in the painting being like the Xs on the napkin. Or the full moon turning into the collar on the woman in Early's dream."

"Maybe the pieces we need to recognize have identities, like pentomino pieces. Identities that're out of place." Calder looked around at the group.

"Hmm," Tommy said. "You and I were talking about the men with black jackets after we saw five of them that morning we met in Powell's — and then we saw five crows land on a tree. And Eagle was reading Mother Goose to Jubie and then characters from the rhymes kept popping into our heads when we went downtown with Ms. Hussey. Plus, crows might as well be blackbirds. But it could all be silly, you know?"

"Not if there's enough of it," Petra said.

"I wish we could make it work with the *F-A* hint," Early said. "Maybe if we put that next to our dreams . . ." Her voice trailed off as she doodled *F*s and *A*s down the margin of her pad.

Zoomy banged the table. "Scaz! What if *F-A* really is for Farmer, like we thought at first, and the stolen art wants us to find it and bring it back to its comfortable building!"

"Well, duh," Tommy said, but not in an unfriendly way.

"Or maybe it's hidden *in* the building," Early said.

"Yeah, but that means no one stole it!" Calder pointed out.

"Maybe they stole it but got scared when the window banged, and stuffed it in a closet," Early suggested. "Things go wrong, you know? And there must be a ton of hidey-holes in there."

"Maybe," Petra said, jamming her hair behind both ears, "William Swift Chase had an *F-A* message slip into his mind, the way we've gotten messages from these dreams. Maybe it was the *art* talking, not him. It might've just happened because he was about to die." Petra bit her lip. "Not that we're about to die . . . Oh, never mind. Let's open the box."

The paintings, sculpture, carvings, and miscellaneous treasures, photographed in happier times, made the building look endlessly colorful and fresh. Windows and doors stood open, and the courtyard was awash in flowers. There were snapshots of Mrs. Farmer beaming at the camera from the chair in front of her Vermeer, the beanbag men peeking over her shoulders; Mrs. Farmer welcoming someone who looked like the Queen of England to the museum; Mrs. Farmer shaking hands with a small boy in a soldier's uniform in front of one of the massive fireplaces while flames danced behind them.

"Such a place." Early sighed. "Imagine living there."

"And not being bothered all the time by noisy family." Petra sighed, too.

"If we can get back in the building — and maybe that's what your message was about, Petra — the spirit of the place will —" Early broke off.

"Tell us more? Snap off our noses?" Tommy finished for her. He looked suddenly uncomfortable. "There's something about that visit that I haven't told you guys."

Just as he spoke, the kids heard Ms. Hussey's voice, high and frightened:

"Quick! Help me! It's Mrs. Sharpe!"

◻◻◻ The five flung open the attic door to find Rat-a-tat curled just outside. He was on his feet in less than a second, pouring down the stairs in a furry blur.

"He was listening!" Tommy hissed as the five hurried down, reaching the second floor just as Eagle bounded up from below. They found Ms. Hussey kneeling on the floor of an open bedroom, Mrs. Sharpe lying next to her. The older woman's eyes were closed, and she seemed half her normal size.

She looks like Goldman when he fell on the floor that time, Tommy thought to himself. *Except that Goldman flipped back and forth, and she definitely isn't moving.*

"She fainted," Ms. Hussey said. "But she's breathing regularly. I know this has happened before when she's overtired, and she's said it isn't serious — just low blood pressure. Still, I think we should take her to the hospital."

Eagle nodded. "I'll pull my van up in front, and maybe by then she'll be awake and you and I can help her in."

He dashed down the stairs as Ratty strolled in. Zoomy leaned close. "Still got his collar," he muttered.

"Oh, poor Mrs. Sharpe," murmured Ms. Hussey. "This has all been overwhelming. Too much stress."

The kids sat around awkwardly, trying not to be too obvious about checking out Mrs. Sharpe's bedroom. She had a huge canopied bed covered with a mountain of tasseled pillows. A Vermeer-like rug, all royal blues and reds, covered the entire floor.

"She got up to show me something over there." Ms. Hussey waved an arm toward the corner of the room, a wall near a dormer window. "Then she blacked out."

"It's *The Concert!*" Petra gasped, feeling as though she might pass out as well. She had a dizzying moment when questions flashed like lightning through her mind. Had Mrs. Sharpe hung Vermeer's painting in her bedroom, and did Ms. Hussey know it? If so, who had stolen it from the Farmer? Was it possible that the trustees actually *had* taken the thirteen pieces of art and scattered them around in their houses, pretending to the outside world that they'd been stolen? Was that what Mr. Cracken and the others had been up to? Had she and Early blundered on one of the days when they gathered most of the art in one place, in order to —

"It's a beautiful copy. An almost perfect duplication." Ms. Hussey smiled sadly, not noticing Petra's strange expression, which was a mash-up of extreme relief and deep disappointment. "She told me once that her husband bought this painting for her in Delft, the city Vermeer lived in, many years ago. He told her it was the best copy of a Vermeer he'd ever seen and that she looked just like the young woman playing the harpsichord."

Petra gasped again and looked around at the other four.

"I *knew* that," she said quietly, sinking down on a nearby chair. "It was in my dream."

"Mrs. Sharpe really looked that good?" Tommy asked, studying the painting closely.

Calder elbowed him. "Whadda you think *you'll* look like in fifty or sixty years?" he asked.

Even more of a toad, Tommy thought, but wasn't about to say it.

"Lemme see," Zoomy piped up, turning away from the painting to bend over Mrs. Sharpe. "I'm good on faces up close, and I know that painting by heart now. Yup, that's the same big forehead, I'd recognize it anywhere."

Ms. Hussey cleared her throat. "I don't know if she can hear you . . ." she murmured.

Eagle's steps clumped upstairs. "Okay — I think it's best if I scoop her up," he said, bending down. "That's right, cover her with that light blanket," he told Ms. Hussey. "Can you tuck it under her feet and then across my shoulder?"

They almost look like they're hugging now, Mrs. Sharpe is so small between them, Tommy thought.

He peered around Eagle to see Mrs. Sharpe's eye open the tiniest crack and then shut.

Was that a *wink*?

"I'm coming with you," Ms. Hussey announced. "I'll drive and you slide into the back with her. And kids — you can bring those cookies on the kitchen table up to your meeting room. Just be careful about mess. I'll call with news. Lock the front door behind us."

"And don't touch anything on the way up," Eagle added. "Rat-ty's lis-ten-ing," he murmured in a singsong voice.

"Of course not," Calder said stiffly.

As the van pulled away, the five stood inside the door for a moment, looking at one another.

"Told you," Zoomy whispered. "The cat's his spy. We'd better put him outside."

They glanced around, but Ratty had already vanished.

"Let's split up and find him. Then we can speak freely," Early suggested.

"I'm kind of glad we have an excuse to check this place out," Petra whispered. "I mean, who's to say what we might find? But be careful not to knock over tippy art or flowers — this has to be an expert, silent search, for either a cat or stolen art."

"Or both," Zoomy prompted.

Calder headed for the top of the house and the rear of the second floor; Petra and Early explored the bedrooms; and Zoomy and Tommy tackled the first floor, which had the greatest number of objects. Because of possible grabbers, Zoomy stayed on all fours and crawled from one side of the living room to the other, feeling around under tables and sofas. Tommy moved with extra care, peering into cupboards and behind art.

Half an hour later, there was still no cat. The five met in

the kitchen. "Whew, this is a large house!" Calder sighed. "We'd better hurry. They may not be gone too long."

"She has a lot of nice bedrooms," Early said softly. "I'm jealous. All this space and just one old lady."

"Plus her mysterious son, at least right now," Petra added.

"*I* know!" Zoomy said suddenly. "Ratty's just like us — he needs a treat. Let's find one, do the kitty-kitty thing, and then grab him when he shows up."

The kids opened cabinets and pulled out a bag of crunchy cat food. They rattled it, hoping for a response. Nothing.

"Ooh, a can of sardines." Early pointed. "Now we're talkin'."

"Watch out," Petra cautioned. "Sardines are super stinky. We *can't* spill any of this oil! Seriously. Mrs. Sharpe would chop off our heads."

At the sound of the sardine tin being opened, Ratty streaked out of his hiding place and into the kitchen. He reared up, pawing at the edge of the counter.

"Whoa, man," mumbled Tommy. "He's like one of the lions on the napkins. I'm glad Goldman doesn't have to see me feeding a cat dead fish. How do we do this, guys?"

"Here," Calder said, reaching for the can. A second later, Ratty rocketed onto the counter. Tommy jumped back, Calder lost his grip, and the can landed upside down on the kitchen floor.

Scazzes buzzed through the kitchen as Ratty grabbed a fish from the mess, flipped it into the air like a circus lion, and swallowed it in one gulp.

"We'd better get him outside before we run out of bait," Calder croaked as Ratty plunged back into the fishy mess. He started to pick up the cat, who whipped around and snapped at his arm.

"Yeow!" Calder jerked back his elbow and jabbed Zoomy, who then stumbled directly into the pool of fish oil.

"We need a lure, quick!" Petra said. Crouching in front of what was left, she stuffed the remaining sardines into the can and headed for the front door. Ratty rushed after her, and as soon as the door was opened, leaped at Petra's hand, baring his teeth. She shrieked and flung the can across the porch and into the bushes, leaving a greasy trail. Ratty raced after it.

Once they'd slammed the front door, the five whooped, fist-bumped, and then looked around. It was a horror scene. Fat drops of oil glistened on Mrs. Sharpe's living room carpet. A nasty puddle complete with ragged guts and tails was sinking into the wood on her kitchen floor. Zoomy had taken off his sneaker and dropped it into the kitchen sink.

Early was the first to recover. "Okay, she must have some good cleaning supplies," she said, "and baking soda. Baking soda is a miracle worker on nasty smells. I know, because we've used it a million times at home."

Soon Petra was crawling along the carpet with a sponge and a bowl of soapy water, the three boys were working on the kitchen floor, and Early had ducked outside to wash off the oil that snaked across the porch. Ratty lay on the sidewalk out front, cleaning his whiskers and grinning pleasantly as if nothing much had happened.

The five took a break fifteen minutes later. "I hope it smells okay in here," Petra said, wrinkling her nose.

"Whew, we'd make a good oil spill clean-up team, anyway," Tommy said, spread-eagled on the living room rug.

"Yeah, us five," Zoomy said happily, sitting cross-legged on the floor.

"So now that we're finally alone in here," Petra said, "did anyone run across anything suspicious anyplace else in the house? Boy, what a shock, seeing that copy of *The Concert*! I thought for a moment that we'd found the real Vermeer — a terrible moment, actually. But you know what? It kind of jolted me into a suspicion that's been slowly coming together in my mind. What if this Eagle Devlin guy is Mrs. Sharpe's son but also — well, somehow *seriously* bad? You know Mrs. Sharpe didn't want Ms. Hussey to meet him, or she would've mentioned him. Maybe Mrs. Sharpe *does* love him like a mother, but knows he's a truly dangerous kind of person. And you know the way he's kind of prickly, as if he wants to keep us all on our toes."

"We know he's in the art storage business," Calder said. "Which means he probably knows places to hide paintings and sculptures. And Ms. Hussey told us he didn't want the Farmer art to go to Washington, but Mrs. Sharpe did. *She* thought it would be safer there, and *he* believed it was wrong to move it from its home."

"I wonder why Mrs. Sharpe had a basement dehumidifier put in, right when Eagle came back," Early said. "Do you think something needed to be stashed down there?"

"Just what I was thinking," Petra said.

"But stolen art?" Zoomy said, sniffing his wet sneaker dubiously. "I read that it needs to stay not too damp or too dry."

"Maybe that's Mrs. Sharpe's 'sting' thing," Early murmured. "She didn't want to, but she's helping to cover up for her son. It's what families do. Maybe he got into something bad and pulled her into it."

"Yeah." Calder nodded. "Like what just happened with the sardines."

"What if Eagle murdered his adoptive father years ago, in order to get closer to Mrs. Sharpe's money?" Petra asked.

"*Seriously?*" Early squeaked.

Petra shrugged. "Not really, but investigators need everything to feel possible."

"Right. Let's go down to the basement." Tommy was already on his feet and looking around for the door. "We owe it to Vermeer, Rembrandt, and all the other artists." He paused. "We owe it to the world," he added, flinging one arm out in a dramatic pose.

"And if we five solve the mystery," Zoomy added, "we'll be superheroes."

Petra had her doubts about what they'd find, but she didn't want to ruin Zoomy's enthusiasm. "Fine, it's worth a look," she said, then stuck out her tongue. "I hate basements. So many creepy-crawlies."

"I'll guard the stairs and bang on the wall if I hear anyone outside the front door," Zoomy offered. "You know I've got hound dog ears. Who wants to stay up here with me?"

When no one answered, he sighed and held out his fist for bumps as the others shuffled past him toward the basement.

▯▢▯ The light switch was broken, but there were four flashlights neatly lined up on a shelf inside the basement door. Amazingly, they all seemed to work.

"Almost like the basement is expecting us," Tommy said. "Spooky."

The kids did a round of rock-paper-scissors to see who would go down the basement stairs first. Calder was the scissors and lost to three rocks.

"Scaz," he muttered. "Been nice knowing you guys," he added as he stepped down onto the first stair.

Screee went the wood. The next step was no better. *Creeeeeep!* it moaned.

The other three followed.

The basement was cold and looked huge and shadowy when seen only by flashlight. Petra stumbled into a stack of heavy metal pails. They tipped and rolled, spilling sponges. The clatter on the concrete floor was deafening.

"Scaz!" she shrieked, and just at that moment a clothes rack in the corner trembled. Small black shapes with wings boomeranged around the room, first one way and then the other. *Shrunken blackbirds?* The three kids dropped to a crouch. Early pulled the back of her sweatshirt over her head.

"Must be bats!" Tommy shouted. "They're more frightened than we are," he said into his armpit. "At least, that's what a grown-up would say."

"Can't we cover our faces and heads with something solid?" Early squeaked. "See any football helmets?"

"Yeah, right," Calder muttered.

Tommy was the first to lift his head. "How about the pails?"

"Good thing no one can see us," Petra said as she grabbed for a pail and plopped it on her head, the handle under her chin. The other three did the same, keeping one hand up to prevent the pail-helmet from sinking down to their necks.

"It'll be good protection for almost anything," Early pointed out.

"Pah!" Petra spat. "Dirty junk, right in my mouth! Well, at least we won't break our crowns if we fall down."

"Reassuring," Tommy said under his breath. *Why was she thinking about Jack and Jill, anyway?* he wondered. *Jack was the one who broke his crown.*

They crept into the next room. It had nothing in it but old packing boxes, a broken chair, and the furnace. A door in the far wall, cracked and peeling, stood open.

"Dracula would love this," Petra said. "Who'd want all these rooms down here? It's like a dungeon."

The last room had a dusty pile of suitcases, an old croquet set, and a stack of lawn furniture. Just as the kids crept forward, there was a terrific *thump!* from behind the pile, causing the four to drop to the floor. Next came a distant *bang!* from upstairs. Petra's hand slipped off her pail and it slammed down on the top of her head, covering her face entirely.

"Wah, help!" she shouted as Tommy lifted it up.

Calder was already creeping forward, saying, "It's just the dehumidifier and Zoomy bumping into something upstairs, guys." Then he stopped moving. "Come here," he whispered.

The three gathered around a huge metal box. On the side were the words SAFE ART. Attached was a device that had one needle measuring humidity and another tracking temperature. It fed into a square unit that plugged into a wall socket.

"Whoa!" Petra gasped, whipping off her pail. The others did the same. Calder was already running his fingers along the smooth metal surface, looking for a way to open the box.

A huge buckle that stretched the length of one side was clipped shut but didn't look locked. Calder pushed. It began to give, then flipped back with a gentle thud.

The four leaned forward, lifting the heavy lid as if it were made of glass.

☐ ☐ ☐ The basement door was shut. Zoomy had left it open.

Through the door, the four kids could hear Ms. Hussey's voice.

"What did you think . . . How could you . . . What if burbledy-burble . . ." She sounded scary.

"I haven't heard Ms. Hussey sound like that since nasty Denise poured glue in her purse in sixth grade," Calder muttered.

"We'd better help Zoomy," Petra whispered.

As they peeked around the door, Ms. Hussey whipped it open. "I ought to leave you guys down there for a while!" she snapped.

Eagle had picked up Ratty and was cradling him in one arm. "Guess there's more than a little distrust around here," he murmured. "Distrust and fish oil. Did you get the box open? There are more on the other side of the room."

He's frighteningly calm, Tommy thought. *Like a cat who's just caught his mouse.*

"What are you saying?" Ms. Hussey whirled on Eagle now. "This is partly *your* fault. For — for — turning up! Poor Mrs. Sharpe, not feeling well, and now the stress of balancing everything and then the kids sneaking around her house." She paused. "*What* box? I mean, boxes?"

"I thought you knew," Eagle said mildly. "We're trying out some of my storage systems in the basement here, in case I want to use the space for business overflow. But they're empty. Isn't that right, kids?"

Reluctantly, the four who'd gone into the basement nodded. They looked disappointed — and so did Zoomy when he heard the news.

Ms. Hussey sank down on the sofa next to Zoomy, who bent over his notebook. "I give up," she said. "I thought this was about finding the art stolen from the Farmer."

"Life sometimes pulls together things that don't look like they should fit." Eagle's voice was soothing. "All is not always what it seems."

"Great, thanks for the news," Ms. Hussey said under her breath.

"Sorry we went down there," Petra said.

"Just being good investigators," Calder added.

Ms. Hussey nodded and sighed. "And sorry I shouted at you, Zoomy. It's been a hard few days."

"Hodilly-hum," Zoomy replied, staring straight ahead, his notebook open on his lap. He'd written, *-stinky spill, Rat-a-tat attack, empty boxes.* On the next line, *-Mrs. Sharpe gone. Like sardines.*

"Is Mrs. Sharpe okay?" Tommy asked. Suddenly he had a flash of her dying like Mr. Chase, and Ms. Hussey living in this house.

As if reading his mind, Ms. Hussey said evenly, "She's fine, nothing to worry about. They'll release her in an hour or so. For whatever reason, she insisted on being alone until the doctors say it's okay for her to leave. In the meantime, you guys should get going. We have a whole lot to do before the trustees arrive, including getting more of that sardine smell out of here. Couldn't you guys find the cookies?"

This was her first joke since coming back to the house, and the five were relieved.

"Sorry — we fed Ratty. We didn't mean to make a mess. And I left some notes in the attic, next to the box of photographs," Early said, shifting her weight from one foot to the other. "Should I get them?"

"Another time," Ms. Hussey said firmly.

"We'll leave *that* box undisturbed," Eagle added, as if talking to the cat's collar.

"And you, my man, are quite a wordsmith. I like that Ratty entry," Ms. Hussey said to Zoomy, who grinned.

As they left the house, Calder said, "I think Ratty's name fits Eagle better."

Tommy was busy thinking about the way Eagle and Ms. Hussey talked. "*We, we, we,*" he muttered. "One minute it seems the two of them are friends, and the next minute they're not. Same with Mrs. Sharpe, so it's really a triangle. You can't always tell who likes who."

"They're an uncomfortable threesome who're stuck together," Early said. "Mrs. Sharpe thinks she's in control, but so does Eagle and so does Ms. Hussey. It's obvious that everyone wants *someone* to find the stolen art, but the three grown-ups aren't sure whether to trust each other."

"Or us," Zoomy added.

Petra suddenly stopped dead. *"For art, this building —* Mrs. Sharpe's words in my dream, you know? Maybe she's talking about the art going into her basement, into that storage box! But *why*? Why on earth would she ever get the art from a thief and put it in her basement?"

"If her son is the thief, she might be willing to take the art and then pretend *she* stole it. So he could go free!" Tommy blurted. Suddenly he felt taller and smarter. "That would be the *sting* she talked about when we were first at her house! A move that fooled other people, right in front of their faces!"

"Yeah! Maybe she's ready to be sacrificed, like a sardine," Zoomy said.

"I think you guys are nuts," Calder said. "But I do think the art is trying to get us to do something. Like my pentominoes talk to me, you know?"

They walked several yards in silence, each wrestling with his or her own confusions.

It was Tommy who next stopped the group. "I was about to ask you guys something when Mrs. Sharpe fainted." He kicked at the sidewalk. "Did — ah — anyone else think Mrs. Farmer was sort of there with us, in the museum?"

"Sure," Zoomy said immediately. "I saw her shoe. And she showed me some lions. My grandma has seen ghosts before — she thinks it's pretty normal."

Early stuffed both hands in her jacket pockets. "After we left the Dutch Room, I looked back. Someone in a long dress whisked around a chair; it was just the fastest *whish*, like a skirt moving if someone was playing hide-and-seek. But I knew the room was empty, so — well, I didn't say anything."

"We're sure she likes kids," Petra said slowly. "And that she didn't care for the guard too much."

"That cold touch . . ." Calder murmured. "And the tweaks!"

"She's waiting for us to go back," Petra said. "I'm not sure I want to, but — I can feel the pull. She's *waiting*, you know?"

"Yeah," Calder said. "Hate to say it, but I feel the same thing. Like all those guys on the boat are yelling their heads off all this time, waiting to be rescued."

"What if we asked Eagle to take us?" Zoomy said. "I'll bet you a million bucks he has a key. And if he tries to do anything bad in there, Mrs. Farmer will protect us."

"Scaz," Tommy said mournfully. "I was hoping you guys would tell me you didn't believe in ghosts."

⬚⬚⬚ The five kids spent a long, uncomfortable hour in the alleyway behind Mrs. Sharpe's house, sandwiched between a splintery cedar fence and the trashcans. Peering through knotholes one eye at a time, they saw Eagle and Ms. Hussey's heads move around in the kitchen. The two seemed to be talking, and at one point Ms. Hussey looked straight up, her hand over her mouth, and then Eagle moved behind her, arms raised — what! Now Ms. Hussey spun around and they were nose to nose. Yikes, what next? Were they about to *kiss*? Then Ms. Hussey disappeared from sight and came up wearing yellow rubber gloves.

"I feel bad about that oil spill," Calder said. "She's still cleaning."

Zoomy could only observe the deeps, but the others gave him a running account. Everyone felt as if they needed glasses by the time Eagle stepped out the kitchen door, closed it with a bang, and headed for his van. Ms. Hussey wasn't with him.

"Quick!" Tommy called as they took off at a run, hoping to stop the vehicle as it turned the corner toward the hospital. Early got there first and waved Eagle down.

The driver's side window opened. "You guys still hanging around? Not much to see," Eagle said calmly, as the kids gathered in a breathless group. Tommy had led Zoomy along by the sleeve of his sweatshirt, calling out, "Dip, three steps" and "Crack, four!"

"We're getting good at this," Zoomy mumbled, and Tommy nodded.

"Mrs. Farmer —" began Petra. "She likes kids. We need to get back, but without — you know, interference."

"And how will you do that?" Eagle asked, his voice still alarmingly smooth.

"Someone could let us in," Calder said, scratching his head with the F pentomino. "Someone who's good at alarms. And devices, like dehumidifiers."

"Ahhh . . . and you think Ms. Hussey and your parents would be comfortable with this?"

Just then two young men in black jackets crossed the street at the end of the block and seemed to pause midstride when they saw the van surrounded by kids. Eagle nodded in their direction and they hurried on.

Is he communicating with them? Tommy wondered. He glanced at three of his four friends to see if they'd noticed.

"Hinige sinigigninigaliniged tinigo blinigack jinigackinigets!" Tommy said quietly.

"Ooooh, well, I'll leave you guys to it." Eagle smiled. "Always loved codes myself. Mother Goose has its own cryptic language that works with our world. Like blackbirds being similar to people dressed in black leather. Stuff like that."

I'm not the only one who sees that, Tommy thought to himself.

The five stood back quietly as he started to roll forward. "Wait!" Petra blurted. The van stopped. "We didn't mean to be rude. We were just trying out a language we made up. Can you get us back into the Farmer, Eagle? Please? We might pick up something that's missing in how everyone's thinking about the *F-A* stuff. You know Mrs. Farmer wanted kids to feel welcome in her home, and —"

Eagle laughed softly. "I always felt welcome there, as a kid. I went whenever I could. It was strange. I almost felt as if I belonged there."

"That basement door, the one that all the trustees have a key to — could you open it for us?" Early asked breathlessly.

Good timing. Wish I could cut to the chase like that. Tommy shot her an impressed glance.

"And what about the guards and the police?" Eagle asked. "Shall we drug them with poisoned doughnuts and . . . hmm, tie them up? Then sit down and do a Ouija board?"

The kids' mouths were all open now.

"Wait," Petra said. "Do *you* believe in ghosts?"

"I believe in what Sarah Chase Farmer believed in. Like you kids, I'm open to ideas. Why do you think I bought a Ouija board for you after our visit the other day?"

"Seriously?" squeaked Tommy. "You're not just making that up?"

Eagle winked at them and recited:

"Wire, briar, limber lock,
Five geese in a flock,
Sit and sing by a spring,
O-U-T and in again."

He grinned. "You guys remember that one? Do you mean to tell me you didn't spot the Ouija board up in the attic this morning? I tucked it in between some old games. Didn't want to be too obvious."

Seems like he's always a step ahead, Tommy thought to himself. *And winks are usually a sign of someone trying to get away with something.*

"As long as we don't end up like Willie running around the beehive," he mumbled. "Isn't there a Mother Goose rhyme about running away from bees?"

"If you can run, you won't get stung," Eagle said evenly. "Meet me back here at seven tomorrow evening, and wear dark clothing. I'll research the guard setup, both inside and out. Tell your parents — and grandma — that you're having a work dinner at Mrs. Sharpe's."

As the van accelerated slowly, the kids felt as though they'd signed on for something that could be as dangerous as tying their sneaker laces to the bumper.

"Scinigaz," Petra said. "Inigarinige winige stinigupinigid?"

◻◻◻ Knowing they weren't expected home yet, four of the five called their parents for permission and then headed downtown. Gam wouldn't agree to Zoomy going with the others, not without Ms. Hussey along, and Zoomy decided to pick his battles: He was needed as a part of the expedition the next night, so he'd lie low until then. Plus, he couldn't fool Gam twice.

"Gam and me, we'll go to Powell's and read some more

Mother Goose. I'll see what else might fit with Eagle and how he views things. Maybe catch some clues."

"Excellent," Petra agreed. "And we'll check out another piece of art with a face, one my mom suggested at dinner last night: Picasso's huge outdoor lady. Might be the solution that no one has investigated. Hidden but in plain sight!"

Calder, Tommy, and Early didn't feel as hopeful, but it was an investigation, a job to keep them busy. After dropping Zoomy at the guesthouse, the four hurried on toward the train station at 56th Street.

When they reached the wall outside the entrance, beneath the tracks, Early stopped.

"Hey, guys! My family calls this the Story Wall, and it's covered with faces. *Real* faces, portraits from the neighborhood. And look, there's a heavy metal box on the bank up there, one I never noticed before! Probably just has track equipment, but it *is* behind the faces! If the art's in there, that'd be faces behind faces, for real!"

At the top of the wall mural were the words *Where Are You Going?* and *Where Are You Coming From?* Early explained that the artist, Olivia Gude, had photographed and talked with a bunch of everyday people who happened to walk by on one particular day here, over twenty years ago. She'd recorded them in paint, including some of their answers to her two questions. Most looked directly at the viewer. A few hurried past. What they shared were mostly heartfelt experiences, like coming to the US from another country, trying to find a way out of poverty, building a life through education and family. One answer was simply, "I'm walking in a circle." The words they left behind spelled out dreams, disappointments, work, routines, hope, happiness, desperation, and faith.

"My dad says it's like an open book with pictures, a living story for everyone, out in all weather," Early said.

"It makes me think of all the art people in the Farmer," Petra said, "but they can't speak. Except in dreams," she added hurriedly.

"Funny how plain old folks get important when they're turned into art," Early said.

"I wouldn't mind having my picture up there," Calder said. "Holding a pentomino."

"Heads up!" Tommy's voice was strangely muffled.

Calder, horrified, watched his buddy scramble up the bank, clinging to bushes and clumps of dead grass. The other two glanced around nervously, expecting a shout from someone driving by.

"Hurry up, man!" Calder called. "A train is coming!"

"Oh, no," groaned Early. "My bad idea!"

Tommy crouched by the box, which was several feet from the tracks and tagged with spray graffiti. He ran his hands around the sides and whooped, "There's a door! This could be it!" The moment the words were out of his mouth, he had a flash of the open door in his dream, the door in the big tree.

"HEY, KID!" bellowed a voice. "Get away from there! You could get fried!"

Tommy jumped to his feet, lost his balance, belly-surfed down the bank, and shot off the wall at the base, landing in a painful pile on the sidewalk.

The girls and Calder hurried over. Tommy sat up and checked his elbow and a hole in the knee of his jeans. "Scaz," he muttered.

A face peered over from the top of the bank. "Trust me, kid, stay off the tracks. Bad way to go," the man growled.

It wasn't until the train arrived and they were safely onboard that Tommy muttered, "He didn't have on an orange vest. Could've been anyone."

The four looked at one another and then around the train. "Yeah," murmured Calder, glancing at a guy in a black jacket several seats away. "Good guys, bad guys — who can tell?"

Without Zoomy there, the boy-girl balance felt awkward; somehow, Zoomy's presence put small things in perspective. Now Petra was aware of sitting next to a girl who had thighs that were half the size of hers, and Tommy was aware of a new Krakatoa simmering on the side of his nose.

"Sorry I gave you the idea, Tommy," Early said abruptly. "That box wouldn't be a very protected place to stash great paintings from the biggest art theft in US history, would it?"

As Tommy opened his mouth to answer, Petra cut across

him. "Thieves have unloaded stolen art in all kinds of crazy spots — a tree house, bathrooms, even the trash."

"I was gonna say, it could be anywhere," Tommy agreed, glaring at Petra.

"Or spread all over, like the black jackets are," Calder said. "Don't forget, it's thirteen pieces of art and thirteen people, now that Mr. Chase is gone."

"Your point?" Tommy said. "That prime numbers can sneak around?"

"No, just that once something goes wrong, like a person dying —"

"The art will run away and *cry?*" Tommy snickered, not quite sure why he felt so mean.

Calder shrugged. "Think about it: Who has the best ideas — us, the Hussey-Sharpe-Devlin threesome, the trustees, or the faces in the art? It's thirteen to thirteen now, art to people. That's all I meant. And the *F-A* clue was important, but maybe no one will ever know what the old man meant."

"Dead to alive," Petra muttered.

"Alive to dead, you mean." Early's hand trembled as she fiddled with a button on her sleeve.

I've never heard Calder blat on so much, ever, Tommy thought to himself. His knee was beginning to really hurt. *Is this just growing up, or noticing that girls like you more if you talk about stuff?*

"So why did Mrs. Sharpe pull us into the group?" Tommy said loudly. "It wasn't our idea. And it can't be because we're so amazing." He glared at Calder.

"Maybe we're the fish baiting the hook," Early said. "Although I don't know what I mean — I just said it." She tucked her hair nervously behind her ears.

Glad Goldman didn't hear that one, Tommy thought to himself. *He'd never want her near his bowl again, not even with the juiciest baloney sandwich on the planet. And why was I thinking that Mrs. Sharpe looked like a fish when there was a huge cat in the house? And right after that, the cat was snapping up real fins and tails . . .*

"Seems like there's fish everywhere. And cats," Tommy said.

"Plus snakes and blackbirds and rats," Early added.

Calder pulled the T pentomino out of his pocket. "T keeps coming up. *Thieves . . . together . . . thirteen . . . test . . . testimony.*"

Talk talk talk, Tommy thought but didn't say. "Maybe your pentominoes need a rest. Some snooze time." Tommy elbowed his old buddy, who seemed like he was showing off.

"T for *time*, and yours is up," Calder said. Tommy slid down in his seat, knowing that his friend was right. He was acting pretty terrible.

"And we're worried about all that but not about going to the Farmer tomorrow night with Eagle — what are we, crazy?" Petra crossed her legs, her thighs rubbing with a miserable *shreee* sound. When everyone looked down, she kicked Tommy on his sore knee by mistake.

"Sorry!" she muttered just as he yelped, "Scaz!" Both looked out the window as if something out there could rescue them.

Stepping off the train, the four glanced around. No black jackets on the platform. The March air had a bite to it and loose garbage blew sideways across their path.

Relieved not to be facing one another, the kids walked several blocks in silence. When they reached the huge Picasso sculpture, set in Daley Plaza in the midst of skyscrapers, Tommy spoke first. "Pretty ugly, isn't she? Like a gigantic hunk of rusty playground equipment, but for giants. Or a huge harp — if you like strings that go between someone's nose and their hairdo."

Early snickered.

Score. Things were looking up. Tommy shifted his feet farther apart and straightened his shoulders.

"Her eyes are awful close together," Calder said.

"*I* don't think she's so bad," Petra said. "I looked up some stuff about her. She's untitled, been here since 1967, and was given to the city by Pablo Picasso. She's about fifty feet tall and weighs something like a hundred and sixty tons. She's Cubist. You know, that art style that chops up what you see and rearranges it."

"That why she also looks like a dog?"

"No, a baboon!" Tommy and Calder were now shoving each other.

"How about a stinging insect?" Early added, and Petra stiffened.

She turned away and walked quickly toward the sculpture, as if to say, *Too bad for you guys, none of you get it.* Seconds after disappearing around the back, she popped out again.

"Hurry!" she called. "Hinigidiniging plinigacinige!"

CHAPTER EIGHTEEN   WHOSE JOKE?

◻◻◻ Zoomy didn't want to worry his grandma, but when he reached the children's section in Powell's, there was the little red book — once again not at all where it was supposed to be.

Gam didn't notice his surprise, having spotted several copies of Mother Goose. Zoomy was down on his knees in front of the shelf and placed his finger right on the spine: *The Truth About My Art*. He pulled out the book and brought it over to Mr. Watch, who was behind the front counter.

"This book has a mind of its own," Mr. Watch joked, but Zoomy didn't think that was too funny. After all, Petra had found it and then someone had moved it seconds after she and the other kids walked away, then it turned up on its shelf again the next day — or so Mr. Watch had said — and now it was hidden in the kids' section.

"Maybe you should keep an eye on it," Zoomy suggested.

Had Eagle moved it there, after it had reappeared? If so, why? And if the man was such a jokester, why were the five of them trusting him to take them to the Farmer tomorrow night? Zoomy tried not to worry, but the questions buzzed noisily in his mind.

He sat down and began tap-tapping his chin.

"Notebook," Gam reminded him. She sat on a stool not far from his.

Zoomy found his purple pen and notebook, and wrote, *~whose joke?* After a moment he wrote, *~who is hiding what?* Was it part of Petra's pattern thing that Mrs. Farmer's book was tucked in next to the Mother Goose books? Like a coincidence that seemed too close to be an accident?

Gam had dragged out the large Baring-Gould *Annotated Mother Goose*, a copy that contained several versions of the old book. She was reading, following the lines with a finger.

"Wow, this Mother Goose idea is ancient," she declared. "News to me! No one's sure who first wrote down the rhymes or songs, but it seems they've been around for centuries. Some people say the *eeny-meeny-miney-mo* types of jingles were used by northern peoples thousands of years ago when choosing a victim for human sacrifice. Oh, my. Hmm, and William Shakespeare must've heard these rhymes as a boy in the 1600s, because snippets got into his plays. And there are university types who think Mother Goose was really King Charlemagne's mother, back in the 700s. She had big feet, like a goose. Mm, we would have liked each other. Kind of surprising that the Mother Goose stuff has been around for so long, don't you think, Zoomy?"

He nodded, still wondering who had moved the red book. Could it have been one of the black jacket guys, the ones who were all over Hyde Park? If so, who *were* they? Suddenly he pictured a very different man in a black jacket, the one in his dream. *You'll understand this message*, he had seemed to be telling Zoomy. *And when the moment comes . . .* The man's eyes were bright and sure, and as Zoomy closed his for a moment, he could feel the truth of what the man was saying. *I will,* Zoomy promised, *I will.*

"Hey, listen to this alphabet rhyme," Gam went on, all excited. "From a collection that was published in Boston in 1761, but — funny thing, the middle numbers just change places — first heard and quoted in 1671. This fits all the mess and fighting around the Farmer collection, the theft and Mr. Chase's death:

> *"A was an apple pie,*
> *B bit it,*
> *C cut it,*
> *D dealt it,*
> *E eat it,*
> *F fought for it,*
> *G got it,*
> *H had it,*
> *I inspected it,*
> *J jumped for it,*
> *K kept it,*
> *L longed for it,*
> *M mourned for it,*
> *N nodded at it,*
> *O opened it*
> *P peeped in it,*

Q quartered it,
R ran for it,
S stole it,
T took it,
U upset it,
V viewed it,
W wanted it,
X, Y, Z, and ampersand
All wished for a piece in hand."

"What do you think of that, Zoomy?" Gam sounded pleased. "Though I'm not sure what *ampersand* is. Are you?"

Zoomy shook his head. "How did you know about all the fighting and disagreeing?" he asked. Gam had a way of knowing an awful lot about what was going on in life.

"Don't stolen art and valuables always make people behave badly?" Gam asked. "Plus I picked up a few things in the Farmer the other day."

"Like what?" Zoomy asked.

"Like, the trustees are meaner to each other and everyone else than barn cats fighting over a newly hatched chick. Like, Eagle Devlin knows his way around that place. He came in late the other day, told the guards in front that he was in a hurry and then looked around as if checking to be sure everything was still there. He even ducked into the empty security room for a moment when the guard in there stepped out for a smoke. But then when he went upstairs, he pretended he'd just arrived. I could hear. It's the little things, you know — the best berries are under the leaves, hodilly-hum."

Zoomy nodded. "Do you think Mrs. Farmer likes Eagle?" he blurted.

Gam looked up from the book. "I expect she'd have let me know if she didn't," she said comfortably. "I think she took kind of a shine to you and me."

Zoomy heard that as permission to move ahead with their plan the next night — Gam wouldn't mind a little trespassing as long as the owner wasn't bothered.

Plus, as his grandma had said, Mrs. Farmer liked Eagle. A ghost wouldn't welcome a slippery guy to her home, would she? Unless, that is, she was fooled by him. And if Eagle could fool a ghost, he could fool Mrs. Sharpe and Ms. Hussey . . .

"Everything okay, Zoomy?" Gam asked.

"Just thinking about people who seem fine but might have a history, like some of the rhymes. An ugly history."

Gam nodded. "A snake with a bump in its middle."

Zoomy thought again about his friend in the stolen Manet painting, the man who hid part of what he was doing with his hand, even as he waited for Zoomy to understand. Even he had a past, a mysterious past — and was Zoomy right to trust him?

Of course he was!

Sitting in Powell's and thinking about the missing art, especially the piece he had dreamed about, Zoomy was quiet. He'd never known, before this whole adventure began, how alive art really was. He'd never realized that once you communicate with a piece of art, it responds and then you're a part of *its* world as well as your own.

Or, like the Mother Goose alphabet said, once the pie is opened, everyone wants a piece. Once you've made friends with someone in a stolen painting and they're relying on you, there's no going back.

You'll understand this message . . . Being needed in this way was a new experience for Zoomy, and at that moment he felt a rush of confidence, almost as if the deeps were not quite as deep and he could do anything the other four could do.

⬚ ⬚ ⬚ Four faces peered into the dark opening behind and beneath the Picasso.

"Whoa," Tommy breathed. "Good job, Petra! Look — recent scrape marks, and a place where a huge box could've been bolted in, way out of sight. It's a natural!" He spat on his hand and rubbed it on the metal. "Look, it's cleaner where something heavy was dragged, like it just happened!"

"But nothing's there," Calder said flatly. "We missed it, whatever it was."

"Too bad we can't ask someone," Early said.

"Yeah, like one of the pigeons around here," Petra said glumly.

The four turned away, somehow feeling worse for having found a likely spot. A familiar back hurried away from them, across the street.

Ms. Hussey?

▯ ▢ ▯ "What? Where —" Ms. Hussey said lamely, looking from face to face. She wasn't happy to see them, and didn't seem to know what to say.

The kids had rushed over and peppered her with questions. She answered with more questions, but mostly ones that didn't need an answer. After all, the kids were just doing what she'd told them to do.

"Okay, you guys," Petra finally said. "Let her catch her breath. Are you headed back to Hyde Park, Ms. Hussey?"

She nodded yes, then shook her head no. "Going into the bank down the street," she said. "Doing some business for Mrs. Sharpe."

The four were quiet. Weren't the trustees at Mrs. Sharpe's house right now?

"Be careful you're not the red herring on the hook," Tommy blurted. *Nice*, he thought happily. *Smooth comment.*

Ms. Hussey glanced quickly around after he'd said this, and looked truly frightened. "Go home," she said as she backed away. Then she pivoted and hurried around the nearest corner.

Petra turned on Tommy. "Why did you say that? You made her run away!"

"Early said it, not me," he muttered.

"But not about her. About *us*," Early corrected.

I hate girls, Tommy thought furiously.

"I think Tommy said the right thing," Calder said. "Why shouldn't we be warning Ms. Hussey? She looked so jittery, and maybe that's what she needed to hear."

"I was thinking about Eagle, but didn't have time to say it," Tommy added. *Actually, I just thought of him, but who cares.*

"Yes, you did have time," Petra said meanly.

"So did you," Tommy snapped back, but didn't really know what he meant.

"Scaz," Calder said, as if he could see through his buddy and thought he should be quiet.

The four walked back to the train station in a stiff silence. Luckily, the return ride was crowded and their seats were separate.

Petra thought about the lady at the harpsichord and the pull of *X*s behind the man's back . . . *For art, this building. This comfort* . . . Well, they *were* going to the building, but the plan didn't feel comfortable. Was it okay that they were being pulled? She wasn't sure.

Now a startling question came to mind: The red square on the back of the chair — could that be Mrs. Farmer's book? What if she'd chosen a red cover to match Vermeer's red? What if this was a warning, a flag of truth for all who got too close? Everything about Mrs. Farmer had seemed so delightful, but now Petra wondered — was there a darker side to the five of them dreaming about her art?

Calder thought of how it had felt to roll across that boat in the storm, and the sounds of men screaming. He clutched the back of the seat in front of him.

Hold tight, he found himself thinking, and remembered the Rembrandt-like face looking steadily out at the black water. *If he could stay calm, then I can, too.* Calder stirred his pentominoes, relieved that they'd be onboard tomorrow night.

Early imagined that peaceful room in which the man and the woman waited. She wouldn't let them down. Good things would come for them all if she could be what she was meant to be. She'd sit on that chair with the red cushion and make herself ready for the right moment.

She thought back to the delicate loop of pearls in the woman's hair and the lace around her wrists, the details standing out against — Wait, oh, *no*! Both figures in the painting were wearing black! Black like the black jackets.

A flash of irrational panic made Early's heart pound. Once in that room, how would she get out if she didn't want to stay? What if she couldn't figure out what they wanted her to do?

Tommy thought about the Flinck landscape again and wondered if Chicago had ever looked like that. And if it had, did that mean the art belonged to the soul of this city, and was somewhere nearby? That the landscape was a clue in the theft? But Chicago was so big . . . that tree was so big . . . and the opening in the trunk was so dark. For the first time, Tommy wondered if stepping into these paintings had been a lure, like fish dangling before the nose of a cat. He remembered how fast Ratty had snapped at the sardines and wondered if the five of them had all been trapped, like so many cats, into going back to the Farmer. Lured back, and to a building filled with lions . . .

When they stepped off the train in Hyde Park, no one looked up at the box behind the Story Wall as they headed south toward everyone's homes. If they had, they would have seen that the man who had shouted at Tommy was crouched in front of it listening to a cell phone, a black leather jacket draped over one shoulder.

◻◻◻ "Hello?" Early never got calls at night. Her family watched her answer the phone.

"Good idea, will do," she told the caller. "And that's okay, it was a long day."

"Ooooh, you talking to a boyyyy?" Jubie squeaked wickedly.

"None of your business," Early said.

"Oh, yeah," Jubie crooned. "Boy, boy!"

Early sighed. Her parents hadn't said anything, but the question was in the air. "That was Petra. She suggested that the five of us take a break tomorrow, before we go to Mrs. Sharpe's for dinner."

"Sounds like a good idea," Summer said. "You guys have done a lot together this week."

"One, two, three, boys in a tree!" sang Jubie. "Little Miss Muffet, sitting on a tuffet!"

"That's not very nice, Jubie," Summer laughed.

"Please stay away from the spider," Dash added, looking at his daughter. "And you, my man, are a poet but you don't know it."

"I do!" Jubie shouted. "And I like Mother Goose! Like the girls!"

"Afraid he does," Early muttered. "Just watch you don't trip and break your crown," she added.

As Jubie's arm flew up to cover his head, Summer said, "Early!"

"Well, if he likes Mother Goose, he'd better get used to how violent it is," she said. She clapped her book shut, marched into the bathroom, and slammed the door.

Her parents looked at each other and sighed, a ripple of worry crossing the room between them.

❏❑❏ "Can you talk?" Petra asked when Calder answered his phone that night.

"Sure," he said. "What's up?"

"It's about us five and what we're doing tomorrow night. I'm worried."

There was silence on the other end as Calder dumped his pentominoes onto his desk.

"I think" — Petra paused during the clatter and then went on — "the reason we got so grumpy today was that maybe we all know this is a pretty bad idea. This trip to the Farmer with Eagle, I mean. And maybe the five of us don't always have great judgment together, like, oh, opening that can of sardines or Tommy climbing up the bank by the train. Like we egg each other on and also show off for each other."

"Huh," Calder said. "But think how rotten we'd feel if we gave up." Suddenly he pictured the men onboard that Rembrandt ship, howling with fear.

"Do you *really* think we'll be able to rescue this art?" Petra's voice was almost teary. "I mean, five goofball thirteen-year-olds like us? Maybe the grown-ups around us think we're more capable than we really are. Or maybe they're just using us for some sort of camouflage — except for Ms. Hussey, of course."

"That's silly," Calder announced.

"Well, it just felt *different* when you and I found *A Lady Writing* a couple of years ago — like we knew what we were doing. We've had some definite glories in the past, but what if we're about to become part of a horrible, five-way joke?"

"Don't forget that thirteen is a stronger age than eleven or twelve," Calder said.

"Don't say because it's a prime."

"I wasn't going to." The pentominoes clacked some more.

"So how come I don't feel more confident?" Petra asked.

The two were quiet for a beat, thinking of all the things thirteen-year-old friends didn't necessarily talk about but that made them feel rotten, like zits or treacherous body behavior or cracking voices. Like the boy-girl thing, which always seemed to be lurking in the background.

"We'll be fine," Calder muttered. The pentominoes clacked even more. "T for *thirteen*. And F for *five*. T-F equals *toward fame*."

"More likely, *toward the farmer*," Petra said with a smile.

"Okay, okay."

After ending the call, both kids felt a twinge of nostalgia — a longing for a time when the world was easier to decipher, and perhaps a longing for a time when you only chased trouble with one friend, not four others.

Five might be prime, Petra thought to herself, but it wasn't as easy as two.

▯▯▯ The light the next day was a gentle, opalescent cream, like the light in Vermeer's paintings, and the wind had died down. The kids felt restless and a bit sad that they had written off a day they could have spent together, but none of the five made a morning call and suggested they change the plan, perhaps afraid that he or she would be the only one. That would look desperate, which was worse than being lonely.

Petra mooned around her house, remaining shut in her bedroom as much as possible. "Working!" she growled when her younger brothers begged her to play with trucks. Notebook open, she watched out her window for trains and the flash-by of faces in windows, a sight that used to connect her with stories. No words came. She picked up a book but somehow couldn't pay attention.

Next she scrutinized the printout of the thirteen stolen pieces, the one Ms. Hussey had given them. If Calder were there, he'd be counting. She went through the five paintings chosen by the five kids, and came up with twenty-two faces. They needed one more to make a prime, and now she found herself looking at the Rembrandt self-portrait. *He'd be a perfect one*, she mused. *He fits. And if he fits, whose dreams has he been in?*

◻◻◻ Calder watched his mom make soup out of everything in the fridge and sat, elbow on table and cheek on palm, moving his pentominoes around. His brain felt numb. "No, thanks," he said to everything she asked.

Once up in his bedroom, he, too, pulled out the pictures of the stolen art and flipped through them. If his pentominoes made him stronger, maybe they'd make the stolen art stronger, too, and easier to find.

Hey! he thought. *What if one or two are already hidden inside the art?*

Ten minutes later, Calder had found *V*s all over the Vermeer (mostly on skirts and sleeves), as well as a *P* and a *Z* (both on the chair), an *L*, and of course the three *X*s on the floor. The *W* popped right out of the clouds above Rembrandt's ship as the *T* became the mast. In the Flinck, the obelisk was an obvious *I* and the bridge looked like a curved *U*. And in the Manet, wasn't that a *Z* in the glass of wine and a *Y* by the man's right shoulder? Rembrandt's Lady and Gentleman were harder, but there was a *T* on the floor, an *L* on the stairs, and what might be a bunch of *N*s on that ruffled collar. And look — an *F* hiding in the man's dangling glove! And if you allowed a thirteenth pentomino, say an *M*, there was a perfect one shining from the ribbon in Vermeer's harpsichord player's hair.

Calder sat back, satisfied that the pentominoes were already helping.

☐☐☐ Early picked up their family copy of *The Annotated Mother Goose* and looked for the alphabet that Zoomy had described to the others by phone yesterday afternoon. And what was that about him finding Mrs. Farmer's red book in the kids' section? There were so many weird pieces that didn't fit — why weren't she and the others together this morning, sharing their ideas instead of working on this separately? Didn't the others realize that people always get irritated with each other when they're frightened? Next week they'd all be back in school and sorry they hadn't been together today, but she'd never be the one to point that out.

❏❑❏ Tommy and Goldman peered out the window. A dog went by, and then a couple of kids, talking together. *Why did we get so stupid with one another yesterday?* he wondered. He didn't feel the tiniest bit mad now.

He was too proud to call, but maybe he'd just stop by Zoomy's place and see if he wanted to take a walk. And if they took a walk, maybe they'd go by Mr. Cracken's house. The penguin butler with the knife had sure sounded interesting yesterday — and why should the girls get all the thrills? Plus, what if the stolen paintings really *were* inside, and he and Zoomy were the ones to crack this mystery? They'd be stars, and then — then he'd be even with Calder and Petra, who had found that other Vermeer when he hadn't been around.

When Tommy knocked on Zoomy's door, his new friend and Gam had just finished their third game of cards and looked pleased to see him. Ten minutes later, he and Zoomy stood quietly across the street from the spooky, crimson house on Blackstone.

The blinds were closed and there was no sign of life inside.

"Let's check the garbage," Zoomy said.

"Huh?" Tommy replied. "Why?"

"Maybe the wrappings for all that art will be in there, and then we'll know it's inside — or maybe we'll see a name or a company. Some clue."

The boys crept around to the back of the house, but no trash cans stood in the alley. "Scaz," muttered Tommy. "It's not pick-up day."

Zoomy was still for a moment, his head on one side, then walked slowly away from his friend. He paused outside the closest garage door.

"Where're you going, man?" Tommy asked, hurrying into the alley after him.

"I hear a crunching-paper sound coming from inside," Zoomy whispered. "Listen!"

Tommy didn't hear a thing, but right then a side door to the garage burst open, and a man in a black-and-white uniform popped out, his arms filled with a neatly folded stack of brown paper.

Realizing it was a now-or-never moment and that Zoomy probably couldn't see what the man was carrying, Tommy said, "Wait! Sir! We're looking for paper for our school science project! This is perfect — can we use that bundle you're carrying?"

Zoomy stood motionless by Tommy's side as the man hesitated, looking from one boy to the other. "I was just going to tuck it into our recycling," he muttered.

"I don't see too well, so I do a lot of spilling," Zoomy said, sounding younger than he was. "I need that extra paper, or my teacher might not let me do this with the other kids. My buddy's trying to help."

Tommy sucked in his cheeks, admiring Zoomy's lie.

"I see." The man was silent for a second or two, then muttered, "Why not, why not?" He thrust the paper at Tommy, who thanked him with such enthusiasm that the man frowned. He watched as the boys walked quickly away.

When Zoomy and Tommy fist-bumped at the end of the alley, the man wondered, *Was that little kid with the thick glasses faking an eye problem? Nah. Kids! They were just excited they'd gotten something for free. Must be nice to be that young and innocent.*

He shrugged and headed back inside the Cracken garage.

The boys rushed the stack of paper around the corner to Bixler Park, where they spread the sheets out on the grass under a tree, carefully flipping and turning them.

"No company name on anything, at least not yet," Tommy said. "But look — you can see rectangles pressed into the paper where it was folded. Like the shape of a picture frame, you know?"

Zoomy suddenly leaned close, his nose right on the pile. "Smell this," he ordered Tommy. "I recognize it."

Tommy did, then rocked back on his heels. "Whoa," he said slowly. "It's Mrs. Sharpe!"

❐ ❑ ❐ After carefully refolding the paper into a neat bundle, the boys called the other three, who were excited to hear they had news.

"We'll tell all tonight," Tommy promised Calder, Early, and Petra, enjoying his power.

By the time the five kids met at Zoomy's place at a quarter to seven, everyone was more than happy to be back together as a team.

"Okay you guys, let's have it," Calder said, a little insulted that the other boys had gotten together without him.

Zoomy explained that they'd taken a walk and just kind of stumbled on the paper used to wrap whatever the girls had seen in the Cracken house the day before.

"But you were the one to *hear* this clue and then *smell* it!" Tommy added. "I just grabbed it."

"My grandpa would call that a one-two," Zoomy said.

"Maybe the perfume smell is something lots of rich old ladies use," Petra said. "Like, it could be Winnifred Whacker's perfume."

"So, I guess this discovery means that whatever was wrapped in the paper is inside that house," Calder said in a flat tone. "And that some rich lady was nearby."

"But how does perfume get onto paper like that, unless some lady was carrying the packages pressed against her — ah, upper body?" Tommy asked.

The five were silent for a moment, each trying to picture either Mrs. Sharpe or one of the other old ladies juggling a load of heavy art, their jewelry flashing and jingling.

"However it got that smell, the paper could be a message that the art is inside the Cracken house, like Calder said and like Petra and I suspected," Early mused. "Or it could already have been transferred to another place! Sometimes thieves move valuables by hiding them in one type of thing after another. And think of all those empty storage boxes in Mrs. Sharpe's basement."

Petra didn't *want* to think about that. What if the Vermeer they'd seen at Mrs. Sharpe's really was *The Concert?* What if the old lady wanted the kids to see that and turn her in? What if she was at the mercy of Eagle — and so was Ms. Hussey? Petra's mind was racing.

Or, what if the perfume on the paper meant their elderly friend had been involved in stealing and handling a whole bunch of the paintings, cane and all? What if the kids had blown a great opportunity when they'd been alone in the house — blown it by spilling sardines all over and crawling through the basement with pails on their heads?

"I stashed it in a closet at my place," Tommy said. Petra, for a startled moment, thought he meant the Vermeer. "Frightened Goldman with all the scrunching."

"Let's keep the paper caper to ourselves tonight, seeing as Eagle is Mrs. Sharpe's son and all," Zoomy said. He pulled a Baggie with five squashed dilly beans from his pocket and they each had one, talking busily every step of the way to Mrs. Sharpe's. It was only as they reached the alley behind her house that the cheerful tone changed.

"I'm nervous," Zoomy announced, licking his fingers.

"So am I," Early said.

"Me, too," Calder admitted.

"It'll be okay," Tommy chimed in, even though he, too, had worries.

"Sure hope so," Petra murmured.

When Eagle's van rolled quietly around the corner, the five climbed in and were greeted by a warm waft of pizza. The kids relaxed, at least a bit; it was hard to feel jittery when things smelled so good, and the scent of pizza was a thousand times better than any perfume.

Eagle explained the plan. "First, we drive over and park a block from the Farmer. Next: a car picnic with pizza and Coke. After all, this was supposed to be dinner at Mrs. Sharpe's, right? Investigating on an empty stomach is never a good idea."

"Thanks for getting the supplies," Petra said. "Ms. Hussey says that, too. Does she know we're here?"

Eagle squinted through the windshield, his attention on the road.

"Nice of you to feed us," added Tommy. *How bad could the guy be?*

"I smell pepperoni," said Calder.

"Hodilly-hum," Zoomy muttered.

"Mm-hmm," Eagle said evenly, and Petra decided not to ask again.

When the van was parked around the corner from the museum, Eagle turned in his seat. "Okay, let's eat. Napkins are with the drinks."

He's eating, too, Tommy thought. *So the food can't be poisoned.*

"I have a question for you," Petra said. "Each of us had a dream the other night, about one of the stolen works of art. We wanted that to happen — I mean, we were thinking about the art really hard, but then it was kind of like one painting picked each of us. If *you* picked one of the thirteen stolen pieces to dream about, or rather if it picked you, which one would it be?"

The chewing and burping stopped. Would he tell?

Eagle turned away from the kids and looked out a window into the dark sky. "Easy," he said. "There's one piece I think of all the time."

"The Vermeer?" Petra asked.

Eagle shook his head.

"The eagle?" Zoomy guessed.

"Nooo." Eagle laughed.

"Please tell us," Early asked.

Her tone is the kind that gets people to spill secrets, Tommy thought to himself. *How does she do that?*

"The Rembrandt self-portrait," Eagle confided. "His face is gentle but filled with solutions, and, well — if I'd had a father as a kid, I would have wanted him to look like that. Like he wasn't shocked by anything and was there for me all the time."

"Your hat!" Petra crowed. "Now I know why it looked familiar. It's just like Rembrandt's!" So maybe *that* was who had been dreaming about that face!

Feeling shaken but somehow relieved that it was Eagle —
and after all, how bad could any art-dreamer be? — she
wondered, *But what does this mean? I wish I could tell the
others.*

Eagle ducked his head. "Got me," he said. "Silly, huh? But
if you grow up in an orphanage, you make your own family out of what life offers, and I've always been so attached
to that image. Somehow, Rembrandt's face feels familiar to me."

"Mrs. Farmer liked kids," Tommy said.

"*Likes*," Zoomy corrected.

"Which brings us to what we're trying to do here," Eagle
said. "I know my mother — Mrs. Sharpe — feels there's an
advantage you guys may have with Sarah Chase Farmer.
That is, her spirit may allow you to get closer to the people
in her art than any adults."

"I kind of felt the Vermeer pulling me in," Petra confessed. Even now, she was feeling the pull.

"Exactly," Eagle said. "As long as it doesn't pull you into a
place with a farmer's wife who cuts off the tails of blind
mice," he added with a grin that chilled the recent coziness
in the car.

Seeing the kids' expressions, Eagle said quickly, "Just
kidding, bad habit, and nothing to do with you, Zoomy.
Guess I'm ruffling feathers to be sure everyone's alert. It's
the hunter in me, or perhaps the bird of prey — I never can
resist the comfort of a scare.

"Now, are you guys ready? I've timed this so that the hourly guard rotation around the outside of the building will allow us access to the basement, and then, once inside . . . well, we'll see how it goes. The two guards in the security room take turns walking through the building several times a night. I've disabled the camera that covers the area we'll be in, but they're used to those old cameras not working perfectly so no one will think it's unusual to see a blank lens. I hear a new security system is being installed next week, so we're just in time.

"First, we clip ourselves together so we can't be separated. Second — not a word once we're underway, not until we're inside."

Eagle passed out heavy spring clips, each fastened to a length of thin rope. Then he fastened his sleeve to Tommy's, Tommy clipped himself to Zoomy, then Zoomy to Early. Next came Petra, and finally Calder. "You okay at the end, buddy?" Eagle asked, and Calder nodded. Circling the group, Eagle tested the knots and clips, pulling lightly on each one. Next he opened the trunk of the car, pulled out a backpack, and slipped it over his free shoulder.

Calder found himself thinking that this was oddly perfect, as they were all linked to the art they'd dreamed about, and now they were *truly* linked — to each other. Maybe this meant the art would be easier to find, with this double click. Maybe it also meant the five of them would always stay friends.

"I wish the moon weren't quite so bright," Eagle muttered. "We could use a few clouds."

"I live with the deeps whether it's night or day, so this is normal for me," Zoomy announced. "And my hearing's excellent, so I'll be the first to know if someone's coming, like a farmer's wife."

"You're quite the kid," Eagle said. "Sorry about that joke."

As they crossed the deserted street and crawled under a fence, Tommy glanced up at the moon.

I wish I were up there — it looks so safe, he found himself thinking.

Next he wished he were on Calder's Rembrandt boat, in the terrible storm — anyplace but here, tied to a man who was taking them into a building with a ghost.

Early tried not to think about how worried her parents would be if they knew what she was doing. They had a healthy respect for how dangerous it was to get too near stolen goods, especially if you had no idea where they were hidden.

Petra found herself silently reaching out to the woman at the harpsichord, thinking, *Oh,* please *tell me! What did you mean,* For art, this building — this comfort? *Is it this building?*

And then there were Eagle's careless words: *the comfort of a scare.* It was another echo, and this time a twisted one.

The Concert *isn't silent*, Petra thought suddenly. *Speaking of echoes, it's filled with music — singing, strings, old-fashioned wood-wind instruments lying around and one in the hands of the man with his back turned. Is it about the art of music, or painting, or people?*

Comfort . . . Mrs. Farmer was all about comfort, comfort and secrets. Petra felt the forceful pull of the Vermeer again.

They moved in a tight, careful group so that no one pulled anyone else. Crossing a huge lawn, the six ducked under towering bushes, shuffled along a bumpy brick path, and finally stood in a line facing the back wall of the Farmer. As Eagle had promised, there were no guards in sight. The building loomed, looking more like a shadowy castle than a modern-day museum.

"I disabled one of the exterior alarms," Eagle whispered. "Just the one covering the basement door. I'll reactivate it when we go."

Glad to hear we'll be leaving at some point, Tommy thought.

"If someone else has set it again, which I very much doubt, we'll run like crazy. And if we're caught, tell the cops we were having a fun adventure. Got it?" Eagle was already pulling the key from his pocket. "Stole this from my mother, needless to say." As he grinned, the moon caught his teeth, lending them a scary brightness.

Who smiles about stealing from their mother? Tommy wondered.

The five kids were now wishing they hadn't come, but something about being fastened to each other kept the peace. Hearts pounded, sweat broke out, and Zoomy whispered, "Scaz," just as the key clicked and the door swung open.

CHAPTER NINETEEN   AN OLD OUIJA BOARD

▯ ▢ ▯ As they stepped cautiously into the basement, Eagle pulled them forward and then eased the heavy metal door closed. He clicked a bolt above the lock.

Locking us in, Tommy thought, fighting panic.

"That for them or us?" he blurted.

"Depends on who's 'them' and who's 'us,'" Eagle said pleasantly. A single bulb lit the cavernous area, a light that seemed to create more shadow than clarity. Eyes became holes in faces, mowers and cleaning equipment looked like medieval torture devices, brooms and shovels became weapons. Tommy wished he hadn't seen so many scary movies, the kind where people crept around in the dark and prisoners were chained to dripping walls. His mom loved that stuff.

Reaching into the backpack, Eagle pulled out six very small flashlights and passed them around. *Not even big enough to bop someone on the head and confuse him*, Tommy thought, turning his over in his hand. *And because we're all clipped together, no one can run without everyone else. Clever.*

"These are pocket lights, really more to make you feel comfortable than anything else," Eagle was saying. "They can't be seen from the outside, which is why you have them. Now. No time to waste, and as soon as you step out of this basement, which is quite soundproof, there'll be no communication except in whispers.

"The best place for us all is the heart of the building, which I believe is in the center of the courtyard and of the mosaic, close to Medusa's head. That isn't really allowed these days, but I'm sure Mrs. Farmer won't mind," Eagle said.

"How do you know?" Petra asked.

Eagle paused. "Time spent here. Knowing her home and her art is knowing *her*, you know?"

Petra nodded. Somehow, what he said felt true.

"Plus, you'll want to record what she says, and she'll know you need some moonlight to do that. Here's the plan: As soon as you five are settled cross-legged around Medusa, I'll run upstairs in my socks in order to find Mrs. Farmer's Ouija board. I put the new one in my backpack just in case, but I have a feeling she'd prefer to have us use her own."

"What's a Ouija board?" Early asked. She could tell from the look on everyone else's faces that she should already know the answer — but she didn't.

"Ouija boards were popular around the time Mrs. Farmer built the museum, and although she never wrote much about these experiences, feeling they were private, she used to invite select friends to come over and use her 'talking board' near the art. A small table would be set up in one of the rooms and guests came for tea and questions.

"There was nothing spooky or devilish about the game in those days — it was thought of as a way to contact the spirit world. The Ouija board has a darker reputation now, but not so much then. We're only going to use it to talk to her ghost."

Only! Tommy thought.

Eagle continued, "When you saw Ms. Hussey downtown — yes, she told me — I was having a chat with the trustees. I needed to do that without her there.

"I had to ask those old folks if any knew what had become of Sarah Chase Farmer's much-loved Ouija board. Well, it worked: Hurley Stabbler, the oldest trustee, remembered seeing her pull it out of the bottom of a china cupboard up in her apartment. As a neighborhood boy, he'd been invited over for tea and a session with the art, something Mrs. Farmer loved to do with boys and girls from the area. He said he never forgot: The pointer jumped across the board and told them all sorts of things about a painting with a maze in it."

"Hey, I like that one!" Calder whispered.

"Of course you do," Eagle said smoothly. "And Mrs. Sharpe understood that I had you five in mind when I asked about the board, although I'm not sure any of the other trustees did. We both knew how important Mrs. Farmer felt children were, and how much she enjoyed having them in her museum. And we knew Ms. Hussey would probably *not* allow me to involve you."

Dear Ms. Hussey, Petra thought, blinking.

"What if we hear one of the guards coming?" Zoomy asked.

"Ah, good question," Eagle said. "Duck and roll. You'll have to pretend Medusa caught you. That courtyard has so many statues and plants, it should be easy to hide."

Passing piles of fold-up chairs and stacks of small tables, the group moved silently through the rest of the basement and up a steep flight of stairs. Eagle pushed open a heavy wooden door and they stepped into a rush of sweet, damp smells — faintly fragrant and somehow delicious. Everyone's shoulders relaxed.

Standing at the edge of the courtyard in the dark, none of the kids even wanted to turn on a light. The moon shone down through the greenhouse roof, casting a complex net of shadows. Leaves and fronds stretched curious fingers toward the group, and a shimmer of lines crossed faces, confusing skin with stone.

Zoomy took a step forward. "Nice deeps," he whispered.

Eagle led the way to Medusa and stopped. Unclipping himself from the group, he said quietly, "You guys settle in a circle, right here, and remember that Mrs. Farmer is surely pleased to have you in her home tonight. I'll be right back."

Eagle put down the backpack, slipped his boots into it, and walked softly and quickly out of the courtyard and up the stairs, his silhouette fading into the darkness.

The kids could hear the distant buzz of a radio coming from the security room at the end of a long hall beyond the courtyard.

"Hinigere winige arinige," Zoomy said.

"Now I'm getting a glimpse of what it's like to see like you," Early murmured to him. "There's a ton of deeps around here."

"Which can be a good thing," Zoomy said comfortably.

"Better scout where you're each gonna hide if we hear a guard coming," Calder whispered.

Tommy pointed to a giant fern not far from where Zoomy was sitting. "Hey, man," he whispered. "There's your cover, a plant five steps to the left."

"Got it." Zoomy nodded.

A chill ran down Petra's spine and she whispered, "I wish we were sitting against a wall instead of out in the open; I'd feel better."

"Just think about the art," Tommy murmured, surprising himself. "It's alone in here every night." This wasn't the kind of thought he usually had.

They sat quietly, trying not to feel afraid now they knew for sure that Ms. Hussey wouldn't have let them come *and* didn't know they were here. No one spoke and the pocket flashlights stayed off. *It's as if someone's listening and watching*, Tommy thought. *Someone who isn't a guard and isn't one of us.*

Suddenly Zoomy tilted his head. "Hear that?" he asked.

The others held their breath. "Yes," breathed Early. "It's not the radio; more like a faraway party!"

The faintest laughter and the irregular tinkle of glasses . . . the scrape of chairs, and now the plink of a harpsichord . . . a woman singing, or was it just the sigh of wind through a broken window?

"She had concerts here, you know," Petra whispered. "She loved classical music."

Calder turned and dug in Eagle's backpack. He pulled out the new Ouija board box and opened it up. "Let's set it up while Eagle's looking for the old one," he hissed excitedly. "What if that sound of music is, you know, coming from the Vermeer painting? Could mean it's someplace nearby!"

The kids placed the board flat on the mosaic, over Medusa's head. They pulled out the small pointer and placed it on top.

Instantly, a gust of wind lifted the board, swirling it overhead like an autumn leaf. Mouths open, four of the five kids watched it sail through the moonlight and land with a splash in the biggest of the fountains, at the feet of the marble woman dancing. *Pish!* The small pointer landed seconds later on one of the gravel paths.

"Yikes," squeaked Calder. "Mistake!"

Tommy lifted his head. "Sorry," he whispered quickly. "Sorry, sorry, sorry," he added, turning his head in all directions.

"Yeah, me, too. That was rude of us," Petra added, her voice shaky.

"We just wanted to join in," Early whispered.

"Hodilly-hum," Zoomy breathed. "And sorry to the thirty-one lions around here."

The place became deadly quiet — no distant chatter or music, nothing but the fountain's subdued burble on the other side of the courtyard, the faint hum of the radio and an occasional nervous swallowing sound from one of the kids.

"Everyone's waiting," Petra whispered. No one asked her what she meant.

Before they'd had a chance to retrieve the pieces of the Ouija set, they heard the heavy clump of boots and a man's voice saying, "Off I go, John. Back in a jiffy." A dancing circle of light was headed their way.

⧉ ⧉ ⧉ In the scramble to move, the five realized they were still clipped to one another.

How stupid could we be? Calder thought as they stumbled to their feet. He grabbed at the backpack.

The Ouija board! In plain sight! Petra almost groaned aloud as she bumped along between her friends.

There wasn't time to do anything but hide in a big heap, so they squashed themselves beneath the fern that was supposed to shelter Zoomy alone.

If the moment wasn't so frightening, it would have been beyond embarrassing. Noses were mashed into knees, hair got snarled in zippers, feet landed behind ears, rear ends met bellies, and hands had to hide wherever possible. Each one of the kids could only hope they'd become invisible, and tried not to twitch or even breathe.

The guard was humming, his feet moving slowly and heavily around the perimeter of the courtyard.

Don't look in the middle, don't look, Early pleaded silently.

Wish I hadn't eaten that dilly bean, Tommy couldn't help thinking. *If I do something rude, the girls will think I'm disgusting forever.*

Mrs. Farmer, Zoomy thought. *Mrs. Farmer! Pleeeeeeease help us!*

Instantly, the guard slapped his face, growling, "Ow, what was *that*? Insects in this gol-darn garden already? It's barely spring!" He sped up, practically trotting away from the courtyard and toward the stairs to the second floor, muttering, "*Ow!* Never heard of a bee that stings in the dark!"

As soon as the guard was out of sight, the five crept out of the shadows and hurried to unclip themselves, too shaken to laugh.

"I hope Eagle hears him coming," Early said.

"Plenty of places up there to hide," Calder said, hurrying over to the fountain and fishing out the soggy Ouija board. He stuffed it into the backpack.

Petra retrieved the pointer. "I can't believe he didn't see us — or these," she whispered.

"Mrs. Farmer helped," Zoomy murmured comfortably, as if commenting on the weather.

"Oh," breathed Tommy. "*Oh.*"

The five waited in silence for the man to return, hoping they'd only hear one set of feet coming down the stairs. If the guard spotted Eagle, the game was up.

After what felt like an eternity, they heard the *clump-clump* of the guard's boots returning and a tuneless whistling.

Tommy leaped into the huge stone sarcophagus. Zoomy re-hugged the pot beneath the giant fern; Calder squashed himself into a bed of flowers and hoped he wouldn't sneeze. Petra crouched in some vines on the far side of the fountain, and Early wedged herself between the base of the stone seat and some tall planters, hoping nothing with wings and legs would join her.

Pausing at the foot of the stairs, the guard shone his light across the courtyard and then suddenly dropped the flashlight with a curse.

"*Another* sting!" he burst out. "Must be my aftershave." The kids heard him grunt as he leaned over to pick up the now-broken flashlight, which rattled harmlessly. The man hurried toward the distant light of the security room, calling, "Jack, you there? I'm not doin' that again tonight! Not if they promised me double!" The door to the room closed with a thud, cutting off the faint hum of the radio.

The five crept out of hiding and resettled around Medusa, doing a silent fist bump. Waiting in the sweet-smelling dark with Mrs. Farmer and the moon now felt perfect.

Soon they heard the faint sound of Eagle's breathing as he hurried back down the stairs.

❑ ❑ ❑ The wooden board was beautiful. Much heavier than the new version, it had the familiar double-arc of the alphabet, and beneath that, 1 to 9, then 0. YES and NO each had a corner at the top, and at the bottom, in the center, the simple GOOD BYE.

After catching up on the news and fishing his boots out of the backpack, Eagle crouched behind the group.

"Okay, you experts — and I mean that! — everyone's fingertips rest lightly on the pointer, or *planchette*, as she would have called it." A generous, heart-shaped piece of wood with a glass window in the center, the planchette was smooth to the touch.

"Lightly, lightly," Eagle cautioned. "This isn't something to lean on. Now. I believe eyes remain closed while the pointer is moving, and the first questions are usually Yes and No ones. And keep your voices really low, even though the security room door is shut. Ideas?" He looked around at the kids.

"Let's ask if the stolen art is in Chicago," Calder whispered. The others nodded.

"Go ahead." Eagle pulled a small notebook and pen out of his pocket. "Ask."

Calder did, and the five closed their eyes, fingers ready.

Instantly, the planchette began to move. It scooted across the board and stopped.

"You can look now," Eagle said.

"Whoa! It's Yes, and right in the center!" Early marveled.

"Is it *here*, hidden in this building?" Tommy blurted. The planchette flew across the board to the NO.

A garble of disappointed *ohs* followed.

"You didn't really think —" Eagle began as Petra cut across him.

"Mrs. Farmer, does *F-A* spell a word?"

"Right." Eagle nodded, and everyone got back in position and closed their eyes. This time, the pointer traveled a shorter distance and stopped.

"It's the *F*," Eagle said, sounding more surprised than they'd ever heard him. "I think you're getting a message. Keep going!" The kids heard the scritch of his pen as he began taking notes.

At the end of a few minutes, the planchette stopped its spelling and the kids sat back, shaking their arms and fingers.

"Wow," Eagle breathed. "You have *F-I-N* and then either *D* or *E*, I couldn't tell. After that, *A-R-T-S*. Then a 6."

"But," Early began, "that's just 'find arts' or 'fine arts,' and both are so obvious! Plus a six, which could mean us. That doesn't tell us a thing!"

"The six could also mean the trustees," Calder said slowly. "Remember when they said they'd been fighting about whether to do an 'event' at the museum themselves, to get attention?"

Eagle sat back, his face hard to read in the play of shadows. "Odd, that *D* or *E* thing — it stopped right on top of one and then the other. Almost as if it couldn't make up its mind."

"Those're your initials," Calder announced.

"Oh," Eagle said. "Huh."

"Maybe you should ask the next question," Early suggested.

"I'm not sure she'll talk to an adult," Eagle said. "But, well, okay. Back in position, guys. Here we go: Will this message help to find your stolen art?"

Instantly the planchette shot across the board, so quickly that Zoomy's fingers fell off it. Everyone opened their eyes.

The answer was Yes.

"Whoa, you guys!" Petra called out. "It's happening! She's helping us!"

"You mean, helping us *again*," Zoomy said. "We would've been goners if she hadn't stung the guard and broken his flashlight."

Eagle laughed, a low chuckle. "Your turn, Zoomy."

Zoomy was quiet for a moment, his face lifted at an angle that turned his glasses into mirrors, a greenhouse with a tiny moon on each eye.

"The people in the art. Are they alive like you're alive?"

The pointer jumped into action, and there was a murmur of "whoa" and "yikes" as the kids hurried to keep their fingers in place.

Eagle, leaning forward, read the letters. *"A-L-I-V-E-N-O-T-A-L-O-N-E."*

"They're alive and not alone!" Early beamed at the darkness. "Oh, thank you, Mrs. Farmer!"

"This means our dreams were *real* — and the art knows we're looking," Petra marveled. "I knew it, I knew it!"

"Think that means they're in a crowd of other pieces of art? Like the 'faces' thing? Or just that they're together?" Calder asked. "Or wait — maybe it means they're alive and not alone because of *us*."

"I think it means ghosts are real," Tommy muttered.

"I think it means we never see all if we're alive, like she says in her *Truth* book, and that keeps us looking and finding." Early paused.

Zoomy said instantly, "Exactly, like when you pick crops, you have to peek under and around. And the not-alone part could be when you share what you find."

"I always liked Mrs. Farmer's ideas about not being alone, too," Eagle said, looking up at the floors of dark windows.

"Do you have your own copy of the red book?" Petra asked.

"I'm a careful reader," he said evenly. "Hate to say it, but we have to stop now in order to get by the guards outside. I'm going to ask whether we can borrow her Ouija equipment."

The answer, again, was a swift Yes, followed by a Good Bye.

"That's it." Eagle reached over and whisked the old board and planchette into his backpack next to the soggy set. "We need to get going, before someone figures out you're not where you're supposed to be. But first let's thank her for welcoming us."

The kids did, realizing how comfortable they'd become in this dark web of fountains, ferns, and ancient things.

Early suddenly had a clear flash of the Rembrandt painting with the man and woman, and felt she was ready — ready to do whatever it took to rescue the art stolen from Mrs. Farmer's home. Ready to protect the people in *all* of these paintings, plus the brass eagle and Ku. Ready to keep them safe, the ones waiting calmly as well as the ones in the storm.

She felt powerful, and that felt good.

"I don't want to leave," Tommy said.

Zoomy nodded. "Yeah, we could have a great campout in here."

As the six stepped out of the basement door and back into the yard, congratulating one another quietly on a job well done, all gasped.

No!

A blinding spotlight snapped on in their faces, its circular beam a violent echo of the round and distant moon.

"You're under arrest," boomed a deep voice. The five kids and the man with the backpack found themselves surrounded by police.

CHAPTER TWENTY   PASSION AND CRUMBS

▯ ▢ ▯ When in trouble, people feel bad for many reasons and in many ways, and feeling bad with friends is different from feeling bad inside a family. Trust stretches and sometimes breaks within both groups, and explanations can't always be public. Humiliation and disappointment turn to anger, and uncertainty becomes suspicion. It would have been impossible to say which person, from within the four decades represented in the police station that night, felt the worst.

A dog walker had spotted a window opening and then closing on the top floor of the Farmer that night and alerted the police, who had then phoned the guards at the Farmer. They, in turn, had called for reinforcements and an extra patrol unit, despite rumors about a faulty window lock. One mentioned a "difficulty" that night in the courtyard but refused to provide details, adding a general sense of urgency and panic. The external patrol and the backup team had been about to unlock the basement door when it opened on its own, releasing the kids and Eagle.

Parents scowled and scolded. Gam looked sad, which made Zoomy look sadder. The other kids grew quiet but defensive. Ms. Hussey was deathly pale. Eagle, oddly, was the only one who didn't look upset.

He was booked by the police for trespassing and theft of

the Ouija board, and then released on bail by Mrs. Sharpe, who had been driven to the police station by Ms. Hussey. Armed with her lion's head cane, the old woman appeared in a long nightgown covered by her elegant red coat. Early's dad, who didn't have a car, was picked up by Petra's mom, who also picked up Tommy's mom and Gam.

The antique Ouija board and planchette were slipped into a box labeled EVIDENCE, with a promise from the police that they'd be returned to the Farmer as soon as possible.

That night, beneath a dented moon, the five kids lay awake thinking, their questions floating out across Hyde Park.

Did they really have to stop this investigation? They'd promised the police, but how could they abandon Mrs. Farmer? And what about the stolen art? What if it was counting on them? Hadn't that art, after all, reached out to each of the kids, each painting in its own way? Didn't that prove the power of Sarah Chase Farmer's ideas?

They hadn't talked about a ghost while in the police station, especially after the detective had accused them of doing "nonsense voodoo" in there. But it wasn't voodoo and it wasn't nonsense, any more than Mrs. Farmer's writing about art was nonsense. It was rude to even question how real she was, wasn't it? They'd never behave like the rich trustees who'd ignored Ms. Hussey's hand on that first visit to the museum, when she'd held it out to steady anyone who needed it. Hadn't Mrs. Farmer held out her hand to them tonight? How could they turn away?

Everyone was in the deeps now, and didn't that make things clearer? A ghost had interacted with the living, that much was obvious, and Mrs. Farmer had definitely had something to say. But maybe they'd gotten her *confused*. Maybe they should have asked her where the art *was*, instead of asking what her great-nephew had tried so hard to say before he died. Would a ghost know what someone else in her family was thinking?

Oh, no, a horrible thought — what if Eagle had somehow made up the messages he recorded in that dark courtyard? After all, the kids couldn't really see the center of the planchette each time it stopped. And what if Eagle had opened that window on the top floor and a draft had made the Ouija board and pointer fly off? What if he'd played a soft recording to make them think they were hearing ghostly sounds? What if . . . and if so, why?

What could the message mean? If you wrote it out, it would look like this:

FIND (or FINE) ARTS 6. Of course they were trying to find the fine arts! And why the 6? Was it the six of them in that building, the six trustees, or yet another six? *F* was the sixth letter in the alphabet . . . But why would the dying man, Mr. Chase, spell out *F* and then *A* if he was trying to communicate two complete words? It didn't make sense. He should have said *F-I*. Wouldn't *F-A* be the start of a single word, and not the first letters of two words?

In one house in Hyde Park that night, a cat curled on the

sofa between an old person and someone much younger. They sat up late, talking.

When they finally headed to bed, the cat meowed, stretched, and followed one of the two upstairs. There he sharpened his claws happily on an old quilt covered with musicians and instruments. *Rip!* He popped threads, and then circled twice before settling down.

❑ ❑ ❑ Gam's cell phone rang before Zoomy was even awake. "A good-bye tea?" she asked. "Well, perhaps . . . Yes, I'm glad you caught us before we headed home . . . Not at all, this has been an amazing experience for my grandson . . . Two o'clock then, we'll be out front."

Next, phones rang in four households in the neighborhood, disturbing spoons lifted over cold cereal and dishes piled around sinks.

"I see . . . chaperoned . . ."

"Well, I'm still concerned, but . . ."

"As long as that Eagle fellow doesn't go . . ."

The invitation and the responses that followed made the morning light a little less gloomy to the five kids. Perhaps it *was* possible for five thirteen-year-olds to move past the humiliation and shock of being hauled off to the police station in the middle of the night. This humiliation had an extra sting — no police had wanted to hear what the kids believed were game-changing messages. They'd tried, but no one official had listened.

Although the five had been grounded and weren't allowed to meet before Mrs. Sharpe picked them up in a limousine hours later, they *were* allowed to use their cell phones, and they did. Soon the world began to feel a little less unfair and heartless; tea with Mrs. Sharpe and Ms. Hussey would mean, of course, tea plus a sharing of ideas. Having a chance to talk about what had just happened in the Farmer meant not giving up on the investigation — at least, not yet.

"I went back to *The Truth About My Art*," Petra told Tommy over the phone. "Listen to this:

"Some of the pieces in this building symbolize, to me at least, Chicago and her history. I am thinking about events and a variety of moments, both good and bad. Call me a collector of postcards who does not pack bags or travel. Chicago is my voyage, and this home, my ship. This city has welcomed my family for generations, and this museum is my way of saying thank you.

"Right or wrong, I see Chicago through the lens of my art collection, and vice versa."

Tommy sighed. "You think someone should try to match up the stolen items with Chicago history and culture, like one of those two-column work sheets where little kids draw a line between the things that match. Smart — if you believe it'll help."

Petra grinned, not noticing his tone. "Thanks. And remember when Ms. Hussey asked the trustees if they believed the theft was personal? Maybe that's what this is about: the Chicago connections!"

"You know we promised the police to stop working on this heist," Tommy said. "I feel better that we're gonna have this tea later today and a chance to sort through what really happened with people who will get it, but . . . maybe this is where we give up trying to be such hotshot detectives, you know?"

"Huh?" Petra asked. "You mean, abandon the art? You're kidding!"

"Easy for you to say, Miss Smarty-pants," Tommy said meanly. "I feel like enough of an idiot as it is. Did you hear the police calling us Teen Nancy Drews? That was horrible!"

"What's the matter with you?" Petra asked. "Who cares? I'm telling the others!" she barked, and hung up before Tommy could say another word.

Minutes later, Early said to Tommy, "What if we stop trying to guess who took it and try to figure out *why* those thirteen pieces. Like, how they fit with their home city? That kind of lets us off the hook on chasing criminals."

"I'm not psyched about it," Tommy said. "And I don't feel like looking up more stuff."

For the next half hour, Tommy's phone was silent and he wondered what he'd done.

Zoomy was the next to call. "Of course it'll tell us something," he said. "You don't have to see to see *that*. And you can't let the rest of us down. We need you."

"You do?" Tommy had said. None of the other four had put it that way.

"Yeah, of course," Zoomy replied. "What's five minus one? Pathetic, that's what! A fox with no tail!" This made Tommy smile.

Calder was on next. "What if the art has been trying to show us all along? And then just when we collect some real clues, like we did last night, we turn our backs on it?" he asked. "I didn't like being called a retro girl detective either, but what matters more: finishing what we started, or playing it safe by wimping out?" No one could see him fishing nervously for a pentomino as he spoke. "I don't see how we can quit," he added.

"You wouldn't quit with me?" Tommy asked.

"It's too late to quit," Calder said. "You'd feel like a Nancy Drew who got bullied."

"Quit calling me a girl!"

"You started it. Actually the cops did, but they didn't really mean it. Plus, we both know that girls can sometimes be better at scoping out the big picture than boys. Like Petra with this Chicago link. I think it *might* uncover something."

"Okay, okay," Tommy said. "I'm back."

▣ ▢ ▢ Only close friends could have managed the network of calls that followed. Early worked by cell phone with Petra, and Zoomy with Tommy, then they changed partners. Calder did online research — his home computer had the fastest service — and spoke to everyone. Mrs. Sharpe, amazingly, responded to a number of unexpected questions, most of which involved Sarah Chase Farmer's life. Having been the closest of all the trustees to William Swift Chase, Mrs. Sharpe agreed that she was a valuable resource.

"Call me a walking encyclopedia," she sniffed cheerfully to Petra, after her third call. "A relic."

This time, Petra pulled together the notes. Her list, after a couple of hours, looked like this:

— **Vermeer's <u>The Concert</u>**: Bought by Sarah Farmer to symbolize the 1904 building of Orchestra Hall by Daniel Burnham. Chicago was famous for this state-of-the-art classical performance space.

—**Rembrandt's Ship at Sea**: Bought to commemorate the 1915 sinking of Chicago's SS <u>Eastland</u>, a disaster in which 844 people died. One of the ten greatest shipping disasters in US history. Chicago was a place for water commerce.

—**Rembrandt's <u>A Lady and Gentleman</u>**: Bought shortly after Mrs. Farmer's marriage, to commemorate the couple's love of parties and dress balls.

— **Rembrandt's <u>Self-Portrait</u>:** Perhaps a signature nod — by the thief — to William Chase's importance as Sarah Farmer's relative. Mr. Chase was a ringer for Rembrandt.

— **Flinck <u>Landscape</u>:** Memorializes Frederick Law Olmsted's many Chicago parks and the Chicago Exposition of 1893.

— **Manet's <u>Chez Tortoni</u>:** A symbol of Chicago's many early twentieth-century writers, like Sinclair Lewis, L. Frank Baum, Sherwood Anderson, and Carl Sandburg.

— **Degas's sketches of a walking procession, horse racing, musical instruments, dancing, and boat masts in a harbor:** Early in the last century, Chicago had many racetracks. Add to that music, theater, dance, sailboats, and parks — all a part of Chicago's landscape.

— **Bronze eagle:** Sculptor Lorado Taft was famous at the time Mrs. Farmer was alive. He created the bronze <u>Fountain of the Great Lakes</u> sculpture, which sits outside the Art Institute, and <u>Fountain of Time</u>, a huge, hundred-person concrete sculpture at the end of the Midway, in Hyde Park. It's still there, and his studio was not far away. He began something called the Eagle's Nest Art Colony, a summer place that supported artists from the University of Chicago and the School of the Art Institute of Chicago.

— **Ku:** This drinking goblet could refer to the rough Prohibition days in Chicago, which of course happened mostly after Mrs. Farmer's death, but played a big part in Chicago's history. That would be a nod to Al Capone and the other gangsters.

The kids had to agree that the thief or thieves had chosen pieces that weren't simply valuable — they also sent a message that said, *Chicago! Chicago!* Only someone who knew the city and Sarah Chase Farmer's ideas could have chosen the thirteen, which would make this a *coded* theft.

And if this was right, the art was probably hidden someplace that was symbolically important.

But *why?* Who would do such a thing? Someone who thought the art belonged to Chicago for all time?

The reason wasn't even partway clear. Why would anyone who cared about Mrs. Farmer's art steal it, to begin with?

☐☐☐ The mirrors in Hyde Park were busy that afternoon as the five kids washed, combed, tried on their nicest clothing, and made themselves as neat and clean as possible. Calder found some deodorant; Petra's mom helped her with a little makeup and two new, sparkly hair clips; Gam found Zoomy an *I Love Chicago* kid-sized necktie in the local drugstore; and Early's mom braided her hair with ribbons, making an elegant do. Tommy slicked back his hair, which made him feel — at least with the bathroom light off — as though he looked more than a little like Johnny Depp.

Stepping into the stretch limousine, the kids were almost shy with each other and the adults. Gam had on her Sunday best — a green dress and white cardigan sweater — and Ms. Hussey wore a long purple skirt, a lavender top, and an array of tiny, multicolored pearls in her ears. Mrs. Sharpe wore a blue dress edged with sparkles and a shawl with swirls of peacock feathers.

"Well, here we are," Ms. Hussey said, looking around at the group. "You five have done some valuable thinking this spring break, and it's too bad it had to end in the police station."

"We practically forced Eagle to bring us back to the Farmer," Petra said. "Like we said that night, it was really our fault."

"Mmm," Mrs. Sharpe said. "You *are* a force to be reckoned with."

"Where's Eagle today?" Calder asked.

"Busy," Mrs. Sharpe said in a voice that invited no further questions.

"We talked to Mrs. Farmer that night," Early said quietly.

"So I heard, so I heard." The old lady nodded.

"And we think we now understand what the thirteen stolen items stand for, all key stuff about Chicago, but not why they were taken. I mean, who would want to hurt the

Farmer or disturb the art if they understood what both meant to Sarah Chase Farmer?"

"Who indeed?" Mrs. Sharpe murmured.

Maybe the old lady did *take it*, Tommy thought to himself, remembering the familiar perfume in that packing paper. *And made Eagle come visit and set up those art cases in the basement . . . But wait, the cases were empty.*

A similar ripple of ooh-maybe-but-guess-not expressions crossed the others' faces.

"Seriously, Mrs. Sharpe: Do you think someone *will* find the art one day? This is such a crazy theft!" Petra blurted. "It's like the people who would know to take what was taken couldn't have done it! *Wouldn't* have done it."

Mrs. Sharpe blinked her eyes for a moment, one hand to her throat, and then sat straighter in her seat. "Hard to say what people will do. I've always loved this Henry James quote," she said. "'*We work in the dark — we do what we can — we give what we have. Our doubt is our passion, and our passion is our task. The rest is the madness of art.*' Henry James was a contemporary of Sarah Chase Farmer. I imagine they may have met."

"*We* worked in the dark," Zoomy said mournfully.

"And there was madness," Tommy added. "Things got a bit weird."

"And method to your madness, I might add," Mrs. Sharpe said brusquely. "But it's critical to foresee consequence and keep an eye on where you're headed. This afternoon, I'm taking you to the Blackstone Hotel, one of Chicago's landmarks and certainly a spot Sarah Chase Farmer visited. Twelve United States presidents have stayed there, and all in the past century — it was built between 1908 and 1910, right around the time the Farmer Museum and the Robie House were built. It fell into disrepair in the 1990s, but is now fully renovated, I'm told, and back to some of its old grandeur."

"And I'll bet tea, in this hotel, means china teacups and silver," Ms. Hussey said. "I hope you're hungry."

"Always," Calder murmured.

The limousine stopped in front of the Blackstone, and a doorman rushed out to open the door. He helped the ladies first, and then nodded to each of the five kids as they scrambled out of the interior.

"Your tea room?" Mrs. Sharpe asked after climbing the stairs.

She always sounds like royalty, Tommy noted. *It's kind of embarrassing.*

"Oh," the doorman said, "If you want coffee, there's a small Starbucks downstairs, and then the Artist's Cafe is just down the street. Our only restaurant now has a prize-winning Spanish menu. The chef is from Barcelona. Olives to die for, and all those little plates of whatchamacallits."

"What!" Mrs. Sharpe thumped her cane on the rug, which looked plushy but far from Victorian. "No tea? In one of Chicago's most elegant historic hotels?"

"Sorry, ma'am."

Ms. Hussey placed her hand lightly on Mrs. Sharpe's arm. "Let's take them to the Artist's Cafe! That's a great building as well, and has a charm of its own."

Back they piled into the limousine, Mrs. Sharpe muttering, "Imagine offering us olives to die for! No taste, none at all!" and drove two blocks north on Michigan Avenue.

The Artist's Cafe was not exactly fancy but bright and clean. A huge array of pies and cakes lined the shelves behind the counter. Stepping inside, the kids smelled hot chocolate, cinnamon, vanilla, and butter.

"Mmm," Zoomy said. "This smells like birthdays."

"Best place we could have gone," crowed Petra. "Yum!"

"My dad took my brother and me here once for a treat, after going to the Harold Washington Library. It's part of the Fine Arts" — Early broke off, her eyes widening — "Building," she said slowly.

"Finigininige inigarts," Calder muttered, looking around at the other four.

"Whatever language you're speaking, it's rude to do that in front of your hostess," Mrs. Sharpe said icily as Ms. Hussey helped her out of her coat.

"Right she is," Ms. Hussey agreed.

"Hodilly-hum," Gam added.

Mrs. Sharpe looked at the ceiling, as if wondering what form of word mangling would come next.

What followed was a dream tea. The kids were told to

order whatever they'd like, so the table was soon covered with tea, hot chocolate, cherry pie, German chocolate cake, berry crumble, apple strudel, warm pecan pie with vanilla ice cream, and a plate of assorted cookies for those who needed an extra bite.

Even Mrs. Sharpe had a crumb on one cheek after they'd finished. It was more dessert than anyone there had tasted in many moons, if ever.

"On reflection, this is a more appropriate spot for this gathering than the Blackstone Hotel," Mrs. Sharpe said. "I'm very pleased that things worked out this way. Did you children know that the Fine Arts Building is the oldest studio arts building in the country? It was built in 1885, and by 1898 was filled with artists' workspaces. It has been of continuous service to the arts ever since. It still has the original interior detail — brass and ironwork, old clocks, stone columns and floors, the manual elevators — and, at the top of the building, some marvelous Beaux Arts murals done by artists who worked here at the turn of the century. I believe Frank Lloyd Wright had a studio here at one time, and W. W. Denslow, the illustrator of L. Frank Baum's *Wizard of Oz*, worked here. It's still used by architects, artists of all kinds, musicians, and those who practice repair and restoration of the finest woodwind instruments."

Mrs. Sharpe took a much-needed breath, then continued, "I'm sure that Sarah Chase Farmer was here at many a soiree, either listening to a recital or visiting an artist's studio. Lorado Taft worked here for a while. And, if I remember correctly, there is an interior Venetian courtyard, one that Mrs. Farmer no doubt knew. It may even have influenced the design of her museum, which wasn't complete until long after this one. Goodness, that's a thought that never occurred to me before. Oddly appropriate, our being here. Shall we venture in?"

"You bet," Calder murmured, just as Early said, "Absolutely," and Zoomy, looking straight ahead, whispered, "Think Mrs. Farmer will show?"

Tommy smiled. "We'll keep an eye out for her boot."

Early, standing next to Petra at the back of the group, said quietly, "First we get the Fine Arts message, and then we're here. It's another one of your echoes, or maybe a pull. Like a trail of crumbs."

"It would be difficult to leave a bigger trail than the one we left in the cafe," Ms. Hussey said comfortably, only half listening to what Early had said.

As if to check the trail, Ms. Hussey glanced back and saw a black jacket very similar to Eagle's on someone chatting with the limousine chauffeur at the curb. She squinted, unable to see clearly through the double set of doors, then frowned.

She'd noticed more black jackets around Hyde Park than usual, as the kids had. More crows, as well. She shrugged, reminding herself that it was all a sign of spring. Did crows turn up for murderous reasons when nesting season for the smaller birds began? Well, at least there hadn't been any crows popping out of the pies today.

Ms. Hussey smiled and shrugged, but a sharp sliver of doubt had lodged in her mind. She did a quick field-trip survey of the little group, counting to seven twice.

[] ☐ [] The lobby was straight from another era, as Mrs. Sharpe had said it would be. Arched columns and old lamps, an expanse of polished stone on walls and underfoot, even an old post box; countless undisturbed details gleamed in a dim interior light.

On the wall above the second set of front doors was a boldly lettered statement:

ALL PASSES — ART ALONE ENDURES.

"Where to, ma'am?" asked the one elevator operator in sight. He held back an intricate metal gate as Mrs. Sharpe stepped inside, obviously pleased that all was looking and sounding as it should.

"The top," Mrs. Sharpe replied. "Tenth floor. Everyone should start there." The elevator wasn't much more than a closet, and only five of them fit comfortably inside.

"I'm the only operator at this time of day," the man apologized. "Not like old times."

Ms. Hussey stayed downstairs with Petra and Tommy. "Meet you up there," she called cheerfully.

As the gate latched, they heard Mrs. Sharpe saying, "Cast bronze elevator doors on every floor, such style. They will surely outlive —" The door clicked shut, ending her sentence.

"Ms. Hussey," Petra said slowly to her old teacher. "Would you say it's a good or bad sign if we keep noticing echoes? Things that are coincidences but not quite, because they feel less random — like, well, they've happened because of something else?"

The young woman frowned, studying Petra's face. "Good or bad? Well, I guess when I notice a human pattern it usually seems as though it's connected to something I want to know."

Tommy, looking up at the statement ART ALONE ENDURES on the wall, suddenly felt as if someone had flashed a camera in his face. *FIND ARTS FINE ARTS . . . FIND ARTS FINE ARTS 6 . . .*

"Scinigaz!" he shouted. As he turned happily first to Petra and then to Ms. Hussey, he opened his mouth to speak and then snapped it shut again.

Someone had stepped through the front doors behind Ms. Hussey, and that person had the soft, wary tread of a large cat.

Ms. Hussey jumped when she heard the words, "Well, if this isn't a popular spot today!"

"You stay right here," she ordered Tommy and Petra. Grabbing Eagle's arm, she turned him before he and the two kids had even said hello. The adults walked several steps away.

Eagle glanced over Ms. Hussey's shoulder at the kids and winked. Looking down at Ms. Hussey, he shrugged and spread his hands, as if to say, *Not my fault.*

"I've got something to tell you, something *big*," Tommy whispered to Petra. She shifted her gaze from the two adults to her friend. "I'm so glad you didn't let me quit this morning!"

"What?" she asked, but before Tommy could say another word, Ms. Hussey was back at their side and Eagle was gone.

"Where'd he go?" Petra asked, looking around. "That was a fast visit!"

"Cinigarinigefinigul," Tommy whispered.

Ms. Hussey raised her eyebrows but didn't ask. She wasn't, after all, in a position to, having just said something to Eagle that she didn't want the kids to hear.

◘ ☐ ◘ The elevator ride up to the top of the Fine Arts Building was silent. The floors shot by, one after the other, as Tommy thought impatiently, *All passes, all passes . . .*

Petra was busy wondering what both Tommy and Ms. Hussey knew, Ms. Hussey was busy wondering about what a number of other people knew, and Tommy wondered what to do — or not to do.

◘ ☐ ◘ "Ms. Hussey! Hurry!"

Halfway down the hall, the other kids clustered around a wooden bench, and on the bench, Mrs. Sharpe leaned against Gam, who fanned her with a handful of gallery invitations.

"Just a spell," Mrs. Sharpe muttered as Ms. Hussey ran over. "Little fresh air . . . You two bring me down, and we'll wait for the kids in the limo. I want them to see . . . while here . . ."

"Oh, dear," Ms. Hussey said. "I just saw Eagle and sent him away. Let's try to get her to her feet," she said to Gam, who handed her large purse to Zoomy, freeing both hands.

Soon the three adults were headed downstairs in the elevator. As the gate closed, Ms. Hussey called out, "Twenty minutes tops! You can walk down the ten stories and see the building that way. And keep your phones on."

"Hold on to that bag and don't forget that all raisins are really grapes," called Gam as the doors closed.

"What does *that* mean?" Tommy asked.

"Just that old people are as smart as young ones." Zoomy was looking dubiously at the purse. "She always says that when she wants me to behave and not do something dangerous." He clicked the pocketbook open. "Oh, a Baggie of dillies."

As Zoomy opened it, Calder groaned. "I'm still too full of cake and pie, aren't you?"

"For good luck," Zoomy said in such a firm voice that the other four obediently took a small bite from the one bean he passed around. "Hodilly-hum," he said, closing the purse and tucking it under one arm. "Come on."

"Wait, guys." Tommy then spilled his "FIND ARTS FINE ARTS 6" flash, and the others responded with a satisfying buzz of ideas and questions. Both Petra and Early patted him on the back — a definite first — and he blushed happily.

In the next half minute, the group agreed on several things: One, they had almost no time to disagree. Two, they needed to get to the sixth floor but also do a quick survey of the other seven, not counting the first floor, which was mostly lobby. Three, if there was a manager's office for all these studios, they needed to get inside it, and fast. Separating — with phones in pockets — was the only option.

Zoomy and Tommy headed for the sixth floor. They would explore and listen at each of the doors. Calder, Petra, and Early would split up and cover the other floors, reading signs outside the studios and hunting for the main office. Feet thumped off in all directions.

Petra, exploring the top floors, found signs outside Frank Lloyd Wright's old studio and Lorado Taft's. She also paused for a moment to admire some huge paintings that looked like the wall murals Mrs. Sharpe had mentioned: Ladies in long, flowing dresses danced through flowery landscapes and around admiring men. She thought of the mysterious party sounds they'd heard at the Farmer, and wondered what *this* building sounded like when empty at night. Maybe art and ghosts went together.

Calder and Early passed rooms with signs for printmakers, painters, architects, sculptors, and jewelers. Each heard singing from behind a number of doors, and sounds of violin, guitar, and piano lessons. A few doors had no identification on the outside. There were benches in most of the halls and small tables covered with takeaway cards and brochures.

Zoomy and Tommy had found three unmarked doors on the sixth floor. Of the marked doors, some belonged to pianists, who were making a wonderful amount of noise. Others belonged to small arts organizations whose names the boys didn't recognize.

It was Calder who stumbled on the Fine Arts Management office, a wooden door in the middle of the third floor hallway. He turned the knob and stepped inside.

"Yes?" asked someone who looked like an artist, a student, or both. Calder's mouth fell open, studying this young woman's face tattoos and spiky blue hair. Was that a cat playing a fiddle on one cheek and a dish and spoon holding hands on the other?

"Oh!" Calder said, wishing he'd called one of the girls to help. "Ah, I'm interested in recent studio rentals. Like, within the last month."

"You're looking for someone specific?"

"Their sign must not be up yet and I'm not sure what name they used." Calder blundered on. "Could I see the list of recent renters?"

"Doesn't sound like something I should do, does it?" The girl smiled, which made the dish lean toward the spoon. "But if you give me a hint . . ."

As Calder stirred his pentominoes, the girl peered over the edge of the counter to see what he was doing. "Sorry, just a math tool I carry," he blurted. "Great for thinking. And, oh, this person said they're on the sixth floor."

The girl turned toward her computer and scrolled through some names. "Not too much lately. Any idea what size studio space or what they wanted it for?"

"Not too large. Good temperature controls. For storage and, ah, work on some largish art pieces." The computer was, frustratingly, turned at an angle that he couldn't quite see. Calder's pentominoes clacked some more.

"What *are* those?" the young woman asked. "I like math games. I use them in my art."

Calder spilled his pentominoes onto the counter with a full-arm flourish that he hoped would knock the computer screen in his direction. It did. "Oops, I'm so clumsy!"

In the confusion that followed, the girl picked several of the pieces off the floor and Calder read the screen as fast as he possibly could. There was only one recent rental, and it had been made the week before the theft, in early March:

SALLY STAYZ, 619

"Here, you can keep these, a present," Calder said before rushing back out the door. Maybe this would distract her from realizing she'd just handed him a giant clue. Minutes later, the five were gathered outside 619, which had no sign and was quiet inside.

Calder was bright with excitement. "It's here. I know it!" It was like being on that Rembrandt shipwreck and seeing help on the way — he could practically taste the rescue.

"Lucky you found that room number *after* I put the big picture together," Tommy reminded him.

"And after *I* realized there might be something special about the *Fine Arts* Building." Early smiled.

Tommy turned her way, suddenly remembering the girl sitting frozen in Mrs. Sharpe's living room, the one with the flying cookies on her lap. *One of the best things about friends,* he thought to himself, *is that you stay around each other long enough to get cooler — and to live through the lemme-outta-here, uncool moments.*

"Scaz." He grinned at her.

"Shhh, you've all done great work, but keep your voices down! These are open stairwells and anyone can hear us." Petra tapped her watch. "We're down to five minutes."

Tommy turned the door handle. It was locked.

"Wait, *listen,*" Zoomy hissed to the group, his ear against the door. "I just heard a beep from inside there, like a cell phone sound."

"Whoa," muttered Tommy. "I wish we knew how to pick locks."

"The person you talked with, Calder — she must have a

master key to all the studios," Zoomy pointed out. "For fire and stuff, you know?"

"She's not gonna just give it to us!" Calder protested.

"We could call Eagle," Early volunteered. "I'll bet *he* could figure out how to pick that lock. He's probably good at criminal stuff. And what if we can't get back here ourselves? We're all grounded right now. But do we trust him to come back here without us?"

"Not exactly." Petra was frowning. "Tommy and I saw him come into the building just now, as if he didn't know he'd find us. Ms. Hussey sort of steered him away. Then he left without saying good-bye. In fact, she kept us apart."

"And guess what?" Calder added. "I forgot to give Tattoo Cheeks the T pentomino, it's still in my pocket. T for *turn*. It's a sign that we *have* to return!"

Hurrying back to the office, the group concocted a drama that they hoped would get them into the studio.

As their voices spiraled down a couple of stories, a young man in a black jacket peered out of a doorway on the sixth floor. Glancing in both directions, he spoke quietly into a phone, one trembly hand cupped over his mouth.

▯ ▯ ▯ Inspired by Mrs. Sharpe's spells during the past couple of days, the five piled into the office and Petra flopped down on the floor in what she hoped looked like a faint.

"Now we *really* need help," Calder said, trying to sound

panicky. "And here's the T," he added, dropping it on the counter. "T for *trust*."

"Goodness!" The girl shot him an odd glance but jumped to her feet. "Want some water? There's a fountain just outside in the hall."

"Do you have a cup of some kind?" Early asked, scanning the office.

"Let's see." Tattoo Cheeks spun to the left and right. "You can have my coffee mug — here, I'll wash it out." She vanished into an inner room, leaving the door open.

At the sound of water running, Calder and Early both lunged over the counter, cracking foreheads in the process. Tommy mashed Zoomy's toe when he reached over to sweep fingers along the area that wasn't visible beneath the overhang. No keys were found.

A minute later, they helped Petra to her feet and piled back out the door, leaving the girl with blue hair looking worried.

"Can I ask if you found the person you were looking for?" she asked Calder.

"Oh!" Calder squeaked. "Yeah."

"See you," she muttered, dropping the T pentomino into her pocket.

When the five kids emerged from the building minutes later, they were out of breath and glassy-eyed. Zoomy, Gam's purse under his arm, had a definite limp.

"Good visit?" Mrs. Sharpe asked, her head against the seat. "I am feeling slightly better, and I thank you all for your patience." She nodded to the five, Gam, and Ms. Hussey.

"You kids look like you've accomplished something," Ms. Hussey said, with an edge of hope-you've-stayed-out-of-trouble in her voice. "Well, it's a lovely end to a very busy spring break, and — I'm sure the art will turn up. Meanwhile, you've seen lots of other great art," she finished lamely.

"The key," muttered Mrs. Sharpe.

"Which kind of key?" blurted Petra.

Mrs. Sharpe's eyes glittered, as if Petra had surprised her.

More of those weird echoes, Tommy thought. *Petra's right, it's strange. Wonder what made the old lady say that minutes after we'd been trying to get hold of a key?*

When there was no answer, Petra pressed on with, "We love the meeting room on the top floor in your house. Um, could we possibly come back and do some more brainstorming about the theft? Like maybe one day after school this week?"

Mrs. Sharpe then startled everyone with her response. "It isn't locked and tomorrow is Saturday," she said. "Please stay another night," she murmured to Gam, "and the five kids can wrap up their work."

"Well, I guess we can do that," Gam said, gripping her purse and eyeing Zoomy's foot. "You've been so kind. Sure you're well enough for this noisy group?"

"We've all been stung at one time or another," Mrs. Sharpe murmured, "and this is no time for faintness. If art alone endures — all passes, as you know — we can press on for another day."

Sitting up, she turned toward the kids. "You've been quite fearless," she said, and the kids felt a rush of shock and pride. "And," Mrs. Sharpe continued, lingering on the word, "there's work still to be done. I doubt that any of us can put Humpty Dumpty together again, but good things can come from such a fall — if, that is, the right pieces are lined up, like a nose finding its place between two eyes. Or a key finding the right lock."

The rest of the ride was silent, as all ages wondered what she meant and thought about strange puzzles made from eggshells, keys, and faces. Ms. Hussey, chilled, pictured the huge Picasso lady downtown. She hadn't meant to pull the kids into so much danger. If she had only known . . .

The kids, for their part, felt as though Mrs. Sharpe knew more of what they'd been up to in the Fine Arts than she was letting on. But how? Had someone been spying on them just now?

Why does Mother Goose keep popping up? Early wondered. *Does she mean William Chase? Is he the smashed egg? Or is it the Farmer? And what's that Mother Goose rhyme about a lock and a key?*

The Fine Arts is a perfect hiding spot, Petra thought slowly. *And if Mrs. Sharpe has had the key all along, what should the five of us do?*

Tommy thought back to Ms. Hussey grabbing Eagle's arm in the lobby. *There's a piece missing here, something we can't see. Does the old lady want us to figure out something before Eagle or Ms. Hussey does? And what if Ms. Hussey has gotten too close to Eagle and doesn't know it?*

Mrs. Sharpe wouldn't let anything bad happen to any of us, would she? Calder was struck suddenly by the suspicion that Mrs. Sharpe had left them in the Fine Arts just now on purpose. *How much does the art matter to Mrs. Sharpe — more than certain people in her life, people like us five? Are we in danger of getting a sting?*

Looking out the window, Tommy shivered. His mom would say someone had just stepped on his grave. *The passes quote — does she mean we'll all die one day, but the art will live on? Do we want to die for art?*

CHAPTER TWENTY-TWO   A NEW CHASE

❏❏❏ After dark that night, a car that had been parked outside Mrs. Sharpe's place drove slowly through the empty streets. It pulled up to the garage outside William Chase's mansion, several blocks from the Farmer.

A man and a woman climbed out and moved slowly toward the side door, pausing every few steps to be sure they were alone. The woman pulled a key from her pocket and opened the door. They slipped inside and the door closed soundlessly.

Lights went on and curtains were drawn in the study. No one passing thought this odd, as Mr. Chase was a private man and may have left descendants, friends, lawyers, or detectives who now had access to his home. Residences in that area all belonged to the rich, and few knew each other's business.

Inside, the woman sat down at his desk and began methodically sorting through its contents. The man paced around the room, examining framed photographs.

An hour later, the two left the house and the streets surrounding the Farmer were once again quiet, the moon peeking between branches as if to say, *I'm looking, can't you see?*

❏❏❏ "Wish we could check out Eagle's basement hidey-hole again," Tommy said. "We got interrupted just when we got the first box open."

The five were back in Mrs. Sharpe's attic.

"Who started all the Mother Goose talk?" Calder said. "And how come all of the adults know it?"

Early bit down on her lower lip. "Eagle started it when he read aloud to Jubie, that day in Powell's. And it's familiar because it's the most famous bunch of kids' rhymes and songs in the English language. I'll bet older folks who grew up with less entertainment practically know them by heart."

She paused for a beat. "Last night I looked up the rhyme about a lock and key. But I need one of you to say it with me."

Tommy rolled his eyes, as if this was too silly for words. "I will," he said, dragging out the I. *I'm such a good guy*, he thought to himself.

Early grinned. "You sure?"

Tommy nodded.

"Okay," she went on, "repeat each line after me, but substitute *key* for *lock*."

"Whatever you say."

"I am a gold lock," Early began.

"I am a gold key," Tommy said, now looking guarded.

Next Early substituted *silver* for *gold*, then they moved through *brass* and *lead* and finally *don*.

"I won't say it! I knew this was going nowhere good," Tommy growled.

"But maybe that's what Mrs. Sharpe was *saying* . . . Everyone knows that if there's a lock there has to be a key." Early sat back. "Even if it's a don-key!"

Tommy tried to look bored, but thought suddenly of the donkey in his Flinck landscape. *Not funny*, he found himself thinking.

"Do you think it's odd that Eagle's so comfortable with these rhymes when he isn't that old and grew up in an orphanage?" Calder asked the others.

Petra shrugged. "Maybe they only had a small library in there, and Mother Goose was part of it. I'll bet he was the type to read everything. Plus, it may just be more of the echoes."

"Forget Mother Goose! How on earth will we get back to the Fine Arts and into that room?" Tommy groaned. "We were *so close!*"

"If it even means anything, this Sally Stayz thing," Early said gloomily. Tommy glared at her, but she didn't seem to notice. "We don't have any proof that the sixth floor is right. Hey, did any of you guys look up that name last night to see if it's a real person?"

"I did," Calder said. "No one pops up, not in the computer anyway. Or the phone book. Maybe we just want things to fit so badly that we're inventing clues."

"Sally Stayz, Sally Stayz," murmured Early.

"HEY," shouted Zoomy. "I've got it!"

◻◻◻ "Sally is short for Sarah — I know that from our neighbor in Three Oaks. And she *stays*, which means —"

"She stays in Chicago!" Petra shrieked, hugging Zoomy and knocking his glasses sideways.

"And whoever rented that room is *explaining* the *crime!*" Early yodeled. The others had never heard her so loud. "It's a *double* coded message, coded by the Farmer fight and the city itself!"

"Now *that's* good thinking," Calder agreed happily.

"This makes us rock stars!" Tommy whooped, hopping to his feet and pretending he was singing into a microphone. Calder elbowed him and he flopped back down on the floor.

"We're loud enough, that's for sure." Petra giggled.

As if on cue, there was a light tapping on the attic door, followed by a *scritch-scritch*.

"Scaz," Petra muttered. "Sorry about the noise," she said as she opened the door.

Eagle stood outside while Ratty squeezed through, sniffing to be sure there weren't any leftover sardines.

"May I come in?" Eagle asked simply. "I just heard your latest Fine Arts deduction, and can't pretend I didn't!"

Zoomy scratched Ratty behind the ears. "Were you listening through his collar all week?" he asked abruptly.

Eagle sat down. "Come here, Rat-a-tat," he ordered. As Ratty leaned happily against his master's knee, Eagle unbuckled the collar and passed it around. "That thick part is a homing device that feeds the animal's location to a cell phone, nothing more." Eagle looked around at the group and shrugged. "Sorry if I scared you."

"So how did you know we made any discoveries at the Fine Arts?" Calder asked. "And how do we know we can trust you?"

"How does anyone trust anyone else in this world?" Eagle asked pleasantly. "It's always hard to tell a plain old gesture from what's meaningful, hard to separate plain old errands from spy missions, and hard to separate overhearing from eavesdropping. Let's face it: People are hard to decode. Nursery rhymes, too. But ghosts . . . now, things are different once you've died, don't you think?"

"We wouldn't know," Petra said, biting her lip. "How do you know?"

"Well, some of it is dreams," Eagle said, looking out the window.

"We've had some crazy dreams, too," Calder said. "All of us. About the art."

"I saw that," Eagle said. "From the notes you left on the table here. That's partly why I thought it'd be worthwhile to take all of you to the Farmer and risk an arrest."

"So you spied on us!" Petra said.

"I wouldn't say that," Eagle murmured. "I took advantage of an opportunity. As, I feel sure, all of you did while you were alone in the Fine Arts yesterday. My mother is a great one for providing opportunities. She loved what your grandma said to you yesterday, Zoomy. Louise Coffin Sharpe is truly a grape, even if she's wrinkly enough to be a raisin. She's believed all along that you kids could untangle what's going on, and you have."

"Mostly," Tommy blurted. "We still don't have the loot."

"But you've communicated with the art, then with Mrs. Farmer, and now you've got me. I guess this is where I have to share an odd twist of fate. Perhaps twist is the wrong word — I think it may be more inevitable than that, like the bounce of sound that happens when you clap your hands in a tunnel."

All eyes were on Eagle. Zoomy propped his elbows on the table, rested his chin in his hands, and pushed his glasses tightly against his face with both pinkies. Petra mouthed, "Bounce of sound," as if practicing it.

As Eagle stroked Ratty's head with each statement, the cat purred in agreement, blinking his green eyes as if to say, *See? Simple!*

"I'll start with my birth. Born on St. Patrick's Day, March seventeenth, thirty-one years ago. My natural mother's name was Rose Devlin, and she listed no father on my birth certificate. I'm told she died when I was a few weeks old. The rest of my childhood was spent in an orphanage."

"Did they read Mother Goose to you?" Early interrupted.

"The ladies in there knew most of those songs by heart and sang them to us as bedtime lullabies. It seems like I've been comfortable with the book all my life. Plus, if you're always wondering who you really are in the world, you pay attention to all clues, and I noticed that Mother Goose is full of people and animals with mysterious messages. I mean, the jingles kind of fit lots of situations in life."

"Yeah." Petra nodded. "We see that. Blackbirds, cats, bees, Jack and Jill's pails, maybe even donkeys . . ."

Tommy frowned.

"The rhymes have a way of following the truth," Eagle went on. "Anyway, I always felt at home in the Farmer Museum, after being taken there for a school visit. As soon as I reached my teens and was allowed to go off on my own, that's where I headed — and that's where I met Mr. and Mrs. Sharpe. Long story short, we talked about our shared love for Vermeer. They adopted me at age eighteen and sent me right off to school, as you've probably heard. An amazing gift! And then, when I was nineteen, Leland Sharpe was killed. I went on to finish college, supported by Mrs. Sharpe, and launch my art handling and storage business in New York.

"All was smooth until two years ago, when the trustees at the Farmer began to fight. Their struggle was front and center in the art world: What to do with a priceless collection that was hidden away in a decaying mansion in an out-of-the-way part of Chicago? Mrs. Farmer's will stipulated that the art remain there forever, but her trust no longer covered all the expenses, and the place cried out for modernization. The museum itself was only open two days a week, and there were drafts and leaks. Security was inadequate. The situation was clearly an emergency.

"And then, as you know, the National Gallery of Art stepped in with an amazing offer.

"The seven trustees at the Farmer began tearing each other's throats out over the possibility of a move to Washington, D.C., and that was when my mother and I had a terrible fight. She believed the art should go. I believed it must never leave its Chicago home, as did William Swift Chase. I didn't know why, but it *felt* so wrong, like a betrayal. I believed with all my heart that anything possible should be done to prevent a move. My mother can be determined, as I'm sure you all know by now, and I can be stubborn, too. She ordered me not to communicate with her until I was ready to support the move, until I'd come to my senses. Shortly after that, she met Isabel Hussey, and they became close friends. That's why Isabel hadn't heard about me and vice versa before last week — hurtful but understandable, as my mother refused to discuss the Farmer situation with Isabel, and she and I weren't speaking.

"And then, when the theft happened on my birthday, she called me and apologized. She asked me to come and stay for a while, with Rat-a-tat, and see what could be done.

"After William Chase died a few days ago, I'm sure you've heard that the trustees were surprised to discover that he left an unexpected amount of money for repairs but not enough to get the museum permanently out of trouble. He also left my adoptive mother a note.

"In that note was an extraordinary request. He hoped that she could find his son. He confessed that he had had an unwanted child thirty-one years ago, on March seventeenth. The mother's name was *Rose Devlin* McDonald — I know, this came as a complete shock — and he'd allowed her to leave him without offering support of any kind. He said he'd heard the mother had died shortly after the child was born, and he now deeply regretted having been so uncaring and not having tried harder to find his boy. Searching orphanages under the name McDonald, he never came up with a child whose age fit, and he assumed Rose McDonald had left me with family or friends. McDonald, of course, is a very common name, and Mr. Chase had no leads. Never having married, he'd lived alone for decades by the time he had that final stroke the other night. If found, this boy was, at the discretion of the trustees, to take the place of William Chase in running the Farmer Museum."

The kids gasped.

"Scaz, you're a *Chase*! And a big cheese in the art world now!" Zoomy offered a fist, which Eagle bumped.

"You'll be famous!" Tommy added, forgetting to sulk about donkeys.

"This is sad plus happy, all at the same time," Early said. "I'm sorry you didn't get to meet your dad."

"It's so crazy that you always felt at home in the museum, and even connected to Mrs. Farmer . . ." Calder, unused to absorbing big news without his pentominoes, fished madly in his pocket.

"You're family, like the people in her art!" Petra looked genuinely happy. "That's such a great match!"

Eagle looked at Ratty and said nothing for a few seconds. "I'm not sure what I am or how I feel about the news, to tell you the truth. My mother, Ms. Hussey, and I are all reeling; there's a lot to sort out. Is there any relevance to the theft happening on my birthday? And how odd is it that a piece of art in the Farmer Museum, the Vermeer, brought me together with friends of my birth father, who then brought me even closer to the art?

"After sharing this life-changing letter with me last night, my mother insisted we go over to the Chase mansion and hunt for clues. I wandered around studying family faces and trying to absorb more strange echoes, among them the fact that I *do* look like William Chase, who *did* look quite a bit like that Rembrandt self-portrait as a young man. So if I'd known what to see, I would have recognized that portrait as a key that could have unlocked the mystery of who I am."

"Awesome," Zoomy said.

"While I looked through the pictures, my mother poked around in William Chase's desk and found a handful of keys. Some were house keys, others car or file cabinet keys — and then there was one that had *FA* stamped on it, a heavy, brass one that was set apart in a new plastic bag.

"'*F-A!*' my mother exclaimed, and the pieces began to fall into place. She described your excitement after exploring the Fine Arts on your own, earlier in the day. We realized that you five were already one step ahead of us."

"And the key?" Calder asked.

"As if we know what to do with it," Petra said quickly, not sure yet how much they should reveal.

Eagle held up his hand. "Bear with me," he said quietly. "I'm not quite done. My mother, after finding this oddly marked key, wondered if William Chase had somehow intercepted the thieves and been forced to take charge of the stolen art as well as hold on to the storage key. She wondered if he'd been framed or blackmailed just before his stroke happened, but that hardly made sense. Why would someone go to the trouble of stealing the art and then make it look as though Mrs. Farmer's great-nephew had stolen it? And if so, why wouldn't he call the police immediately?"

The room was quiet for a moment, excepting the sound of Ratty cleaning his whiskers.

"So what were you doing in the Fine Arts Building yesterday afternoon?" Early asked. "Before Mrs. Sharpe found the key?"

"I'd been listening in on some of the kids with black jackets, the ones who're all over Hyde Park, and heard them mentioning a meeting in the Fine Arts. Stupidly, I didn't put it together with William Chase's last *F-A*, but I did know those kids seemed to be following all of us around, and especially after our arrest of the night before, I was suspicious. I thought maybe one of them had seen us sneak into the Farmer, and called the police."

"Oh," breathed Petra. "So it wasn't exactly a coincidence that you were at the Fine Arts yesterday, but more a getting-pulled-in-the-same-direction."

"Yeah, none of *us* knew we were going there, either, it just happened," Tommy blurted. "Because of those olives at the Blackstone Hotel."

"I *was* surprised that you were all there," Eagle said. "So here's where the picture begins to sharpen. I don't take credit for how this has fallen into forms we can read, far from it — there's a definite force at work here, one that has affected us all. I must admit: I had my ear to your door just now — forgive me, please! — and heard 'Sally Stayz 619,' and was so excited I almost burst in. After a few seconds of what-should-I-do, I realized you'd just think I was on the wrong side if you didn't have more background.

"Now you've heard it, I can say what I've been thinking: You five are brilliant! How did you get the name Sally Stayz? Speaking of a pull, I pulled every string I could find yesterday afternoon but made no headway on recent rentals at that Fine Arts office. Nor did Mrs. Sharpe get anywhere."

The kids then told all, including Early's sudden revelation about the name of the building, Tommy's flash on the Ouija board message, Calder's trick with dropped pentominoes, Petra's fake fainting spell, the five-way exploration of all the floors, and Zoomy's listening in at the door to 619.

"My mother was right all along," Eagle said. "You five *are* the key to this puzzle. At least, you're the closest key to a possible fit!"

"Huh?" Tommy said, just as Ms. Hussey knocked at the door. Smiling ear to ear and carrying a plate of grilled cheese sandwiches, she practically floated into the room. Everyone settled around the table and Ms. Hussey assured them that she'd also heard the story of "the most recent member of the Chase family." They filled her in on Sally Stayz 619.

"Real-ly!" she said, in her now-I'm-hooked voice, the one she used when someone in her class came up with a great concept. "Wouldn't that be perfect if the key fit in the door and the art was inside? But . . . I agree that something's very wrong with this picture. I mean, why would the key be in William Chase's desk?"

"If we could just get back there, to 619 . . . but you know we're all grounded. And our parents already stretched the rules, both for the tea and then this last meeting." Calder looked discouraged.

"All the more reason," Ms. Hussey said slowly. "Mrs. Sharpe has asked me to get your permission for another trip to the Fine Arts Building. She is calling herself the Carrier of the Key, and wants Eagle to drive the seven of you in his van. And you *must* be there, even if we invite the cops, which would reassure parents, no?"

The kids were quiet as everyone pictured police bursting in the door of 619.

"What if we were wrong and Sally Stayz is an artist? What if she's in there when we open the door and we give her a heart attack?" Petra asked. "Besides, if Eagle goes, our parents might say no, after what happened in the Farmer. Even though it was really *our* fault," she finished, glancing at Eagle. "We dragged you into that."

"I wanted to do it," he said. "No regrets."

The kids glanced at one another. "What if you came with us, too?" Calder asked Ms. Hussey.

"I'd love to, but couldn't. Whether or not this is a red herring — the key may not even work, you know — I might lose my job. I can see it now: *Teacher Lures Kids on Surprise Field Trip with Police.*"

"You think it's a smart idea to go with the cops, Eagle, and Mrs. Sharpe?" Early asked her. "I don't know, my parents might not be happy about that. Things can go wrong."

"You don't have to, of course," Ms. Hussey said. "But your choices are limited and you want to be there when that sixth floor door is opened. Plus, what parent can object to the police stopping by and whizzing you off on a special investigative trip?"

"Mine," Early said.

"I think Mrs. Sharpe is our best protection," Zoomy piped up. "Raisins seem more innocent than grapes, and Eagle is still on the grape side."

"Thank you," Eagle said with a nod. "I'll take that as a compliment."

"What if you drive us down in your van, Eagle, and Mrs. Sharpe goes inside the building with us?" Petra asked. "The police might not listen to us, plus . . . that all sounds so noisy, we might scare away clues of all kinds as well as blackbirds."

Eagle looked thoughtful. "Could work."

"Hmm." Ms. Hussey shook her bun loose and then recoiled it. "Perhaps I'll call each of your homes and your grandma, Zoomy — take credit for the plan, and promise we'll have you back immediately. I've had to explain more difficult field trips to parents before. Eagle, why don't you let your mother know that the children agree."

"Call it done," he said, and headed downstairs.

Ms. Hussey sat in a corner of the attic and called each household in turn, explaining this latest possibility. "This is an important development, and honors all of the kids' incisive problem solving and ideas. No, perfectly straightforward, I assure you . . . Mrs. Sharpe will be with them at all times. Oh, yes . . . Back in no time."

While Ms. Hussey made the calls, Petra leaned toward her friends. "But *who* would steal the art and hide it in the Fine Arts Building? I mean, isn't this insane as a possibility? It's not exactly a secure place for such valuable things."

"And it isn't Eagle's fault, but everyone will think it's a nutty idea to go on another expedition with him," Tommy said.

Eagle, now back in the doorway, said, "No nuttier than blackbirds popping out of a pie and singing after they've been baked."

Ms. Hussey finished her last call and looked around at the group. "As long as we keep in close touch, we're good," she said. "Don't look so worried," she added.

As if to change the subject, she said brightly, "Eagle, why do you refer to Mother Goose so much?"

He shrugged. "The kids asked me that, too. It fits. My life, your life . . . sometimes we all lose things, like Lucy Locket, or get rocked in a cradle on a branch that might break or sit on high wall and hope we won't roll off. At times the dish has been known to run away with the spoon." Ms. Hussey blinked.

"Plus," Eagle went on, "my birth mother left me her childhood copy of that book."

"Oh! Did she write in it?" Ms. Hussey asked, her head on one side.

"She did. For some reason it always felt like a secret to be savored, which is why I didn't mention it before. Silly to hide that, I know. She wrote, 'For my son, Eagle: Fly, hunt, shine. I will always be with you.'"

"That's beautiful," Ms. Hussey said warmly. "It's wonderful. I hope it's okay that we made you share it."

"It's been my compass," Eagle said quietly, "and with Mrs. Farmer's and the Sharpes' help, I hope I've honored her wishes."

"Why do you think she said 'hunt'?" Tommy asked. "Sounds kind of violent. Like my mom, she calls me a finder but not a hunter."

"Tommy!" Ms. Hussey said.

Now it was Eagle who blinked. "Well, hunters and finders are two kinds of people. Speaking of hunting . . . Mrs. Sharpe is ready for you."

☐☐☐ Mrs. Sharpe sat up in front with Eagle on the trip downtown, leaving the five kids in back.

"Scinigaz," Tommy said. "What if some person is waiting for us to open that door and — I don't know, shoot us with an arrow."

"We'll have a witness, at least," Petra said. "Mrs. Sharpe."

"And she has her lion's head cane," Tommy said, hoping the old lady would smile. She didn't.

Eagle looked at the kids in the mirror and said soberly,

"Robbin-a-Bobbin
Bent his bow,
Shot at a pigeon,
And killed a crow."

"Don't be cruel," Mrs. Sharpe said in a tone that ended conversation. The van rumbled north on Lake Shore Drive, the five kids glancing uncomfortably at each other.

Is this just one of Eagle's jokes or is someone about to be killed? If

Mrs. Sharpe is on edge, shouldn't they be? What if she knows more than she'd shared about all of this? Shouldn't Ms. Hussey be more cautious? Questions darted through Tommy's head.

Petra, with a stab of foreboding, remembered what she and Early had overheard in the Farmer Museum on the day they'd met the trustees, the talk of an "event."

"This is an event to remember," Petra blurted.

Mrs. Sharpe smiled for the first time that day. "That it is, complete with a Carrier of the Key."

CHAPTER TWENTY-THREE   THE MADNESS OF ART

◨ ◻ ◨ "What're *those* guys up to?" Calder asked, his fingers missing his pentominoes dreadfully.

The five kids and Mrs. Sharpe stood outside the front doors to the Fine Arts Building and watched a group of students in black jackets hurry out to a beat-up van with a load of crate-like cardboard boxes.

"Doing what students do, no doubt," Mrs. Sharpe said drily. "Moving art around."

All six squashed into the tiny elevator for the ride up to the sixth floor. Eagle waited outside in the van, having given his cell phone number to the kids.

As the operator opened the elevator gate, his passengers peered anxiously around him. A young man in a black jacket had just locked the door to 619 and was slipping a key into his pocket.

Five mouths dropped open in horror.

The sixth, however, barked out an order, thumping the floor for emphasis. "Young man! Not another step! In the name of William Chase, I command you to wait right there!"

The young man did. "Can I help you?" he asked in a strangled squeak when the group arrived at the door. One eye twitched and he had the worst acne Tommy had ever seen up close. *My occasional Krakatoa is nothing compared to the*

Alps here, he thought with a flood of sympathy. *Things could be worse.*

Mrs. Sharpe said nothing, but produced her key and fit it easily into the lock. Now it was the young man's turn to gape.

He stepped back as the door swung open and the kids crowded into the studio. Mrs. Sharpe blocked his retreat with her cane, waving him inside ahead of her. The space was empty with the exception of a desk and chair, a garbage can filled with food wrappers, and a scrap of heavy cardboard.

Shoulders slumped; a fog of disappointment filled the room.

"We need to talk," Mrs. Sharpe said in her iciest voice. She sank down on the chair. "Now, shut the door," she ordered the young man. He stepped over and placed one hand on the knob, his head down, then flew like lightning around the side of the door and back out into the hallway.

The five kids dashed after him, but he was already pounding down the stairs.

"Quick, call Eagle," Mrs. Sharpe ordered. Petra got through first, and handed the phone to the old woman.

▊ ▢ ▊ By the time they'd crowded out of the elevator on the first floor, Eagle had the young man pinned outside against the corner of the building.

"Believe me, I didn't want any of the money!" he pleaded. "I just did it to help the others. It went on for so long — I was one of the recruits. Relief duty. People had to sleep, you know? And we're supposed to be in school, not watching art, for crimminy's sake!"

Mrs. Sharpe looked at the student as if he were a centipede. "And where *is* the art?" she asked. "Tell me now or we will turn you over to the police."

To everyone's horror, a tear rolled down the student's face. "The art was the happening itself — taking it out that night, moving the crates, keeping watch down here, and then returning it when we got the word. But of course he died . . ." Another tear rolled.

Mrs. Sharpe fished a tissue out of her handbag and handed it over. "Pull yourself together — we're not going to hurt you." Her voice had thawed. "Let's try again. Where, my boy, is the art?"

"One of us heard a sound outside the door yesterday and realized someone was planning to break in. We couldn't decide what to do; we were afraid we'd be blamed for the theft and no one would believe how this happened, so —"

"Yes? So? Get to the point."

The young man looked around for help, found himself alone, then sighed. "We're just students at the School of the Art Institute. Honest! He offered lots of money to carry out his orders and remain silent until he gave the word, and then we were supposed to share the disappearance and reappearance of this great art as an 'event,' an art happening. It seemed like an adventure and a win-win situation. I mean, how many students get to carry out a heist that stuns the world, and then bask in publicity and a generous check when it's all over? It was a staged piece of performance art that he said would safely but effectively highlight ongoing struggles within the art world. A scare that was drama, not reality: Lovers of art all over the world could learn from and enjoy it. He also thought the trustees would realize the value of what they had if it was gone for a little while. But now . . ."

Mrs. Sharpe's face was grim. "Would that 'he' be William Swift Chase?"

The young man nodded. "Nice old man. And we've all been hanging around in the neighborhood since he died, keeping his secret and watching to see where or how we could safely dump the art, as we weren't sure anyone would believe we hadn't really stolen it! There're so many police around the Farmer Museum now, it didn't seem possible to leave it and run. We even watched some of the trustees' houses nearby and thought about unloading it in one of the yards, but that felt much too risky. We saw you kids going inside with the trustees a few days ago, and so we kept an eye on all of you. We followed you down to Millennium Park one day, and watched you around the Bean. Fastening the boxes high inside the sculpture in the middle of the night seemed like a cool idea, but we couldn't find the right brackets or mirrored coating for the cardboard. Whoa, would that have made a terrific TV opportunity, if the art could've been 'found' there . . ."

"Give it to us," Calder said suddenly. "We have a van."

Everyone looked at him.

"Thank you, we most certainly do." Mrs. Sharpe shot Calder an admiring glance.

"And you won't tell?" the young man asked. "There were originally only five students involved, but then, what with all the watching and following, they had to reach out to friends and there're probably two dozen of us Black Jackets now."

"I am a trustee. No questions will be asked," Mrs. Sharpe assured him.

"Dirk!" the student said into his cell phone. "I'm with one of the Farmer trustees. She says she'll take the art, no questions asked. Where are you? *Already?* No one saw you guys?"

The student shrugged apologetically. "Mission accomplished. The boxes were delivered minutes ago to a graveyard in Woodlawn, on the South Side. Oak Woods Cemetery. That's where generations of the Chase family are buried. They're stacked — I mean, the containers — in the huge family tomb, which looks like an open Grecian temple with low walls and columns. Sarah Chase Farmer is there, and that's where William Chase will go. It seemed logical."

"And what if someone from the cemetery grounds department *saw* your van and is over there busily throwing away the crates this very moment?" Eagle asked. "That's one of their biggest and fanciest monuments, and that section is always neatly kept."

Mrs. Sharpe waved her cane toward Eagle's van. "Not a moment. Hurry!" she barked. With Petra on one side and Calder on the other, they hustled her into the front and leaped in the back with the other three, still fastening seat belts as Eagle roared out of his parking spot. As the van zoomed away, the student leaned weakly against the side of the Fine Arts, as if he'd just been released from a den of lions.

"One of you children," Mrs. Sharpe ordered, "call Oak Woods right now, and try to get a living person."

"Right, not one of the dead," Zoomy added in a hodilly-hum tone.

"Actually, I meant not an answering machine."

Tommy tried over and over, as did Petra, but no one picked up. The van careened south on Lake Shore Drive.

"I knew it!" murmured Early. "We *were* being watched."

"By four-and-twenty blackbirds," Petra added.

"After one of them sang!" Calder's voice cracked hideously on the last word.

"And now we get to clobber the pie," Zoomy said happily.

"Hopefully," Tommy bleated.

It was Early who suggested they call Ms. Hussey and send her over there, but then they realized that she didn't have a car to use and by the time she'd called a cab, they'd be at the graveyard.

"Don't call her," ordered Mrs. Sharpe. "She'd probably try running, and it's several miles and those streets can be deserted at the best of times. We'll be home soon."

"Yup, too far on foot," Eagle agreed.

An odd peace settled on the van, as each kid sent thoughts of hope and protection toward the art. Early sat with the *Lady and Gentleman in Black*, keeping them company as they waited; Calder sent rescue vibes to the men caught in *The Storm on the Sea of Galilee*; Tommy felt as though he was trotting purposefully along that inviting path in the Flinck landscape; Zoomy told the man writing to keep right on with what he was doing; Petra was back in the Vermeer, the pull toward the *X*s so strong and clear that she called out, "Mrs. Sharpe!"

"Yes?" The old lady responded.

"Why did you say that to me in the dream? 'For art, this building. This comfort.'"

Mrs. Sharpe turned slowly around from the front seat.

"Where did you hear that?" she asked softly. "I wrote a novel titled *What If He Turns?* It's loosely based on *The Concert*. I pulled out my manuscript the other day, wondering if I should show it to someone — but I haven't as yet. I wrote it in honor of my husband, really as a tribute to him. That was his favorite Vermeer. And in my story, the woman who is singing says those words in her song."

"*Oh*," breathed Petra. "In my dream, the woman at the harpsichord turned her head and said those words to me, and somehow — well, I knew it was you, Mrs. Sharpe."

"*Oh*," Mrs. Sharpe said, echoing Petra.

"Mrs. Farmer told us on the Ouija board that the people

in her art were alive not alone, just like her," Zoomy said. "I think she meant it."

"Marvelous," Mrs. Sharpe said. "Alive not alone . . ."

"Great," Tommy muttered, thinking it wasn't. *Goldman would hate this*, he thought to himself.

Petra looked as though she were walking on air. "Maybe that's why we got the same message, Mrs. Sharpe!"

"It's the madness of art," the old lady murmured.

◻◻◻ The Chase tomb was located beneath a huge oak tree, in the fanciest part of the cemetery.

Eagle careened around the corner of that section of the drive just in time to see a maintenance truck pulling up from the other side.

"Whoa!" he shouted out the van window. "We're here to pick up those boxes!"

The groundskeeper crossed his arms, watching with surprise as Mrs. Sharpe, Eagle, and the five kids spilled out.

Mrs. Sharpe peered into the tomb, looking with obvious distaste at the cardboard crates. "Hardly adequate packing and storage materials," she sniffed. "William was carried away by his clever idea but didn't handle things appropriately. How like him! Probably regretted it terribly, poor man," she added.

"And who are *you*?" The man stared at Mrs. Sharpe and Eagle. "We're required to dispose of all packaged goods and trash left on this property. No pickups allowed."

"I am Louise Coffin Sharpe, a trustee of the Farmer Museum," Mrs. Sharpe said, standing at her tallest, her cane snarling out in front. "And this, my man, is recently stolen art. We plan to take it and will."

"It is these five kids who are responsible for rescuing it," Eagle added. "And not a moment too soon."

Responsible for rescuing. The words sounded beautiful. Calder, Petra, and Tommy realized with a shock of delight that they'd reached new heights as players; Zoomy was stunned to realize that these thirteen pieces of the world might have taught him to play the game like everyone else; and Early, flying, caught a glimmer of how she fit with all the pieces and players around her, including Mrs. Farmer — fit and belonged.

"And who are you?" the man asked Eagle.

"I'm — well, I'm William Swift Chase's son."

"Well, that's *different*," the man said. "So sorry for your loss." He nodded formally to Eagle.

"Thank you," Eagle said politely. "And now, if you don't mind, we'll load this up."

"Mighty odd spot to find the art." The man shook his head and climbed back into his truck. "Thieves are crazy these days. Nothing's sacred. Well, so long, we'll be seeing you back here in a few days, at the burial."

As Eagle reached down to pick up the closest of the boxes, he jumped back. "Ouch! *Yeow*, something stung me!"

Mrs. Sharpe laughed, a high-pitched creaking sound. "Oh, my," she said. "Oh, my! Too early for bees. I'm sure it's just a reminder of what's what and who's who. And as Mrs. Farmer put it, 'We never see all that we know is there.'" Turning toward the tomb, the old woman said, "Thank you for all, my dear — for watching, helping, and intervening to the best of your abilities. They're on their way back."

The five kids watched, their mouths open.

Eagle touched the box lightly with a finger, braced for a second shock. There wasn't one, and he loaded the pile of boxes with no problem. Soon a packed van headed slowly north to Mrs. Sharpe's house, swerving gently to avoid all potholes. As it pulled up, Ms. Hussey burst out the front door.

"This is the Welcome Home wagon." Eagle smiled. Isabel Hussey peered into the back of the van and shrieked.

□ ▢ □ "Unload the art, Eagle. My decision. I take full responsibility," Mrs. Sharpe said, leading the way into her house.

"Scinigaz," Tommy muttered.

"Inigis shinige stinigeinigaliniging inigit?" Early whispered.

"Really, children!" Mrs. Sharpe whirled around, looking suddenly years younger and happier. "You'll have to do better than that variety of Igpay Atinlay!"

"Guess Gam was right about raisins being grapes," Zoomy said.

Eagle and Ms. Hussey stood quietly by the van, as if not sure what to do.

"Well? Think I've lost all remaining marbles?" Mrs. Sharpe said lightly to them. "I haven't. But your idea of welcoming the art home is just right. The children have earned an unforgettable dinner party, and I, for one, would like to attend."

Eagle did as she said, carrying the boxes into the living room as Ms. Hussey stood guard, looking up and down the street to be sure they weren't being watched. Once they were all inside, she pulled the curtains and closed the blinds.

Mrs. Sharpe sat happily in her corner of the red sofa, although this time she sat straight. "Now. Everyone but Eagle take a seat," she ordered. "Here's what will happen: Isabel dear, would you please call all the parents and explain the situation; we need to keep the children for a couple of hours. Children, you can talk amongst yourselves and decide what kind of feast we shall have. It should, however, be take-out from somewhere close by, in Hyde Park. Mind you, spare no expense. Italian would be fine, or French, Thai, Jamaican, or Middle Eastern, although I draw the line at ribs. My upholstery would never survive. Your choice in ordering, and I repeat: It is critical that everyone remain where they are. No moving around, with the exception of the . . . ah . . . powder room, of course.

"Son. As a trained professional in the world of museum-level storage and as the only relative of Sarah Chase Farmer in this house, I'd like you to unpack her art."

Gasps filled the room. Eagle paused, his head on one side. "Let me get this straight: We all eat together, the living and — I was going to say the dead, but that isn't right — and then we return these treasures to their home tonight, in *my* storage boxes from downstairs. No more cardboard."

"You could call our dinner group the living plus the alive-not-alones," Early suggested.

Tommy noticed at that moment that the sculpture of the naked man wasn't in the living room in its usual spot. *Good thing*, he thought.

"That would include all ghosts, the people in the art, whatever you want to call that crowd," Calder agreed.

"Right." Mrs. Sharpe nodded. "It's a plan."

"So?" Zoomy asked, swinging his legs. "Clobber away, Eagle! I want to meet everyone!"

Ms. Hussey leaned toward her elderly friend and whispered in her ear.

"Due to your range, young man, you'll be allowed closer when the time comes," Mrs. Sharpe announced to Zoomy. "But for obvious reasons, we must keep all spilling and chaos on this side of the room."

As Eagle cut open the boxes with a razor blade, moving ever so slowly, the room was silent. Faces relaxed when he slid out the first of the framed works.

"Amateurish job, but at least nothing touched the surface," he said, holding one of Degas's Jockey sketches up in the air. "Here's to the Black Jackets!"

"Hooray!" the room shouted.

Minutes later, the thirteen pieces were lined up on a white sheet, across the room from where the three adults and five kids sat. The framed art was propped against chair legs so it could be seen; the small Ku and the brass eagle, his wings shining, bracketed the lineup. Mrs. Sharpe had asked Ms. Hussey to find as many candles as she could for the area they were planning to eat in. She ordered Eagle to turn off all the lights, with the exception of two bright reading lamps. These last shone directly at the art from some distance away, bathing it in a soft pool of light.

Whether it was the flickering candles or the excitement of the moment, something very odd then occurred.

As eight pairs of eyes studied the art, soaking in this extraordinary parade of color and detail, the people in the art began to move — just the gleam of a fingernail, a blink, or the twitch of a head. It was as if something unearthly, something at least as powerful as the moon, had pulled the everyday into an irresistible place, one in which every heart was welcome. What had been painted or drawn centuries earlier could now say, *Yes, yes!* to the present. And those sitting in a certain house in Chicago, each framed by their own lives, realized they would never again feel either alone or without the echoes and passions of those who had lived before them.

The Yeses in the room bloomed in silence as everyone tried to absorb a mind-bending variety of thoughts.

Zoomy, down on the carpet in front of Manet's man, saw the writer's ear move ever so slightly as his face relaxed. "I won't tell your secret," Zoomy whispered.

Tommy saw the couple in the Flinck landscape turn toward each other. Light caught on a cheek, a nose, leaves shimmering at the top of the gnarled tree. And was that the burble of running water?

Early caught the promise of a smile from the man who stood waiting. Next, the lady stretched her right hand in just the tiniest of movements. A spark flew outward from the ring on her first finger, as if to say, *Yes! It will happen!*

Petra caught the light dancing in the harpsichord player's earring and thought she heard the rustle of skirts. A fold in that long, cream-colored cascade of fabric deepened into a V, as if to say, *Vermeer! He knows you are here, and all is well! There is no need for him to turn!*

Once again, Calder thought he heard the screaming, the snap of torn rigging, and the slap of the storm. And at that moment he knew the fear in the faces of these men would subside, and the break in the clouds overhead would open outward, spreading calm. As he looked at the one face that stared steadily back — the man in the foreground who many believed was Rembrandt himself — he caught the tiniest nod of thanks.

"Henry James was right," Mrs. Sharpe said suddenly. "You can live with doubt, but what's seen or felt or heard is yours for life. No one can ever take that away."

❑ ❑ ❑ "Do you think the people in the art will miss each other?" Zoomy asked, helping himself to seconds of barbecued chicken pizza and Caesar salad.

"You mean, after all these days of being stuck face to

face in the dark?" Tommy asked. *Scaz, did that sound bad.* Embarrassed, he added, "I mean . . ."

"We get it," Petra said, rolling her eyes. "Yeah, I wonder what happens when no one is looking."

"If being rescued means they can finally relax, I think *my* lady would take off that stiff collar and rub her neck," Early said. "And maybe she's thinking about having a walk in that restful Flinck painting and getting together with friends."

"I like it." Tommy nodded.

"And everyone in the boat but Jesus and Rembrandt are stepping on each other and shouting, 'Me first!' about getting off that thing," Calder said, his cheeks bulging with fettuccini Alfredo.

Ms. Hussey passed him another napkin.

"My Manet man is relieved he can stop writing and have a dilly bean," Zoomy said. "Plus, he's probably taken off that top hat and stepped on it. Must've been like wearing an upside-down cookie jar."

"Or a pail," Petra said.

Tommy nodded. "I think my Flinck man is smiling and he's been dying to do that for centuries."

"Mine, the self-portrait, is shaving those cat whiskers from his face," Eagle said, glancing at Ms. Hussey. "He's been dying to do that, too."

"I don't mind the whiskers," Ms. Hussey said.

"And in *The Concert*," Petra mused, "while those two women are playing lovely music, the mystery man turns and invites the gentleman in Early's painting to play ping-pong. Or maybe hit the basketball court — no one's gotten any exercise for a long time. Meanwhile, all the ladies hang out and yuck it up."

The others laughed. "Yeah, and imagine the welcome-home celebration that will happen in the Farmer after they're back on the walls!" Calder looked around. "I mean, the private party that no one living gets to see. Think of those people in the Dutch Room who were watching the theft from the walls when it happened."

"Now they can cheer and jump up and down," Zoomy finished for him. "They'll probably say stuff like, 'Where the dingleberry have you been?'"

"I think you guys have had enough Coke for one meal," Ms. Hussey said.

"Not me," Eagle said, refilling his glass. "I can't get enough fizz tonight."

Instead of looking irritated, Ms. Hussey grinned and he grinned back, as if all those bubbles were only the beginning.

Saw that, Tommy thought to himself.

Looking up, he caught Mrs. Sharpe's eye. "Could be the dish and the spoon," she murmured.

Encouraged, Tommy blurted a question. "Mrs. Sharpe, do you think Mrs. Farmer heard you out there in the cemetery?"

The room quieted down, excepting the rustle of Calder's fingers in his empty pants pocket. Ms. Hussey had already promised him a box of small teak cubes that he could glue together into a special new set, and he couldn't wait; thinking without pentominoes wasn't easy.

"Well..." Mrs. Sharpe looked thoughtful. "She's buried there, of course. But you remember what she wrote in *The Truth About My Art*: Those paintings became her family, and family connections don't exactly die. More accurately put, they change form."

"Oh." Petra's eyes widened. "Like Eagle finding out he's a Chase, after a lifetime of feeling comfortable in the museum. It's different but not."

Ms. Hussey glanced happily at Eagle, who smiled as if they were the only people in the room.

Jeez, Tommy thought. *Go easy, guys.*

"Mrs. Sharpe," he went on, "are we all coming to William Chase's funeral and burial service?"

"I hope you will," she said. "That cemetery is actually a lovely spot. It's where my husband is buried and —" She paused and swallowed. "Our little son, who died shortly after birth. Plus thousands of soldiers from the Civil War, a number of Chicago mayors, and some senators, scholars, writers, social activists, and scientists, including Ida B. Wells and Enrico Fermi. Quite a crowd."

Ms. Hussey patted her arm. "And now your other son will be able to help you out a bit more. I understand he's thinking of moving back to Chicago."

Mrs. Sharpe tried to hide a smile. "And it's about time," she said briskly, reaching over to pat Rat-a-tat, who rested his head on one of her shoes. He licked his lips and blinked pleasantly. Mrs. Sharpe quietly pushed a small piece of chicken off her plate and — *snap!* — Ratty caught it in midair.

"Since you'll probably want your own place and it might be an apartment, perhaps this ferocious gentleman can stay with me."

"Good thought," Eagle said. "And speaking of good thoughts, I've been thinking ahead about how to explain the reappearance of the art. As we know, the Art Institute blackbirds will be singing about their role in this — what should we call it? — 'fabricated heist' as soon as the news of the return is out. I think the trustees can explain William Chase's basic idea, but it's the recovery that everyone wants to hear about."

Mrs. Sharpe nodded. "And that's when these five kids will explain their excellent work to the press. I have no illusions about the dreadful mess many of my peers are responsible for, a mess we brought on ourselves! If you children hadn't badgered Eagle into taking you to the Farmer that night, you wouldn't have received the messages that led you to recognize the importance of the Fine Arts Building. And if you hadn't managed to finagle a room number and the giveaway name of Sally Stayz — and I'll bet Sarah's collection *will* stay in Chicago now, the donor money will pour in — I hate to think what might have happened. Those Art Institute students were a jittery wreck, and if they hadn't dumped the crates in Oak Woods today, they might have done it tomorrow. Understandably, as their fears of being blamed for the heist were probably justified."

The old woman shuddered. "Let's face it. Because of Mr. Chase's risky behavior and subsequent untimely death, the art might well have ended up in the back of a garbage truck."

"Mrs. Sharpe, Early and I saw something odd at Mr. Cracken's house," Petra began. "A bunch of what looked like wrapped paintings, and some of the trustees were there. Then Tommy and Zoomy got hold of the packing paper when the butler was getting rid of it."

"Ah," Mrs. Sharpe said. "That was an effort to raise money, amongst the trustees. Eagle provided wrapping materials for us all, and we each agreed to contribute whatever art we felt willing to part with, to raise money for the Farmer — and store it at Monument's house."

"And the wrappings smelled like your perfume," Zoomy said flatly.

"Hmm," Mrs. Sharpe said. "Well, I did hold the paper for my son while he unrolled and cut it in sections before the trustees arrived that day, and what with the sardine smell —" She sniffed. "I must say, I squirted quite a bit of my Chanel on the rug in here."

"Whew, good to know," Calder said. "Not that we thought . . ."

Mrs. Sharpe gave him a withering glance. "I may as well tell you that William's sting stung me as well, and I'm glad. I've come to realize that he was right about keeping the art here in Chicago, in the home that Sarah Chase Farmer built for it. I will put my entire available estate toward helping. In hopes of inspiring the other trustees to do the same, I have suggested they each begin to raise money by selling some of their own collections."

A wave of *oh*s, *ah*s, and *great*s swept around the room, and Tommy suddenly understood why the statue of the naked man was missing.

Eagle patted Mrs. Sharpe's shoulder. "It was a winning idea, and I think it'll start the process. Where there's a will, there's a way, and Sally will stay!"

He now turned toward the kids. "So. When we call the police shortly and announce the return of the art tonight, you five will need to come along. Sorry, another trip to the police station, but this time, they'll be treating you like royalty." He grinned. "Hanging on your every word."

The five sat quietly, but the two girls and three boys suddenly looked older, more collected, and as if they were preparing what to share, which they were.

"Needless to say, you can choose your words," Ms. Hussey chimed in. "And as you're all discriminating thinkers, I don't think that will be difficult. Not every dream, cold spot, or suspicion needs airing . . ."

"Speaking of words, I have a question for you wordsmiths," Mrs. Sharpe said. "I understand the principle behind the code you've been using, but what *exactly* is the meaning and derivation of *scaz?*"

The kids told her, explaining carefully that it wasn't really a bad word.

"Feels good to say," Zoomy added. "And no one gets their knickers in a twist."

Mrs. Sharpe paused for a moment, looking around at the candlelit faces in the group and then at the thirteen pieces of art that seemed to shine in their own light.

Closing her eyes, she murmured happily, "*Scazzz!* What a sting!"

AUTHOR'S NOTE: WHAT'S BAKED IN THE PIE

⬚⬚⬚ Fresh, local ingredients are always good. All of the neighborhoods, buildings, institutions, and pieces of art in this mystery are real. Most can be found in Chicago. The Farmer Museum, however, wears a disguise. When writing about it, I imagined The Isabella Stuart Gardner Museum, in Boston, Massachusetts. The structure and art collection are just about identical; the thirteen stolen pieces are, sadly, the same. They can be seen on the FBI site, www.fbi.gov /about-us/investigate/vc_majorthefts/arttheft/isabella or on the Gardner Museum site, at www.gardnermuseum.org/resources /theft.

The real crime occurred in the early hours of March 18, 1990; the art has now been missing for an astounding and tragic twenty-five years. My hope is that someone will read this book and lose their heart — perhaps all over again! — to the missing art. Who's to say what magic or which dreams might help in recovering it?

Sarah Chase Farmer and Isabella Stuart Gardner have much in common, but Mrs. Farmer's book, *The Truth About My Art*, is her own. I have hijacked the marvelous 1894 Anders Zorn portrait, *Isabella Stuart Gardner in Venice* — it appears in *Pieces and Players* as a portrait of Sarah Chase Farmer in Chicago.

Ulrich Boser's excellent book, *The Gardner Heist*, provides a wealth of information about the unsolved Gardner

Museum theft and the long, frustrating search for these missing treasures.

There are elements of this story that might remind readers of the 1990s struggle surrounding the Barnes Foundation, in Philadelphia. The art world is never at a loss for drama and disagreement, which is part of its power and charm.

The two volumes of Mother Goose rhymes that are referenced in this story are *The Real Mother Goose* (Scholastic, 1994) and *The Annotated Mother Goose*, William S. and Ceil Baring-Gould (Bramhall House, 1962).

All characters in this story are fictitious; they do what they do, and I do my best to keep up.

A Note about Pentominoes,
PLUS A PICTURE OF THE PIECES

■ ▫ ◻ A set of pentominoes is a mathematical tool consisting of twelve pieces. Each piece is made up of five squares that share at least one side. Pentominoes are used by mathematicians around the world to explore ideas about geometry and numbers. The set looks like this:

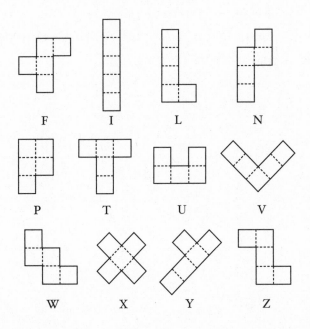

Pentomino pieces are named after letters in the alphabet, although they don't all look exactly like their names. They appear as one of a number of game pieces in this story.